I0664962

TYCHE'S LOST

A SPACE OPERA ADVENTURE EPIC

EZEROC WARS
BOOK 8

RICHARD PARRY

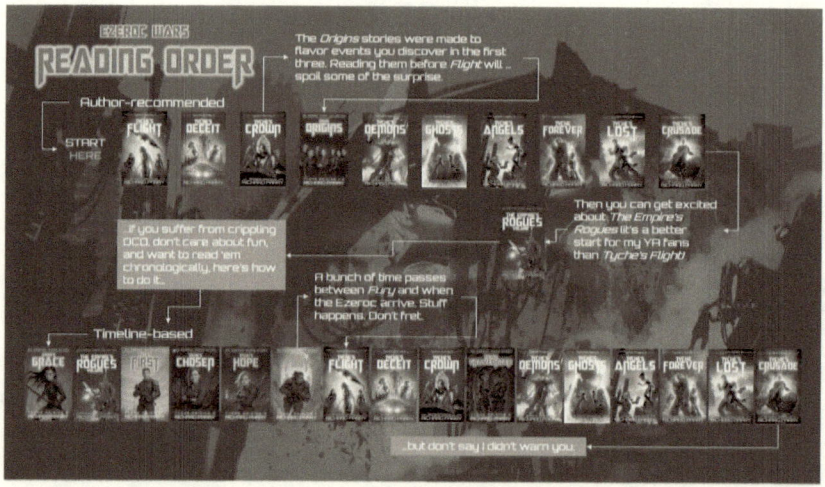

TYCHE'S LOST

SAVERIA'S DIED TWICE BEFORE. THIRD TIME'S THE CHARM.

The *Gravedigger* crashes on an uncharted world, stranding Chad Forradel—Imperial spymaster—and his ward, Saveria. What they find isn't just wreckage. It's a forgotten human colony, twisted by the Ezeroc.

Humanity's oldest enemy has seeded the stars with corruption. The survivors of Viukde were sent back into space not as emissaries, but as **weapons wearing human faces**.

Chad and Saveria must get off-world and warn the Empire. But with no ship, no help, and no time, survival might not be enough.

If they fail, the Ezeroc won't need to invade. **We'll invite them in.**

Tyche's Lost is the intense eighth book in Richard Parry's *Ezeroc Wars* series. If you love gritty space opera with razor-sharp dialogue and desperate stakes, grab your copy today.

YOU'RE AWESOME

You could have picked any book, but you chose this one. That means a lot.

Your support keeps independent authors like me forging ahead, writing the stories we love (and hopefully, the ones you love too). Whether you're here for the characters, the worldbuilding, or just a little escapism, thank you for being part of this journey.

You. Kick. Ass.

ROLL FOR NARRATIVE

WHERE WORLDBUILDING AND
OVERTHINKING COLLIDE

Love stories that linger in your brain long after The End? Ever wonder why some books hit like a natural 20 and others critically fail their way into the 1-star abyss?

Join *Roll for Narrative*, my hub for sci-fi and fantasy lovers. I explore storytelling like a rogue casing a dungeon, review movies, books, and games, and dish out writing tips like a chaotic-good bard with a grudge against bad prose. No spam, just good stuff.

Join the quest:
https://rollfornarrative.parrydox.com

FALLING SKIES

The heavy roil of thunder beat the air. It strummed Forrest's skin, more delicate than the rain that fell like endless tears. The night air smelled alive, the fresh scent of night flowers mingling with the petrichor of thirsty earth.

They stood at Vigil as they did every night. Marla was on the wooden stage, lantern light touching her face. She was a good leader, strong and just, not giving more to the gods than was necessary. She offered them the villainous and evil when she could, the weak and infirm when she couldn't. Forrest would stand in a hundred more thunderstorms if it showed support. When he was close to her it lifted his heart, soothing his fears.

Fifty villagers shared tonight's Vigil. They held clubs and ropes. Sometimes the Vigil was for sharing of thoughts and feelings. Other times it called for an offering to the gods. Forrest glanced at the stone statues surrounding the village square. Taller than two men, they leaned toward the flickering light, as if waiting for the rain to douse the fires. Ten in all, the village's gods watched all, missing nothing. They looked like insect centaurs, mighty against the night. Long stabbing limbs reached through the rain. Forrest shuddered. *I've nothing to fear if I do what's needed.*

Marla stared at the crowd. A wide-brimmed hat protected her straw-colored hair from the worst the storm had to offer, but she squinted as a squall tossed rainwater about. "Tonight, the world changes."

The crowd settled. Forrest tightened his grip on the club he held. Marla often spoke of what was *necessary* to guide them forward. Of the cost to build the Church high enough to challenge the stars. Often, she spoke of change, but she'd never said it was time. He felt his heart quicken as lightning slashed the sky, the boom of thunder touching him again.

"Tonight, evil comes to us. The gods," Marla swept a hand toward the statues on her left, "protect us, but we know they help those who help themselves." A knowing nod, shared by many. "They will come to us with false promises of a better world. We must harden our hearts." She squared her shoulders. "They'll look like us, but make no mistake, they're not our kin. We'll take them to the Altar, and the gods will deliver justice." She glowered. "If we fail, the gods will destroy us all."

The Vigil members shifted, some anxiously, some eagerly. Forrest shared a look with young Tom Baker. *None of us want to die.* He held his hand up. "What must be done?"

"Justice," Marla crowed. "Redemption!"

The crowd cheered, raising clubs and lanterns high. Thunder boomed again, louder, immediate, and sudden. No lightning foretold the sound. Forrest turned to the east. The cloud cover was heavy, a thick blanket hiding the stars from view. Even so, light pushed eager fingers against the storm. Whites, oranges, and reds illuminated the clouds. *The gods are fighting the interlopers.* It was the only explanation.

A long line of fire broke free from the clouds. Forrest thought it must be a chariot of heaven. It burned, fragments of molten fury falling in its wake. Lances of light and anger stabbed skyward even as the chariot fell. The noise pushed Forrest to his knees, shielding his head with a raised hand. A roaring, like a titan in rage and pain, and then a crackling like bottled lightning. Behind the trail of fire, a boulder followed. Forrest knew the boulders carried their gods. Earth above, born of earth below. *The chariot must be the enemy Marla spoke of.*

Marla glanced up, and for a moment the peace of her presence flickered. Forrest felt uncertainty gnaw at him. He wondered how something so majestic and beautiful could be the enemy. Marla's eyes fell back on the waiting Vigil, her teeth bared in a snarl. She stabbed a finger toward the falling star. "Bring them! Hurry!"

Forrest felt his heart swell. He turned, almost slipping in the mud, but his purpose was clear. *Find the invaders. Bring them to the Altar. Sacrifice them for the Church.* He ran, rain lashing at his heels like a thousand tiny whips. He felt joy in holy purpose.

BUT THIS ISN'T how it started.

ONE

Three dead people crewed the ship.

The *Gravedigger* was no stranger to death. She'd flown Navy colors before turning pirate. The evil and the wicked called her home, wreaking all manner of injustice on the innocent. That was before the corvette fell into the hands of a liar, thief, and the most handsome man to walk the stars: Chad Forradel.

Chad's back ached, but not as bad as his skull. It wasn't the Endless jumps. The pain ran deeper, became personal, held his hand at night, and stroked his brow in the morning. It'd been like that since he'd woken from the grave and smelled the burnt air of Earth. Although dead Ezeroc lay stacked like fallen trees, victory for humanity and the constructs in evidence, it was rough for Chad. His esper gifts hadn't worked right since throwing his life aside so the Empress could learn a few tricks.

The tricks saved the Empire, but they left Chad in dire need of a vacation.

The ship hummed, quiet, ready, and almost empty. The bridge itself was a standard design. A holo stage four meters a side sat at his feet. Consoles with empty acceleration couches sat to the sides. Tactical's three couches sat on his right, Comms' two on the left. The starry night lay about them, bridge windows showing all.

One Comm couch held the other dead people. Chad leaned toward her as much as his acceleration couch's harness would allow, steepling his fingers. "This is complicated."

Saveria Complex looked at him. That was about all the reaction he'd been able to get from her. She'd died on Earth right alongside Chad, but if he was being honest, she'd had it worse. The Ezeroc crawled inside her, corrupted her flesh, and stole her mind. Insects made a hatchery of her skull. AI intervention saved Earth when Algernon dropped a nanobot swarm. The nanites churned through Saveria's body, tearing apart the insect tissue. There wasn't enough left of her brain to put in a sippy cup.

We saved a planet at the cost of a woman's life. It didn't feel right at the time, and it feels worse now. Chad looked away from Saveria's stare. There wasn't any life in it. He felt like he was looking at a machine waiting for a program. Which led to the third dead person. Emberlie's mind crystal lay in Saveria's skull. The fallen AI gave thought and action to Saveria's body. Algernon thought Saveria might keep her human memories. He was certain Emberlie was gone, a fracture running through the storage core tossing all she'd been to the emptiness between stars.

That's not all that's empty. All Chad saw since Saveria woke up was that blank stare. She hadn't spoken, following Chad through the *Gravedigger* like a ghost, reminding him of his failings with her silence, sins with her loss, and weakness with her fragile frame. *If you'd been a little stronger, she might still be alive. Saveria's your responsibility, and you've got to do right by her.*

Chad stood, stretched his back, and strode to the windows, pondering their next destination. The stars hung in the hard black. Their ship's drives were quiet and cold. Chad swiveled to Saveria. She looked at him, same as always, patient and empty. "I figure the universe is about done with us." She said nothing. "We need to do something about it." Not even a blink. "I reckon," he stabbed a finger at the stars, "there's a good place for a couple margaritas."

It's like talking to a tree that breathes. He sighed, more from habit, rubbing his forehead. This would be easier if his skull didn't pound like the devil used it for a drum solo. Chad couldn't think straight, let alone use future-sense to chart the stars. All he knew was getting clear from Karkoski was vital. She headed the Admiralty, and since they'd grown closer, she made mistakes. Just like he had. Hers were small matters, the loss of a starship, the failure of command. His were larger, almost costing the Empire their homeworld. It cost Saveria her mind. Chad reckoned in a different universe, one not rich with murderous insects, he and Karkoski might have a chance to be closer.

As it was, the Empire needed their focus. Focus meant distance. Distance meant a vacation.

Algernon said it would take time for Emberlie's cracked crystal to meld with Saveria's brain tissue. Time wasn't a resource in rich supply, but Chad owed Saveria, and while everyone was squaring ledgers, Nate owed Chad some shore leave. He reached out to Saveria's mind, trying to touch her thoughts like he had every day since she woke three weeks ago.

CHAD Hello Saveria, can you hear me

Silence. Not even the sibilant hiss of Ezeroc mind-speech. There wasn't anything there. Or Chad's gifts were so far gone he couldn't talk to a fellow esper five meters distant.

"Good talk. Let's get on, then." He sauntered back to the captain's acceleration couch and slung his lean frame into it. He pulled up the couch's personal console. Viukde System waited for them. Thirty-nine jumps. It was far enough away that the light from Sol was a distant memory. So far away, no one would find them. The weary pair might find a little peace.

THE OBVIOUS SIGN things were amiss was when a rock the size of an autotaxi tore a hole in the *Gravedigger*, but in hindsight Chad should have seen this coming. If he'd still had the gift of future-sense he'd have seen it plain as day. But even a normal would know star systems off the main galactic swirl were bound to be troublesome.

The *Gravedigger* shuddered from the jump, right into a cloud of rocks. Klaxons blared, the bridge lighting turning an urgent, angry red. The bridge holo stuttered, a wireframe of the corvette appearing in lines of orange light. Angry red highlighted the bottom deck. A chunk of the starship labeled *SHIPS STORES* was gone, now mere fragments on the drift. Chad tightened his straps, and ran a hand through his hair. "I meant to do that."

Saveria said nothing.

Chad worked his console. Shaking off Endless fugue was second nature to him. Outside, the expected yellow subgiant star Viukde glowered from a heady distance. The bridge holo updated with system telemetry. Viukde Alpha and Beta were lifeless rocks. Gamma sat the expected 2.65AU from the star. The super-important thing was Viukde Delta was missing.

Another rock hit the hull, midships, directly on a particle beam mount. A tremble tickled his hands through the console as something in the belly of the *Gravedigger* detonated. Chad glared at the holo, expecting sense, or at least workable data. *Planets do not disappear.* It looked like Viukde Delta was no longer a planet, but rather a spectacular asteroid field. The hard black was alive with tumbled hunks of rock. The *Gravedigger's* RADAR and LIDAR painted the void, mapped space, and showed a gazillion rocks in their vicinity. Velocities appeared next to the thousands of pinpricks of light on the holo.

Chad tapped his console. *We've got to get out of this cloud of hell.* The thrum of PDCs shedding tungsten into the hard black vibrated through the decking. He gave Saveria a glance, expecting concern, fear, or confusion. She remained a blank slate. He couldn't tell if she prayed for deliverance or destruction. Or if she remembered how to pray.

The captain's console chimed. The battle computer spied a mini-jump through the asteroid field. The holo churned with warnings. Gravitational interference could destroy the Endless drives. They could impact rocks the ship hadn't mapped, birthing a new sun's worth of energy as they hit at FTL speed. Chad spared another look at Saveria. Neither trusting nor anxious. Empty. *You've got to get her out. You've got to give her the chance.*

He slammed his hand down on the Endless controls.

Ahead, an eternity of faith. Behind, broken trust and promises. A vacant shell traveled at his side. Behind, he'd left the one love the universe gave him. Ahead, death and pain awaited. Impossible, unbelievable acceleration. He couldn't feel it. He was it. He was everything. He was the universe.

Stars stretched, making streaks of light past the bridge windows. They jumped.

STARS SHUDDERED, taking a breath. Smoke drifted on air cycler eddies. It was a promising sign, because they still had air enough to hear, and he still had senses and a mind. They hadn't hit anything at FTL.

Viukde Gamma hung in blue-but-mostly-green calm above and to the left of the bridge. An asteroid, not Ezeroc megaroid-sized, lurked above the planet. It was probably the equivalent of one of their corvettes, an even match for a fully-crewed *Gravedigger*.

"Oh, come *on*." Chad tapped nervous fingers on his console. "Do these fuckers not have a home of their own?"

Saveria turned her gaze from him, eying the Ezeroc ship. He didn't take it personally. If anything, this was a great success. She hadn't looked with that much interest at anything, even his excellent cooking, in the three weeks she'd been awake.

The bridge holo cleared. *ENEMY ORDNANCE INBOUND.* The Ezeroc ship fired a string of rocks at them. Chad sneered, tapped on his console, and told the *Gravedigger* to light 'em up with a particle cannon. Ezeroc threw rocks fast enough, but it was a lazy tumble through the dark compared to near-C of human weapons.

Nothing happened for a moment, then the holo updated. *SYSTEMS DAMAGED. PARTICLE CANNON UNAVAILABLE.* "Oh, *come on*," he hissed. "This isn't fair!" Right about now, he could use an Engineer or two. A couple of people to crawl about the hull, righting wrongs. That made him thing of Hope, which made him think of Saveria, and he clamped his mouth shut with a snap.

Okay, so you don't have a particle cannon. While he thought about options, he told the battle computer to take evasive maneuvers. The rumble of thrust shook the hull, pressing a firm hand on his chest. He sank onto his acceleration couch. *How about a nice bout of railgun fire?* He checked the systems. Sure enough, railguns were ready and willing. He flicked a switch, tapped a few commands, and hit the fire controls.

The railgun mounted on the front of the *Gravedigger* swung about and lined up the Ezeroc craft. Brilliant white stabbed the night, the roar of the gun shaking the deck. It fired fifteen more times. Chad watched the weapon unload on the enemy while the bridge windows auto-tinted the glare to non-painful levels. The firing solution was standard buckshot spread, giving a small chance of hitting a ship even if they initiated evasive maneuvers.

He turned the *Gravedigger* about, and moved to engage the Ezeroc, because Chad wasn't running. Although he had a slim physique, he *hated* cardio. Didn't mind dancing, though.

The holo updated, noting a starship transponder signal on the planet below. He considered it. Normally there would be tens or hundreds. One was bad, because it suggested the Ezeroc were using this planet as a *sashimi* bar, but good because there'd be another hull. He opened the comm. "This is *Gravedigger* actual to the starship," he checked the transponder, "*Ardent Fury*. Nice name, by the way. We are an Empire Navy vessel under fire from an Ezeroc ship. Please send any and all aid." He gave it a couple seconds. Chad double-checked their distance from Viukde Gamma, noting four hundred thousand klicks and change. *Call it three seconds there and back, ten seconds for a half-way competent comm officer to push a button...* At twenty seconds, he knew he wasn't getting an assist.

A railgun round impacted the Ezeroc starship, which surprised Chad almost as much as he figured it surprised the Ezeroc. They hadn't moved out of the way at all. He eyed his wrist. Chad wore no anti-roach bracelet; he had the skills to protect his own mind. He hadn't felt them probing at him, mental claws sliding against his thoughts.

They weren't reading his mind. They didn't know the *Gravedigger* fired. "It's Christmas," he breathed. He pushed the *Gravedigger* harder, the ship roaring toward the Ezeroc. He told the battle computer to keep firing until there was nothing but stray rock out there.

The Ezeroc, for their part no fools, increased their rate of fire. The *Gravedigger* applied lateral thrust, easing out of the way of inbound ordnance, right to the point where the bridge lights failed. Darkness fell, the holo dark. Chad's console died. The lambent orb of the system's star set around Viukde Gamma's horizon. Gloom shrouded Saveria. He could only see the glint of her eyes as weight-lessness took him.

They were adrift, with an inbound salvo of Ezeroc munitions. He spun to Saveria. "Get in the pod." She stared back, unmoving. "No, seriously. I love the mime routine, but it's time for you to wake up and get in the escape pod." Chad nodded to the escape pod annex off the bridge. "We're going to die, but our deaths could be delayed by at least minutes if we eject. And why the hell is there no emergency lighting?"

The glint of her eyes moved left to right and back again as she shook her head. *Well, hell. That's an unexpected level of conscious-ness she hasn't shown in a while. It's a shame she's chosen to manifest independent thought as 'ornery rebellion' right as we're about to die.* Chad unclasped the buckles on his harness, slipping free. A quick tap on the console mounted in his ship suit's sleeve and his boots clunked to the deck as their magnets held him fast. He clanked aft, making his way to a small diagnostic panel. The main difference between this panel and the rest on the bridge was this one still glowed with power.

He cast a quick glance over his shoulder at the view through the windows, then got to work. The panel showed power out to the bridge and major systems. The drives hit emergency shutdown once bridge control vanished. It *should* be a simple matter of rerouting power through the junction nexus down the starboard side of the hull. *Who needs Engineers, anyway?* He tapped the console, telling the system to get on with it.

The bridge lamps came back on for a second, then the ship shook as an explosion tore the starboard side of the *Gravedigger* apart. The shriek of tortured metal and gasp of atmospheric decompression was unmistakable, even though the blow-out was a deck down. He glanced at Saveria. "It's not my fault."

She said nothing but tightened the straps of her harness. Chad ran a hand through his hair, feeling his headache peaking as he glared at the readout. *Focus.* The power relays starboard were gone, but he could do a secondary route back to port, and ... *viola.* The bridge lights came back on, as the holo stage bloomed to life. Gravity clutched at him as errors swarmed the holo. *IMPACT IMMINENT BRACE BRACE BRACE.*

The ship shuddered as rocks cored the hull. Chad stumbled, magboots clanking, making his way back to his chair. He fell into it as a shower of sparks flared from a tactical console. He brought up system telemetry, looking for a way out. The *Gravedigger* watched the starry night, noting another Ezeroc craft joined the first. It was smaller and moving to intercept.

He eyed the planet. It eyed him right back. The *Gravedigger's* main drive shuddered, coughed, and fell quiet. Chad stared *hard* at his console. "Don't worry. The drive will come back on, because otherwise we're going to die."

He didn't expect a reply, but her voice raspy and rusty with disuse, Saveria said, "Maybe we deserve to."

The drive rumbled to life, saving him from an answer. The *Gravedigger* lunged for the planet. He worked his console. They had no flight control. They were destined to impact the ground, no question about it. The smaller Ezeroc craft followed in their wake.

The problem with this particular Navy corvette is it's not atmosphere capable. If the *Gravedigger* entered honest, air-filled skies, she wasn't coming back out again.

Chad worked for a spell trying to get the ship to turn, but he couldn't get control. The drive was on burn, the ship digging her own grave. The bridge holo warned ABORT ATMOSPHERIC ENTRY ABORT. To the side of the main fusillade of errors, he noted, PARTICLE CANNON CONTROL: RESTORED.

He leaned forward, rubbed his eyes, and double-checked. Despite his headache, today wasn't a total loss. They'd take a few roaches down with them. He asked for a firing solution on the Ezeroc ships following them into the planet's gravity well. The *Gravedigger*, no stranger to fisticuffs, obliged. As the tinge of re-entry fire licked the hull, the particle cannons spoke into the night.

Chad got out of his chair, steadying himself as he charted a course toward Saveria. He made it to her acceleration couch as the ship shuddered, metal crying as atmosphere flensed her hull. "We've got to go."

Saveria nodded. He helped her with her harness, taking her hand as they made their way to the escape pod annex. The ship shuddered, rolling like a dying whale as they burned toward Viukde Gamma. The escape pod annex was a short, stubby corridor. Two doors aside, one at the end. Five pods, enough for a full bridge crew. More than enough for the two of them. He opened a door, pushing Saveria into it. "My luck's terrible. Better if you go your own way from here. If I make it, I'll find you."

She shook her head, pulling him after. The pod was big enough for four, but she clung to him anyway. Chad sagged, then grabbed a handhold against the wall. He put a hand on the back of her head as she trembled in primal human fear. He wondered what it would be like to have only half a mind as the fire of assured destruction ate the hull of a starship you last crewed as a pirate. "I'm sorry."

She pushed him into a harness. He helped her with her straps, nodded once, and yanked the launch handle. The pod shuddered as the *Gravedigger* spat them into the stormy night sky of a strange world. The thruster on the pod roared, and the walls shook as they rattled toward the surface.

It wasn't the ground Chad watched as they fell. He looked up through a viewport at the *Gravedigger*, firing at the Ezeroc craft. He told himself he watched to make sure the Ezeroc didn't follow the escape pod. His belly felt hollow, his heart empty as the *Gravedigger* died for their sins.

Viukde Gamma welcomed them with open arms.

TWO

Saveria woke to the gentle hum of the escape pod. Warm, yellow-white light draped the interior of the cabin. She lay on her acceleration couch, facing up. Her view of the outside world was limited to the aperture provided by the pod's eight top windows. Half were behind her, but the other half showed green leaves, dappled with light.

It's called daylight.

Her fingers found the clasps holding her in place. She freed them with a snap of fabric and clatter of metal. Her arm knocked against the acceleration couch beside her. Laying on the couch was a man. Lean, fit-looking, but he wasn't familiar to her. Should she know him? They must have spoken to each other before getting in the escape pod.

Saveria rubbed her arms, the crinkle of her ship suit nudging aside the hush of the air cyclers for a moment. *I don't know who that is. I don't know where I am.*

Was she a prisoner? She didn't have a weapon, but her hands weren't bound. A passenger, perhaps? There must have been an accident. Starships rarely died in the night, but spacers knew how to get into a ship suit fast as thought.

Am I a spacer?

The cant of the escape pod meant she needed to walk up a small slope to get to the hatch. Saveria scrambled for it, hand on the release lever. Outside showed her a glen, with trees and sun. No one waited. She cranked the lever, the explosive bolts *thunk-thunk-thunk-thunking* before the hatch blew, spinning across the clearing.

She clambered free, breathing air clean and sweet. She turned a slow circle, boots whispering through dew-wet grass. The escape pod had *GRAVEDIGGER* emblazoned on the side. It sat in a small circle of scorched earth where the braking thruster slowed their descent. The trees above were snapped, dropped branches scattered about it. The pod itself looked undamaged.

Saveria ran her fingers over the *GRAVEDIGGER* letters. *I know this name, don't I?* Her head felt empty. Soft, like a sponge waiting for moisture. She ran a hand through her hair, pulling strands away. It lay, brown and straight, across the palm of her glove. It wasn't pink.

She should be holding pink hair. Not brown. Saveria shouldn't have hair at all. Her head was burnished gold metal. It wasn't soft, pliable meat.

I don't know who I am.

An insect buzzed past her head, startling her. Saveria followed it, uncertain. A bird chirped. She spied it through the trees, singing. It was olive green. *Anthornis melanura* without a doubt. Saveria held a hand out, but the bird flew away. She drifted after it. It sounded sweet, like tiny bells, and full of joy.

Another bird swooped low. She didn't know what it was. It snatched an insect from the air. She almost couldn't make out what happened. Saveria rubbed her eyes. Where they malfunctioning? The refresh rate felt low.

I don't have a refresh rate.

A crack drew her attention. She spotted a young man watching her through the trees. He was as frozen as her. He was young, but his face was careworn. Scarring marked the line of his jaw. Bright green eyes watched her from a face darkened by days in the sun. He didn't wear a ship suit like her. His jacket was brown leather. He carried a wooden club, but absently, like someone asked him to hang on to it for a spell.

The moment between them held. Did she know him? Was there another escape pod nearby? The man looked to his club, then back to her. He took a step closer. Saveria took a step back, then held herself firm. "Hello. I think my spaceship crashed." Saveria felt like she should have a baseball cap, something to pull lower, to hide her face from what she'd done.

What did I do?

The man turned, hurrying off. Saveria watched him for a moment, then followed. "Wait! I could use your help. There's a..." A what? Was her companion in the pod a friend or enemy? "Another passenger. Wait!" Her lips felt like weak rubber, slow at speaking. Saveria tried to match the man's pace, but her legs lumbered beneath her. She stumbled, catching her balance against a tree. Her gloved fingers rasped against the bark.

Why is my hair not pink?

She pushed off from the tree, hurrying through the forest. It felt alive, an entire organism, not a collection of individual ones. Saveria thought she should be able to sense it, right on the inside. Not with sensors, but something ... *else*. But she couldn't hear anything aside from the crashing ahead as the man tried to get away. Saveria was sure she should be able to ... *touch* it.

With my heart.

She slowed, pausing for breath. She was hot. Saveria peeled the front of the ship suit open. Underneath she wore a sheer bodysuit. *GRAVEDIGGER* was emblazoned above her left breast. She couldn't very well take the ship suit off here. She had boots, but no shoes. She was alone in a forest.

Why am I wearing pirate colors?

The crunch of feet and hurried breathing made Saveria look up.

The young man returned. She met his eyes. *Not so alone after all.* He held his club like he was terrified of her. "You've got to come with me."

Saveria nodded. "I do. I have a," she mentally groped for the right word, "friend who needs help."

"No." He shook his head. "You're for the Altar."

"The what?" He lunged at her, swinging his club like a bat. She ducked underneath it, grabbed the handle, and twisted. He spun through the air, wrist acting like a pivot, and crashed into the ground. Saveria held the club before her eyes while he scrambled back like a crab. It was crude, perhaps machined on a lathe rather than made in a fabricator. She held it out to him. "You dropped this."

He got to his feet, the movement uncertain, like she was a scorpion waiting to strike. Saveria nodded, encouraging, and let him snatch the club. "How did you do that?" He rubbed his wrist.

Krav maga / kendo / karate / judo / jiu jitsu... Saveria sifted through until she worked out what she'd done. "*Aikido.*" Someone taught her *aikido.* He'd touched her inside and given her the gift of knowledge.

"Is that how you'll kill the gods?" He tried for a sneer, but it wouldn't stick.

She watched him for a few moments. "Do you know my name?"

He blinked, mouth slack, then shook his head. "I don't know you at all."

"Neither do I." Saveria looked back the way she'd come. "I have to go."

"Wait." He stepped closer, stopping after a couple of paces. Not wanting to meet *aikido* again, or something else? "I'm Forrest Blake."

She wanted to give him something, but her head was empty. Saveria ran a hand inside her ship suit. Her fingers found the slight rasp of the bodysuit's lettering. "Call me Gravedigger."

"That's your name?"

Saveria frowned. Memories drifted, shapeless. "It's what I am."

A shout rose from where she'd come from. She spun, but Forrest's hand on her arm stopped her. Saveria cycled through a hundred ways to break the brittle parts of his meat before she realized it was concern, not anger, in his eyes. "They'll kill you."

"You can't kill someone who's already dead." Saveria shook herself free, running back through the forest. Leaves and branches slapped her as she ran. She made the small glen. It was as she'd left it, except for one tiny detail.

The escape pod was empty.

The forest loam was churned as if by many feet. They'd blazed a path through the trees. She might catch them if she hurried. Saveria almost ran off, then held herself still. She returned to the escape pod, jimmying the emergency supplies cabinet. Inside was water, ration bars, a small blaster, and good Empire coin. The blaster's battery was dead, but the food and water were good anywhere.

She let coins tinkle to the floor of the escape pod. She needed to know where she was, and who her companion was to her, and *who she was*. Saveria put a hand to her head. It felt lopsided, like it had metal inside, a tiny vault holding her memories close.

Stepping from the escape pod, she looked at the sky, breathed the air, then squared her shoulders. She touched her lips with curious fingers. Someone else touched her like that not long ago. "Where has my Hope gone?"

Aside from the tinkle of the bellbirds, the forest didn't answer. She'd have to get her answers another way.

AFTER A HUNDRED METERS RUNNING, Saveria slowed. Her breath rasped in her throat. She couldn't remember anything earlier than waking in the escape pod, but her body felt weak. Like it hadn't been *used*, forgotten like an old shirt in the bottom of her ship's locker.

Running longer was out of the question. She opened a ration bar, chewing. The chewing action reminded her of—

Mandibles, tearing flesh. Sharp, stabbing limbs, piercing flesh. A chitinous saw, grinding against her skull.

She dropped the ration bar to the forest floor, backing away. Her hands shook. The flash she'd seen felt like prophecy, but she knew it was a memory. She'd been somewhere dark, with living things crawling beneath her skin. For all the forest was warm and light, she felt cold, goosebumps prickling her skin.

"Breathe. Just ... *breathe.*" She didn't know why she said it, or who she'd learned it from. It felt like a trick, something to calm the shaking of a soul too worn to take much more.

The ration bar waited on the ground. She picked it up, brushing dirt away. The crinkle of the wrapper under her fingertips felt familiar and comfortable, like a toy you'd sleep with if monsters threatened from the closet.

This was made by my people. We've crossed the stars. She visored her eyes with a hand. The sun had risen higher, blotting out any hint of space, but she knew it was there. The vast universe waited above. She looked at the ration bar. *We crossed the stars until we met the enemy.*

She took a bite, chewing slowly. She wanted the memory of the dark to return, so she could *see* who the enemy was. Nothing happened. The sun shone on, unconcerned. A gentle breeze stirred her not-pink hair, whispering at the back of her neck. Her heart calmed.

Where am I?

Another bellbird sang to her. She offered it a lopsided smile. "Viukde is a yellow subgiant, radius two point seven eight of Sol's. The solar mass is one point three seven of Earth's star. Temperature..." She closed her eyes. *Remember. Remember this* one *thing.* "Four thousand seven hundred Kelvin. It shines eight point three seven times as bright as Sol. Viukde Gamma is the only terrestrial planet, and the third in the system. It has one point one four Earth gravities."

The bellbird cocked its head, blinked, and flew off. *Everyone's a critic.* Saveria touched her cheek, then ran her fingers to her forehead. Someone else touched her that way with trembling fingers not long ago. Why couldn't she remember?

Saveria knew 1.14G might be why her legs felt clumsier, but her heart said it was something else. Part of her had never used these legs before.

She finished her ration bar, then sipped water. It was warm and tasted like ship's stores. She wanted it to be the clean cool of a running stream but didn't know if she'd ever seen a river in her life.

Spacers don't have streams.

She squared her shoulders, turning to follow the tracks once more. The route through the trees was easy to follow. It wasn't a natural path; tools had been used to hack away the undergrowth. She fingered a broken branch. *A machete?* She found no dropped clues, no handy markers to show who she followed, or if they were friend or foe.

After an hour's walk, she broke from the tree line into a field. Grass grew to her waist, small insects buzzing through the air. The sun felt hotter here. She tugged her arms free of the top half of her ship suit, tying the sleeves about her hips. Sweat marked her body-suit, making it stick to her back. It should feel bad, but she felt alive. Glad to be using her body after weeks of torpor.

You've been asleep for three weeks.

Sleeping, or near enough. She wiped moisture from her brow, then set off through the field. Like the forest, the trail was easy enough to follow here, flattened grasses drawing a line south. She stopped, eying the sun. *Is it south? Does Viukde rise in the east and set in the west on this world?* Saveria allowed herself a wry smile. It didn't matter. 'South' was good enough.

It's close enough for government work.

Who said that? She couldn't remember but knew she'd heard it from a friend.

Once through the field, her magboots crunched on gravel and packed dirt. Dust rose in her wake, drifting on warm air. The dirt looked like an amateur-hour road, rutted in places by what must be thin wheels. Saveria lost the trail here but saw a lazy wisp of smoke rising in the mid-morning light ahead. It was as good a marker as any to chart a course with.

The road wound through a cleft between two small hillocks. Saveria heard rustling from her right and craned her head to see. Above, a man stood framed by blue sky. She smiled. "Forrest Blake."

"Gravedigger." He nodded, sliding down the side of the slope. He stumbled to a halt in front of her. He carried a small bundle, which he offered to her. "Here."

She didn't take the bundle of what looked like rags. "What's that?"

"Clothes." His eyes trailed down her bodysuit, then looked away as if startled by what he saw. "Dressed as you are, they'll take you to Altar."

"Isn't that where you wanted to take me?" She put hands on her hips. "When you attacked me with a stick."

He bowed his head, cheeks flushing in shame. "Aye, that's the truth of it. Marla said we must, but..." He trailed off, like words were a precious resource and he had too few.

Saveria took the bundle of clothes. "Are you taking me to Altar? That doesn't sound," she groped for the right word, "fun."

"The other godkiller with you is already at the village. He'll be put on the Altar and made whole." Forrest risked another look at her, eyes wandering up to her face. "Your face is ... beautiful. I've never seen anything so perfect."

She parsed that a couple of times. "You think because I'm pretty, I shouldn't be laid on your Altar?"

"The Altar is for fixing flawed vessels." He crossed his arms as if cold, despite the warmth of the day. "I think you're already whole." This last was said so quietly she wasn't sure she heard right. Her hearing might be just another faulty system.

"You're helping me?" At his nod, Saveria snorted. "You attacked me."

"Marla said to." He nodded to the clothes. "Please."

Saveria shook the clothes free. Worn pants, perhaps a size too large. A leather jacket like Forrest's, with a slightly different cut. The interior wasn't smooth and clean like she was used to, the stitching rough as if a person made it, not a machine. Shoes tumbled free, simple moccasins that would be easier on her feet than magboots.

Saveria snapped open the clasps on her boots, pulling them free, then tugged her ship suit off. Forrest's eyes almost popped out of his skull before he spun on his heel, taking great interest in the smoke rising in the middle distance. She caught another flush to his cheeks and wondered what that was about. She kept her bodysuit and socks on, pulling the rougher clothes over the top. They felt heavier than her ship suit, but more comfortable for traipsing about uneven ground and non-air-conditioned environments.

She ran fingers through her not-pink hair, pulling it back from her face. "I'm ready."

Forrest turned to her, giving her a once-over, then a second and third once-over. "I'll take you to our village. We'll work something out. Stay with me. Don't talk to anyone." He headed off.

Saveria followed. The smoke in the distance resolved to a couple trails heading skyward. They rose from chimneys. Saveria knew such things were possible, but hadn't seen or heard of anything like it for her entire life. She knew this like she knew water was wet. It was a fundamental truth that endured more than the day she'd been awake, or the three weeks she'd sleep-walked aboard...

Where have I been?

They walked into the village. The verge wasn't clearly demarcated; buildings appeared as if sprouting from the earth singly, then in twos, and finally in clumps. The density increased until they walked among buildings. None were more than two stories tall. People watched them from doorways. Forrest put a hand on Saveria's elbow, pulling her along. They walked down a small alley, around a corner, and shored up beside a low-slung building. He nodded to double doors. "In here."

She put a hand on the wood, pushing the doors wide. Inside was a collection of wooden pens, some with livestock inside. She counted two horses and a cow. Saveria entered, looking at the roof. Light leaked in through small gaps and cracks, and dust hung in the air, making god rays.

Forrest waited at the door. "Stay out of sight. Stay *here*. You've got to remain hidden. Too many people saw you with me already."

She turned to face him. "These are your people?"

He nodded. "I will say you're a pilgrim, and that I sent you to further south." He looked at his feet. "It's a truth that will hold long enough."

"Long enough for what?"

Forrest shook his head. Saveria didn't know if he denied answering the question or had no good answer. He grabbed the doors, drawing them closed. She heard the rattle of wood on wood, and hurried to the doors, trying them. They shifted but wouldn't open. Forrest barred them from the outside.

Saveria looked about what must be a barn. She was a prisoner of a man who'd attacked her with a club, in a place she didn't know. She ran fingers under her borrowed jacket, feeling the lettering of her bodysuit.

At least she had a name. *Gravedigger.*

THREE

Chad didn't wake in the arms of a beautiful woman. He didn't open his eyes to the scent of fresh-baked bread and the delicious aroma of coffee. Chad's eyes fluttered open because the pain in his skull demanded attention, like he had Ezeroc larvae in there and they wanted *out*.

He groaned.

His lips were parched, and he couldn't move. He craned his neck. Straps crossed his body, tethering him to what felt like a bed of nails, but looked like a simple set of wooden boards. He tried for another groan, but it came out as a whimper. Resting his head for a spell, he risked a look around. The room was comfortable enough, if you were into wood decor. He could see a door off to his left. The room felt like five meters aside, which moved it from *cozy bedroom* to *functional lounge*. Maybe wherever 'here' was didn't have a permanent gaol, and thus he was in someone's rumpus.

Those fuckers would get a surprise when he found a blade.

His sword lay out of reach, leaning by the door. Resting on a small table next to it was his blaster. He risked reaching out with his mind to feel the weight of them, but he got nothing but another bolt of pain inside his skull. He panted, closing his eyes for a moment. When he found strength, he cracked 'em open again, continuing his land survey of the room. There was a table in the direction of his boots, adorned with a few knick-knacks which he ignored, and a comm unit which he didn't. The comm unit looked, as Kohl might say, *proper fucked*. The plastic housing was cracked, and the holo stage lay dark and empty.

Chad wondered why he couldn't use his gifts. His head hurt, but not like he'd knocked it in a crash. He figured that's what happened, on account of still wearing a ship suit but not being surrounded by an escape pod. He thought about that for a long time.

Remember your entrance to Viukde System. They'd come in hot and strong, like a good cuppa joe. Asteroids impacted the *Gravedigger*. Best guess had 'em as solar debris from a destroyed Viukde Delta. Were the rocks black? *Everything in space looks black.* But the Emperor's sword was black metal, bonded to tech to be an effective protector against espers. It still let an esper wielder use their own gifts. Was that what the tech did — guided a path through?

He didn't know. It didn't make sense. Hope managed to make bracelets so humans needn't fear the Ezeroc's mind control. She didn't have a stockpile of the black metal of the Emperor's sword. He'd have to speak with her about the specifics, perhaps when he returned from his vacation. *Let's say there's a system-wide ring of asteroid fuckery, suppressing your esper abilities.*

It felt better than the alternative, which was he was done. A normal. Good with a smile, passable with a blade, but without his gifts, worthless to the throne. He thought about Karkoski for a second. No *way* she'd bolt a used-up has-been to her career.

The door opened, and a woman entered. She looked worn like an old broom, but her eyes were clear and bright, like a hawk's. "You're awake."

"And you're observant." Chad nodded as best he could. "I seem to be tied down. Would you mind?"

She barked a laugh. "I don't think so. We held Vigil. You're for the Altar."

Chad heard the capitalization of *Vigil* and *Altar*, like they were holy words. "How about breakfast instead?"

She snorted. "So, this is how you came to kill our gods. With wit and charm." She closed the door behind her. "I should have expected it. The last came with fire. No reason godkillers should try the same trick twice."

He tried for a smile. It felt sickly and unwashed on his face, on account of the pain in his skull. "I'm not here to kill gods. I'm on vacation."

She sniffed. "I'll admit, you don't look like much of a godkiller."

"And you don't look like much of a sociopath, but here we are." Chad tugged his restraints. "I'm Chad."

"I don't care."

"No." Chad *tsk'd*. "This is where you tell me your name. Be nice to know who's planning my imminent demise."

She raised an eyebrow. "Fair enough, Chad. I'm Marla. Folk here reckon me the chief of this village."

"Makes sense. Sociopaths often rise to top management positions." Chad shifted, his left butt cheek going numb. "That comm unit work?"

"Nothing much works. It's how we like it. Simple life, with simple people." She turned, fingering the pommel of his sword, then picked up his blaster. "This is the weapon of a godkiller."

"It's a hand-me-down blaster I won in a game of cards." Chad wiggled his right hand. There was a tiny amount of give in his bindings that side. "I'm going to take a wild guess and assume you're in some way allied with the Ezeroc."

"The who?"

"Big insects. Can't miss 'em." Chad coughed. "If I was laying odds, I'd say they sanded the Republic off this rock aways back, keeping a bunch of inbreeds as livestock."

Marla drew the blaster, examined it, then pointed it at him. "What would happen if I shot you with this?"

"Not a lot, in the galactic sense." Chad tried for a shrug, but the bindings didn't make it easy. Hell, being *nonchalant* while tied to a slab was hard, but he did his best. "Shorter term, I'd say it's a blessing. My head hurts. It's a fresh hell, and I'm not ashamed to admit it."

"You're sick?" She took a step back.

Interesting. Not only are the Ezeroc farming people, but they're not performing good animal husbandry. You expect basic veterinary care in an operation like this. "Not with something you can catch. Pushed myself too hard, is all. Paid the price."

She grunted. "Won't matter soon. You're for the Altar." Marla tossed Chad's blaster to clatter on the little table, dropping the holster beside it. "Make peace in your own way. We'll set off when it's dark." She slipped out the door, pulling it closed behind her.

"So that's a 'no' on the coffee?" he called. No one answered him. *Maybe they don't have coffee here. That's as good a reason to die as any.*

THE ROOM GREW hot as morning walked toward midday. Chad heard a tiny scrape from his right, away from the door. He hadn't managed to get a hand free, but he worked with renewed vigor. If there was one thing the Ezeroc were good at, it was minting tiny roaches to crawl through small apertures to core out your brain.

Speaking of brains, his still hurt, but it was the only one he had. His right wrist felt slick, and he knew he'd chafed the skin to a bloody ruin. The pain gave him an alternative set of hurts to focus on aside from his head.

The scraping continued. It sounded like it was under the floor. Scraping turned to creaking, then with a *chunk-pop*, a floorboard clattered free. It was joined by another, then a third. A kid crawled through the gap. Leather jacket. Scarred face. Needy eyes. Chad disliked him immediately. He didn't need more waifs and strays.

The kid stood. Might be twenty on a good day, late twenties on a bad. He opened his mouth like he was about to say something, so Chad stepped into the silence. "Fuck off."

"What?"

"Fuck," Chad winced at a new lance of pain in his skull, "*off*."

"I'm here to rescue you."

"No, you're not." Chad sniffed. "You're here to get information from me."

"I'm ... how did you know?"

"I'm a spymaster. *The* spymaster, if we're trading truth." Chad stared at the ceiling. "Information's kind of my thing." *Or it was, before you cocked everything up.* "Oldest trick in the book. Break in, look like a friendly face, ply the prisoner for secrets, all using the kind of sob story a needy heart desires." He put a little squeak into his voice. "'Oh, Chad, you're brave and strong. If only I knew where your ship was, I could take you there.'" He glared at the kid. "About right?"

"No." The kid shook his head.

That surprised Chad, but he rallied. "Which part's wrong?"

"Most of it." The kid eyed the door like it was a fire hazard. "Do you know Gravedigger?"

"Course," said Chad. "She's my starship."

"No, the other one."

Chad ran that through his head a time or two more just to see if it made more sense on repeat. "There's only one *Gravedigger*. Or was. Gone now, like all the other good things in life. We crashed on your shitpile planet."

"We?"

Chad squinted. "See, this is how it goes. Get me to loosen up, and I spill the beans. Won't work, kid."

The kid gave a growl of frustration. "She's got honey-brown skin. Warm eyes. Face clear as the dawn on a spring morn. Stares at you like you're the only thing in the world."

"You describing a starship or a pinup model?"

"She said her name was Gravedigger."

Fancy that. "I think you've been hit on the head." Chad wriggled his shoulders. There was a little movement on the right side. "Let's say I know a ... *person* named Gravedigger. What's the deal?"

"She's for the Altar."

"I hear that a lot around here." Chad sighed. "You said you were here to rescue me."

"I lied," admitted the kid. "No way I can get you out. I barely managed to get in."

"Is there a point to this conversation?"

The kid looked around, a curious mix of desperate and anxious. "She can't go to Altar. She's not broken."

Chad laughed. It came from deep in his belly. The kid's wide-eyed look made him laugh harder. "She's the most broken thing there is."

He took a step closer. "Don't say that! How could you know?"

"Because I'm the one who broke her." Chad settled. "Well, let's call it a joint operation. It takes two to break the hardest metal."

"How do I help her?"

"Aside from helping me first?" At the kid's blink, Chad shook his head, then winced. "Stay out of her way. When she remembers who she *really* is, there'll be a reckoning." *And I figured I've earned my part of that.*

CHAD HAD questions and found it difficult to answer any of them tied to a table.

First on his mental list, which he'd had time to re-order at least twenty times, was: *what happened to the* Ardent Fury? Her transponder was still live, a beacon that guided them in. The *Gravedigger* was headed in that general direction as she carved a trail of burning atmosphere toward the dirt. This question felt more important than the rest, because it offered a tantalizing hint at a future off this shitty rock.

Next up was the tricky question of: *where are the Ezeroc?* He'd seen 'em coming down after the *Gravedigger*, but they didn't crawl over this village in the ways he expected. He'd made this question number one on the list a few times but kept demoting it because he had a hunch on the answer. The best explanation his very sore head provided was, *you're in the cattle farm. If a rustler adds two cows to your herd, you don't worry about it.* It's not like Ezeroc ranchers would rumble down here, checking his brands. An alternative answer was: the *Gravedigger* busted their hulls on the way down. It was something to hope for, but not plan on. That way lay madness.

A somewhat guilty third on the list was, *where is Saveria?* If he was a better man, he'd have put this at number one, but he wasn't even close to good. He was good at being bad. Chad was an expert at keeping the dirty secrets of the throne. He didn't make a lot of friends, which was one of the reasons he was lucky to be so handsome. Good looks took you a long distance on the drift.

Sidling next to this was, *who's the damn kid?* He had the angsty look of youth everywhere. Dispossessed, and bound to get underfoot at a moment's notice. He clearly had a thing for Saveria, but Chad had no idea why she named herself after their dead starship. The poor woman had died enough times already. Chad didn't have the heart to tell the kid he didn't stand a chance, on account of batting for the wrong team. Besides, letting out intel like that could torch a valuable ally.

Nearing the bottom was, *what's Marla's game, what's a Vigil, and where's the Altar?* These felt like questions that would answer themselves if Chad let the sands flow through the hourglass long enough.

Perhaps last on the list was, *when will I get my gifts back?* Chad felt like it deserved attention, due to its relative importance in keeping him alive, but the reality was he knew the answer. It was *never,* with a shadow of *and that's assuming hell's already frozen over.*

The wooden room he was in creaked as the sun moved overhead, the timbers shifting in the heat. The kid was long gone, the floor-boards back in place. He'd no doubt be off trying to work out how to get Saveria's comm codes, or whatever the youth called it these days. *Codes would be a worthy pursuit if this mudball had a comm network.* If the *Ardent Fury's* comm systems worked, there might be a chance, but Chad wasn't used to getting lucky. That was the Emperor's whole shtick.

The day drifted toward late afternoon, then early evening. The door opened again, Marla once again leading the charge. With her came two enormous men, sizable enough to make Chad wonder if they'd manage to clone October Kohl. Thinking about Kohl almost made him weep with nostalgia, because he could use a friendly murderer about now. Chad offered a nod to Marla. "Evenin'."

"You're chipper for a man going to his doom." She waved the thugs forward. Chad checked out the detailing. One was bald, head shiny with oil or sweat, but he sported a beard a man could take pride in, his bare chest both furry and packed with muscle. A truncheon hung from his belt and had the look of a device that saw frequent use. The leather handle was worn, the wood pitted and stained. Chad had to admit: the guy represented Team Ginger better than most.

His companion had a shock of unruly black hair, no beard, and shoulders wide enough for two normal humans. He had the common decency to wear a shirt but hadn't been polite enough to leave his weapons at home. The wooden handle of a club poked over his shoulder, and a supplementary billy dangled from his hip.

They moved to either side of Chad. Baldy leaned close. "We gonna have a problem?"

"That depends if you need advice on a good barber. I'm not from around here." Chad glanced at Mop Top. "Maybe you can help. If I wanted a good shave—"

He choked as Baldy's meaty hand found his throat. The giant squeezed for emphasis. "I ask again, are we going to have an issue?" Chad shook his head as best he could. Baldy let him go. "Good." He nodded to Mop Top. They unbound Chad from the table, helped him upright, and set him on his feet.

Chad fell to the ground. His legs were asleep, and the slightly higher than normal gravity didn't help. He held a hand up. "I'm good. I just need a moment."

Baldy grabbed his raised hand, hauling him upright. "I thought we weren't going to have a problem."

"In fairness, I've been strapped to a table all day. I'm not feeling my best." Chad tried for a smile and found no takers. He held his other hand out. "After you."

Marla snorted, grabbed Chad's weapons, and led the way outside. Chad followed, propelled by Mop Top's hand between his shoulders. He staggered outside, squinting at the wan light provided by the setting sun. The building he'd come from was a wooden building with no distinguishing features other than a badly-finished porch. He found himself in an open area that had aspirations on being a town square. A raised platform that didn't look compliant with any building code you'd care to mention stood in the center. Around the square stood a collection of statues, unmistakably Ezeroc in various poses of fighting, stabbing, and killing. A shadowing of humanity, peppered like badly trimmed stubble, held a loose circle at the perimeter. Chad expected haunted eyes and malnourished faces, but most looked happy and healthy. Expectant, even.

Next to the platform sat a rickety cart, with a pair of oxen at the head. Chad turned a slow circle, letting out a whistle. "This is new."

Marla, already half-way to the cart, turned back to him. "Come on. We're wasting time."

Chad held up a hand. Mop Top gave him another shove, causing him to stumble. Chad gave the man a glare, which Mop Top returned tenfold. He sighed. "Hold up, sport." He turned to Marla. "I'm not arguing any particular part. I guess I'd like to know which specific gallows you have in mind." Chad jerked a thumb at a nearby statue. "Gods?"

She nodded, holding up his blaster. "Godkiller."

Chad wobbled his hand back and forth in a *maybe* gesture. "Eh. It's a good enough piece in a jam, but..." He glanced at the Ezeroc statue again. It was remarkably lifelike. He did another slow circle, backing away from the menace presented by Mop Top and Baldy. He pointed at the billy at Mop Top's hip. "Non-lethal weapons. You want me to go to them," he jabbed a finger at the statues, "alive."

Marla nodded. "You're broken. You need to go to Altar."

"You also have non-lethal weapons because your gods don't like threats." He took a step toward Baldy. "What do you weigh? One forty kilos without your shirt? You must be on the protein." Quick as you please, he lifted Baldy's truncheon with nimble fingers, sidestepping the expected lunge. He tapped the big man on the rump with the truncheon as he passed.

The thug stumbled, righted himself, and spun, hands outreached. Chad waggled the truncheon. "Now, now. Let's not get off on the wrong foot." Mop Top made a play behind him. He ducked under the man's swing with his bat, smashing the truncheon into his shins. The giant tumbled with a howl. Chad straightened, facing Marla. "Hey."

She tipped her head in acknowledgement. "You know there's no escape. This planet's landlocked, Chad." She spread her hands, shrugged, and offered him a knowing look that said, *there should be no lies between us.* "There's only the Altar." Baldy and Mop Top righted themselves, taking a few steps back to stand between Chad and Marla.

He gave the truncheon a lazy twirl. "I'll figure something out."

She nodded, like they were still swapping truths. "Perhaps I can find something to motivate you." She put her fingers to her lips, blowing a shrill whistle. A commotion started at the edge of the square, the townsfolk parting. Two more giants came forth, carrying a struggling youth between them. It was the kid.

Chad laughed. "I feel we need to have us an honest conversation. That asshole," he stabbed his truncheon toward the kid, "is working for you. If you figure on using him for an extortion trick, you've got the wrong ammunition in the gun. Simple as that." He raised an eyebrow in Marla's direction. She waited him out. "See, where I've come from, I've done worse things than torture kids. I keep the secrets of the Empire, but worse, I stop those who'd speak against the throne."

Marla nodded. "Speaking false against your lord's a sin, I'll admit."

"I'm not much concerned with the truth of it. They stand against me and mine, I've got no sympathy." Chad glanced at the youth, who was doing a decent job of struggling, but to little avail. "Where *do* you get such large men?"

The village chief settled Chad's sword in the back of the cart, then pointed the blaster at him. "Convince you with this?"

"You don't want me dead."

"I don't mind if you're hurt most of the way there." She gave a lopsided shrug, then pulled the trigger. Nothing happened.

Chad grinned. "Biolocks. Karkoski's idea. Seemed a devilishly tricky thing to implement, but I figure it's working out."

Marla tossed the weapon to the dirt. "Who is Gravedigger?"

That gave Chad pause. "Starship, of no particular import."

She shook her head, pointing at the kid without looking. "Forrest knows a woman using that name. He knows where she is and what she looks like."

Chad squinted. "That's how it is, is it?"

Marla nodded. "That's how it is."

Chad rolled his shoulders, widened his stance, and raised the truncheon. "Come get some." Marla looked shocked for about two seconds, which was how long it took for Chad to cock his arm back, throwing the truncheon between Baldy and Mop Top. It hit her in the forehead, at which point she dropped to the dirt beside his blaster.

Chad knew *people*. He knew the color of their thoughts, the weight of their regard, and how they worked at an almost atomic level. The kid, Forrest, might know where Saveria was, and what she looked like, but he wouldn't give up his One True Love™ without a fight. Which meant Marla was an esper, and if she wasn't, someone nearby was. Taking her out before she could issue commands was priority one.

Baldy and Mop Top roared in unison and charged. The two holding the kid moved to help, at which point the kid got an arm free, swung about, and kicked one of his tormentors in the groin before tear-assing away. The one who'd been kicked in the groin looked like he wanted to give chase but couldn't find the will to live. Chad sympathized, because no way a brutal strike like that went unanswered.

After that he had no more time to consider Forrest or his future fate, because Baldy got to him. Chad ducked a swing, stabbing two fingers into his opponent's eyes. Baldy howled, which distracted Chad enough for him to take an eye-watering gut punch from Mop Top. The asshole put hip into it and everything. The blow lifted Chad off his feet, pushed all the air out of him, and dropped him to the dirt.

Mop Top curled his fingers into Chad's hair, hauling him up. Chad took a leaf from Forrest's tree, swinging a booted foot into Mop Top's groin. The man froze, eyes wide, because Chad kicked him hard enough to rupture his descendant's testicles.

Breathe. Just ... breathe. Chad staggered around Mop Top, making for his fallen blaster. He made it close enough to taste before a massive weight struck him from the side. He tumbled to the ground in some surprise. The kid's remaining assailant reached him with an epic-level tackle. Chad hit the ground, sliding for a spell. The few spoonfuls of air he'd managed to suck in went right back out.

His attacker straddled Chad in what he thought was a power position, laying into Chad with fists. Chad, no stranger to ground fighting, brought his legs around in closed guard, protecting his head with his hands, then grabbed the asshole's collar in what his *jiu jitsu sensei* would have called a textbook collar choke. Chad pushed his elbow toward the sky, knocking his opponent unconscious in no time flat.

Chad wriggled free in time to see Baldy standing between Chad and his blaster, holding Chad's sword. Worse, Baldy was *close*, already extending the rapier in a crude but admittedly effective thrust. Chad squirreled left, but not quite fast enough. The blade found a home in the meat of his side. Chad hollered, chopped Baldy in the throat with a less-textbook *shutō* knife-hand strike. Baldy staggered, tugging the blade free as he went, causing Chad to scream.

He stumbled, leaking red in wet splatters on the thirsty dirt. He fell, and in a stroke of luck, landed by his blaster. Chad snarled, raising his weapon. He pulled the trigger, turning Baldy into burning pieces of man as blue-white plasma *fzzzt-cracked*. Lurching to his feet, Chad wobbled around until he faced Mop Top, who held his groin for all the good it'd do. He was framed by Chad's makeshift jail.

The big man tried for anger but held nothing but fear. "I'll see you in hell."

"Tell them who sent you." Chad shot him too, spraying the badly-made porch with burning meat. As an afterthought, he shot the choked-out man on the ground, blasting pieces of body and clods of dirt to trail smoke through the air.

He clutched his hand to his side. A *lot* of red came through his fingers. Find a bandage, or find Saveria? There was only one option. Chad fetched his sword, belting his scabbard on, and holstering his blaster. It hurt, but that was life. If you wanted to keep on living, you had to learn not to mind the pain.

He stumbled in the direction Forrest ran, holding a hand to his leaking side. If he'd been in better shape, he might have wondered where Marla got to.

FOUR

Forrest sprinted through the streets of a town he knew like the dirt on his soul. Faces watched, intent, hungry, but staying out of his way. If anything, they were distancing themselves. Shutters slammed closed. Doors shut.

He might have known the town well, but he didn't understand it anymore. Breath rasping in his chest, feet skidding on loose dirt, it was an uncomfortable realization. Forrest felt like his mind was clear for the first time. He'd stood at Vigil with the rest, then set out to hunt the godkillers. The Altar wouldn't be denied.

Once he saw Gravedigger, his face heated. Feelings pushed aside *duty*. It wasn't that she was perfect. She was *different*. He tried to help her.

Maybe you shouldn't have locked her up.

They'd caught him as he exited the temporary jail holding the other godkiller. Forrest figured it for a mercy when Marla's hard eyes settled on him. The village chief stroked his scarred jaw as two of her best enforcers held him steady. When she'd stared at him, Forrest felt like she looked *into* him. At his soul, his wants, and the dark desires that distracted him from the duties of Vigil and the needs of the Altar.

So, he'd hidden a tack in his pocket. When he'd pressed the short spike of metal into his side, Forrest felt the pain and truth of his body. Marla hadn't got what she'd wanted. Just stray scraps. It'd been enough for them to hold him ready for the Altar. Forrest needed mending. He felt it himself. Didn't he?

But... I don't want to be fixed.

Forrest ran. Feet pounding on familiar-yet-strange streets, running away from friends-but-hunters. He skidded around a corner, barging past a couple out for an evening stroll. Forrest almost missed the swing of a pole from a doorway, ducking low at the last second. He felt the *whoosh* of air as it passed where his head was a moment before. He kept on, heart pounding, mouth tasting of dirt, the air behind him full of hate.

Blue-white light backscattered against the buildings. It came from the square, accompanied by a *fzzzt-crack* of sound. Forrest spared a glance back. The shadows thrown by the light made it look like the square birthed lightning. The godkillers had fearsome weapons. They weren't people. Not like Forrest, or even Marla. They were perfect, beautiful, and deadly.

What did the prisoner say? *She's the most broken thing there is.* Gravedigger wasn't *right*, and not just because she took his weapon and purpose both without really paying attention. Gravedigger's eyes looked through him, just like Marla's, but instead of the iron will of a ruler, he saw confusion. It was as if she didn't know which gods she'd come to kill.

A man lunged for him from an alley. Forrest skidded sideways, almost lost his footing, and pressed on. *Focus on getting her away from here. That's all that matters.* A baker's awning greeted him ahead. He made for it. The baker was closed, which made the shop ideal. Forrest jumped the railing of a porch, snared a rainwater pail from under a leaky roof, and vaulted down the other side. The baker's shop lay dead ahead. He slowed his run enough to spin, tossing the bucket through the front window. It broke with the crash of sin. Forrest accelerated, jumping through the gap.

The glass and wood splinters still stuck in the frame snared his jacket and cut his face. He barely noticed. Inside the bakery, empty shelves promised fresh bread on the morrow. The back-door hung dark and empty. He made it through as the main door crashed open in a splinter of wood, one of Marla's enforcers shouldering the wood aside like it wasn't important.

The back room led past wood-fired ovens. Forrest grabbed a sack of flour as he ran, upending it in his wake. Hand on the back-door handle, he yanked it open with a rattle of timber and metal. He didn't check whether his pursuer slipped on the flour.

Cooler air greeted him as he made the back alley. He turned right, jumping a crate of supplies, then jinked left through an open window. A hand on the sill, a vault, and he was inside, staring at a family sat down for an eventide meal. He gave them a nod, tossing, "Pardon!" in the wake of his passage as he barged through their home. He caught glimpses of wooden toys scattered on the floor, narrowly avoiding skating on one.

The wall beside his entrance window ruptured inward in a shower of dust and wood. The family screamed as another of Marla's troops slammed through. *A wall! That's hardly fair.* Forrest shored up next to the front door of the house, rattling the handle. It was stuck. He glanced back, taking in the giant grinning in triumph moments before he collapsed on the floor as a toy cart skidded from under his feet.

The door gave, and Forrest was outside. Speaking of carts, there was one parked below the eaves of Old Man McGuire's roof. Forrest ran for it, scrambling up. A hand whispered past his shoulder, almost collaring him. He jumped, grabbed guttering, and hauled himself to the roof. Below, three of Marla's men made to follow. Forrest didn't know how such big men could run so fast, because he wasn't slow by any means. He'd known Marla recruited the best for her soldiers, but their abilities seemed unjust by any measure.

Scampering across the roof, he made the neighboring house, keeping his footsteps light and his speed high as he dared. A holler behind drew his attention, and he spied one of his followers falling through a roof. *Size isn't everything.* He spared a grin for the dusk, then ran on.

Down to the street, left, jump the cat, dodge the barking dog, second right, and straight on. Sweat soaked Forrest's shirt, his jacket feeling the wrong choice for the evening's activities. Ahead lay the barn. All he had to do was get there, let Gravedigger out, and point her to the trees. That was the extent of his plan.

Forrest slid around the corner outside the barn. He slowed, pulling to a halt beside the main door. It was still closed. He took a moment, bracing hands on knees as he sucked air. None of his pursuers were here. It might be safe to open the door. Forrest waited until his breath settled enough to hear more than the bellows of his lungs. *Nothing.*

"Young Forrest Blake." Marla detached herself from a huddle of shadow where roof gave cover from the meager starlight.

Forrest took a step back. "Marla!"

He saw her face was marked, bruising starting on her forehead. Her top lip was bloody, but her eyes held steel and fire despite that. "It's rare one who stands at Vigil would turn on us."

"I didn't... I mean..." Forrest's words ran down, his bucket of thought emptying into the void. Marla's closeness focused his mind, giving him renewed purpose. He hadn't thought to stab himself with a pin. He'd fancied himself free.

"I know. It's not your fault. That's why they can kill gods. Do you see?" Marla stroked his face, running a hand down the scar on his jaw. "We must maintain the Vigil."

"We must maintain the Vigil," he agreed.

She turned away, eying the barn door. "This is the place." Not a question, because she had no need for them. He nodded anyway. "You'll be spared, Forrest. Youth and desire aren't crimes."

He sagged, relief flooding him. "Perhaps I should go to Altar."

She shook her head, still looking at the barn. "We'll have need of a good warrior against the dark." Marla eyed him over her shoulder. "Make no mistake: evil's come to our homestead."

Forrest nodded again. It's what his heart wanted to do. He stepped past her, hand on the barn door. The rough wooden beam that he'd dropped in place earlier today waited for his touch. He hefted it aside, dropping it to the packed dirt of the alley floor. A heave, and it was done. The barn lay in wait.

Lantern light lapped around his ankles. One of Marla's enforcers arrived, carrying a wary flame. It pushed shadows aside. The three of them entered the barn, eyes everywhere.

Two horses. One cow.

Forrest looked up to the roof. Above a horse stable, rotted wood had been pulled aside. Beyond, stars winked at him. Gravedigger was on the wind.

FIVE

The night welcomed Saveria like an old friend, albeit one with a cold handshake. She'd made her getaway from the village not long after Forrest locked her up. She'd had enough of him for now. At a base molecular level, she thought he might be decent, but something darker rode him like a prize stallion. A purpose she didn't understand governed his actions. It wasn't *nice* to hit people with clubs. It wasn't *nice* to lock them up.

While the day got on with its business, she'd wriggled through the barn's roof, then scampered away from rooftop to rooftop. Her feet felt light, her body ready. It was like whatever was in her head making her stumble was coming to an agreement with the machine it piloted. She wasn't sure which way she should go but figured the escape pod's site was a lost cause. She angled farther south, with a little east thrown in for good measure.

Not a soul saw her jump across the roofs above them. The town wasn't large, maybe a couple klicks aside. A good Navy destroyer felt roomier.

How do you know what a destroyer's like? Have you fought another's wars?

That didn't seem right. Saveria shook her head, then dropped from a roof into a goat pen, and set off toward fields that looked very similar to the one she'd crossed earlier. She waded through grass like it was the ocean. She touched her face, wondering if she'd felt salt spray in her life.

Saveria made a copse of trees that became a forest. Day turned to dusk as it tended to. The light faded, which caused her to stumble as her borrowed moccasins collected against something buried in the dirt. She bent, brushing loose soil and tiny plants aside. Her fingers rasped against stone.

It's called ceramicrete.

Saveria looked up. The forest hadn't reclaimed this section of the world. It tried, but Engineers built the best things. A ceramicrete road lay ahead, straight as an arrow, a clear indication of where she should go. Most of it was covered with dirt, fallen leaves, and encroaching vines, but the trees hadn't clambered over the road yet.

The forest encouraged her on. She stood, following the road. Before too long she encountered a crater. The ceramicrete was broken, descending into a basin filled with water. Rocks and dirt formed a small island in the middle, and a single tree grew there.

This was a missile strike.

Birds gave their evensong, cheering on the whispering wind. She spied a pile of lichen-covered rocks.

Those aren't rocks.

She made her way toward them. The 'rocks' turned into three bodies. One wore lichen-covered armor. The other two were below it. All that remained to tell the story of who they were was bones and tattered clothes.

The armored one covered the others with their body.

It hadn't helped. All died in the blast. Saveria put a hand on a shoulder plate, unsure why. The dead didn't need her regard. She stood, leaving the tiny huddle of regret behind her.

The road drew past structures, most sagged to rubble and detritus. The marks of heavy ordnance were visible everywhere. Scattered ceramicrete and metal. Broken armor. Bones, and damaged air cars. The forgotten and lost waited for a redemption that never came.

She passed an archway leading to nowhere, rubble beyond hinting at a building that no longer existed. Saveria ran a hand across the archway's pitted surface, feeling like she should feel its memories, but getting nothing back but the rasp of old stone.

Darkness dogged her steps. She made it to a wide-open area, the trees keeping their distance. Ahead, a starship hunkered against the ground. Saveria walked toward it. Her heart didn't know machines. She'd need an Engineer to know if it could fly again.

Pain lanced her skull. She gasped, dropping to her knees, hands against her head. It felt like liquid lava inside her skull, a fluid made of pure fire coursing inside. Within the flow, she felt something *click*.

Hope Baedeker is the best Engineer in the universe.

"Who is Hope?" she screamed. Her yell fell flat against the empty space. The starship didn't answer. Saveria gasped, hand on the ground in front of her. It shook but held her. Not metal, but flesh. Weak, but good enough. Saveria tasted bile, but the pain passed. She stood.

The starship was the only thing of note here. She moved toward it, then stumbled as her feet passed through what she'd thought was a collection of leaves. Her toe stubbed against something hard and heavy. She moved brushwood aside. Beneath the detritus was a skull. It wasn't human, its massive mandibles looking hungry even in death.

Most of it was damaged and chipped. The skull was cored by a hole. Saveria searched, finding other pieces of scattered chitin.

This is the enemy. They took my Hope from me.

"Who is Hope?" she whispered. Saveria spied the telltale snub of a PDC hanging below one of the starship's wings. A careful examination showed another three visible turrets sprouting from the hull like a promise of things to come.

The ship itself wasn't anything fancy. It didn't have the sleek lines of a racing yacht. Four drive cores at the back, three decks, and two hundred meters nose to tail. The back yawned open, a ramp descending to the landing pad. While the ship murdered alien life forms that got too close, Saveria couldn't see any humans around the verge. It protected nothing but ghosts.

Are the PDCs still live? Will it recognize me as a friend or enemy?

Saveria walked a circle around the craft. She was a hundred meters from it when she'd found the dead alien, so she kept the same distance as she strode the perimeter. The flight deck was visible from the ground, but the interior was dark. Vines climbed the sides of the ship, as if hungry to embrace the hull and draw it into the earth. Through a break in the vegetation she made out the ship's name. *ARDENT FURY*.

It's not a warship. Why is it named like one?

The PDCs didn't track her progress, but that wasn't a sign of safety. They were likely somnolent, waiting for something to trigger their crisis condition. She could just leave the ship here. Walk away, leave the mystery for someone else to solve. But it felt like...

You've killed so many people. You owe the universe.

Her head flared with pain, not as bad as before, but enough to remind her there was something wrong with her. For a moment, she had an image, brighter than the horror show of the insects. She was on a desert world. Sol beamed bright above, a brilliant majesty. She stood with her troops: a people forged of metal and thought. She held a weapon, something her kind made as a warning against their gods.

Saveria spat bile. She was on her knees again. She looked at the *Ardent Fury*, hand outstretched. The ship waited.

Another memory came to her. She was on a space station. Pirates came from across the hard black, in a warship stolen from the Empire. They attacked her home, and she ... *pushed*. Saveria made so many people die. They walked out airlocks or escaped in pods with no destination set. She'd done that, because she was afraid.

Saveria cradled her head in her hands. *What is happening to me?* One part of her remembered standing on a desert planet with machines she called friend. The other lived with humans on a station.

Both these things couldn't be true. Saveria couldn't be both organic and construct.

A whine drew her attention. She looked at the *Ardent Fury*. A PDC woke, the weapon swiveling to track her. She stood, realizing she'd crawled toward the ship in her reverie. Saveria spun, looking for cover, but there wasn't any. Not that it would help. This close, PDCs could turn armored vehicles to gravel.

The gun didn't fire. She eyed it. A red light winked beside the turret. She looked down, seeing a laser cross-hatch played over her body. Mapping her, working out what she was. A second later, the turret shuddered, pointing to the ground.

It knows what humans are and counts them as friends. Saveria wondered if it was an error, then shook her head. Thoughts like that weren't useful. Error or not, the ship was her only path to answers, and a way off this rock.

She jogged toward the extended ramp, heading inside.

INSIDE THE *ARDENT FURY*, light found a home in the gloom through portholes, the circular windows ringing the hold. A few near the extended ramp were covered by the reaching fingers of vines, but farther back the starship looked like what she'd expect. Nature receded, leaving the clean lines of human manufacture.

Saveria spied a bird's nest above. A bellbird watched her, head tipped sideways as it wondered at her intrusion. She moved further in, eyes wide, head up, before stumbling. Glancing down, she saw she'd tripped over the sad remains of a person. The ship suit they wore was unmarked by time, good Guild tech withstanding the wearying march of years without breaking a sweat. The ship suit held a skeleton close, encasing it like a shroud.

The skull looked ... *wrong*. Saveria knelt, and touched the bones as delicately as she could. The skull was devoid of hair or other tissue. The back of it was open, the rim looking gnawed. She searched the body, looking for anything that would identify this person. The ship suit bore a name.

CHAPLAIN MORRIS
UD ARDENT FURY

She traced her fingers over the *UD*. It wasn't an organization she was familiar with, military or otherwise. Near the body was a small personal console, but it didn't wake when she pressed its activation stud. Out of power or broken, it didn't matter. Saveria smoothed the ship suit. "I'm sorry for what happened to you. I'll see if I can fix it, so it doesn't happen to anyone else."

Saveria stood, heading deeper into the ship. Her moccasins made no noise over the metal decking. The cargo bay airlock was open. Beyond the airlock, she found her first complete dead alien. Its fore-limbs were lodged into a wall, stabbing claws piercing the metal. Plasma had chewed holes in its carapace, but did less damage than a blaster would to a person. These aliens were tough.

The enemy had me. Who saved me?

She snarled, kicking the corpse. It rattled, then fell to pieces on the decking. Saveria stood over the remains, wondering what to do next. The bridge would have a ship's log. But before she made it to the bridge, she needed a weapon. PDCs watching outside or not, the monsters made it inside. They'd breached the boundary humans made, killing everyone inside.

They get inside you. That's what they did to me. She touched her head, fingers probing the back of her skull. There were no lumps or lines of scar tissue. But she was sure that's what happened. They'd got inside her, desecrated her flesh, and warped her mind. She stood against her friends and would have killed humanity.

They would have made me kill my Hope.

She groaned. "Who is Hope?" The *Ardent Fury* didn't answer. The ship made no noise at all. Even the air cyclers were quiet. Saveria needed a weapon more than answers.

You are a weapon. It's what they made you.

Saveria shook her head. She padded the corridors of the *Ardent*

Fury, looking for a weapons locker. She found more bodies, different names on the suits but all noting the same two letters: *UD*. She found a ladder heading up and took it. The railings were clean and smooth, no signs of neglect in ship maintenance. The middle deck stretched left and right; left would head aft to Engineering, and right would go to the bridge.

Her heart tugged in her chest. It wanted left. She turned, heading rear. She passed a mess, with a collection of bodies inside. They looked to have died in horrible ways. Two of the alien corpses were among them, clear evidence of a rampage ending here. She wondered at their story, whether it finished in derring-do and bravado, teeth bared and fierce against the storm. *No. They would have died in terror*. Saveria saw no weapons with the dead. It confirmed her suspicions this wasn't a warship. She'd have found at least one blaster by now.

She found Engineering sealed. The door was locked down. Angry red lights watched her from the access panel. Saveria put her hand on it. It chirped, then gave a flat tone. She cast about. Her eye found a loose panel to her right. She ran her fingers around the lip, looking for purchase. It rattled, then popped free to clatter on the decking. The noise echoed down the corridor, dogging her path, reminding her the bridge waited. *If anyone's alive on this ship, they'll have heard that*. Hell, it'd been loud enough to wake the dead.

The fallen panel exposed the wall's interior. A narrow opening ran aft to Engineering. It didn't have the look of human manufacture. Something had clawed its way through the innards of the ship, like they'd done to her body. Chewed, and ate, and made a home. She eased her head into the gap. Roomy enough for her. It looked like something much larger made this. Saveria edged inside, following the tunnel. She passed torn conduit, water and air lines, and chewed support beams. The path didn't travel very far. It made it past the airlock, emerging within Engineering.

Saveria slipped out. All around her lay death, but none of it recent. Empty ship suits. An Engineer's rig, brown stains over the metal. A plasma torch, laying on the deck, a small section of melted metal near the tip. Someone dropped that while it was on, and it chewed into the decking before running out of power.

Saveria found an acceleration couch. The material of the chair had ruptured. Old stains marked the surface. She looked about, trying to find reason within the carnage. A collection of Engineers worked here. Evidence suggested all were dead. But the empty suits held no bodies. She crouched near a ship suit. The side was rent like you'd fillet a fish, the meaty innards removed. Saveria breathed the stale air of Engineering, wondering why the aliens left other bodies but took these ones.

They took you for your skills. Engineers know human tech.

This world was bereft of working things. No gravity elevators or functioning starships. Were the aliens trying to build a way up the gravity well? It didn't make sense. They had ships in orbit. One followed them down.

Saveria felt her heart beat faster. She'd *remembered* something from before the escape pod. She'd been on the bridge of a starship, watching the man she'd woken next to work the controls. The enemy was already here, waiting in orbit.

She moved to the reactors. One still worked, but lights were amber. The other two beside it were dead. She turned the dynamo on one, but got nothing, then did the same to the other. She glanced around, looking for the reactant supply. She found a spare fuel canister in a supply rack, dragging it across the decking with a squeal of metal. It was as heavy as she remembered them being.

When did I last carry a reactor fuel container?

It didn't matter. She couldn't get the canister into the reactor's feed chamber. It was designed to be lifted by a rig. Saveria eyed the one laying on the decking. She picked it up, touching the power icon on the breastplate. It *hummed*, then the signature four limbs articulated out. It clambered on her, encasing her in its machine embrace. The visor slipped over her face, HUD blooming to life. Many, many red warnings. *POWER CRITICAL* was the most significant, but she had to hope it had enough to lift the canister.

She worked the controls set in the arm of the unit, wondering how she knew how to use it. A flash of memory: two sets of limbs tangled together on the deck of a starship. Someone with pink hair lay with her, tracing fingers up Saveria's arm. Her skin shivered in remembered sympathy, goosebumps pricking her arm beneath the rig's protective shell. *Here*, said the woman with pink hair. *You use them like this.* Pointing at the controls set in the arm, then touching Saveria's head. *They know what you want. You just have to know how to ask.*

Saveria wanted to hold the memory, clutch it close, but it left. She saw the person with pink hair. Tasted her skin and felt the heat of her. If she wanted to see her ever again, she needed to get this starship working. Saveria growled, then walked to the fuel canister. She told the rig to heft the canister. Two limbs articulated out, gripping the reactant. Two others braced her on the deck.

Nothing else happened.

You just have to know how to ask.

She didn't know how to use the cognitive interface, but she still had her voice. "Install reactant, please." The rig chimed. One arm left the decking to remove the cover from the reactor. It dropped the fuel canister into the waiting slot, sealing it. Saveria fist-pumped the air, then walked to the rear of the reactor. A few quick spins of the dynamo, and the reactor hummed. Green lights bloomed over the display.

A moment later, the starship groaned in response. The hiss of air cyclers, and the subliminal tones of reticulation systems coming back online. All the happy noises of a hull that would keep humans from death in the hard black.

Her rig blared an error, noting *POWER DEPLETED*, then dropped from her like a shed skin, forming into a small cube as it fell. It clanked to the decking. She hefted it, moving to the acceleration couch. Unspooling cable, she docked it to charge. She might need it later. One thing was certain. She'd need more than a single container of reactant to get off this rock. Endless Drives were hungry.

Saveria settled in the acceleration couch, trying not to think about the rent at her back. She tapped on the console, bringing the holo to life. Saveria found the logs of the ship's Chief Engineer, scrolling to the bottom few, and hit play.

The holo shimmered, cleared, and then filled with the head and shoulders of a woman. Piercing eyes. Strong jaw. Knew what her job was, no mistake. The Chief Engineer looked behind her, as if sensing a threat hidden from the cam, then faced forward. "Chief Engineer Marla Cupicha of the Undying Dawn missionary vessel *Ardent Fury*." A pause, a glance down, and when Marla looked at the cam again, her eyes held fear. "Viukde Gamma is lost, and God has forsaken us."

SIX

Always look on the bright side.

Chad stumbled into the tree line, feeling weaker than a newborn kitten. His side still leaked red, and no amount of cursing fixed it. Since losing his esper gifts he hadn't had torrents of blood running from his nose, eyes, or ears, which was a plus.

He was trying to catch the damn fool, Forrest. The kid set a mean pace through the streets of the city, which meant Chad lost him after the first three corners. He shored up next to a horse trough, gasping while he leaned against a wall. When he disembarked, he left a red handprint. They could call it a *souvenir* for all he cared.

Chad knew the chances of running these people down reduced to zero after he saw them head out of town, riding *oxen*. Horses would be more expected, but no, some group of clowns decided the official transportation animal of Viukde was the humble ox. While oxen weren't known for setting land speed records, they were faster than a slightly-used, very injured Chad.

Which left him on foot, hustling through fields and into this very nice copse of trees. He hoped this planet didn't have ticks. Chad was mildly surprised no one challenged his escape from the village, as plenty of people stood about and watched, but they seemed not to care. Like ambulatory posts, for all the enthusiasm they showed for his capture. *Kazuo would know what's happened to them. He knew all the dark ways of suppressing a mind.*

He caught a glimpse of Marla leading Forrest and a group of serious-looking pieces of humanity into the trees. Chad tried to draw his blaster on them, alarmed at how his hand shook and arm drifted. *Blood loss. You're quietly bleeding to death.*

He tripped on a stone, groaning.

Not so quietly, then.

Chad rested against a tree, breathing ragged, not quite sure how he'd made it this far. He waited for his wind to come back, eying his blaster with trepidation. He knew what he had to do. He aimed the blaster in a random direction, pulled the trigger four times, and squinted as wood debris exploded, trees turning into pyres. Before he could think much about it, he stuck the glowing tip of the blaster in the bleeding wound in his side.

WHEN HE CAME TO, it was only a few minutes later. He was on the floor of the forest, trees still alight, and hadn't burned to death. He remembered the pain of cauterizing his wound and wondered if he'd get disability leave when back in the world.

If dying that one time didn't do it, it's unlikely a little bleeding-plus-burn will do the trick. He picked himself up, squinting against the burning trees' glare. It was likely everyone in a klick radius knew he was here, which meant running was less useful than a good swagger. He tried one on, sauntering through the trees. Chad picked up the trail of oxen without too much difficulty. His side hurt like seven devils, and while he might die of shock, it was less likely he'd bleed to death. You had to work on the problems you could, right?

Chad felt the subtle hiss and scrape of Ezeroc against his mind. He adjusted his sword belt. He'd wondered when they'd show up. It seemed like setting fire to a forest and following a group of people hell-bent on capturing his ward was a good signal flare for the roaches.

The fire well behind him, he sauntered on. The path he followed turned into a road, and not one of these faux ones made of hard-packed dirt. This was honest to God ceramicrete. A little overgrown, a little *used*, but who wasn't? Fifty meters after finding the road, he found two of Marla's giants. They guarded the road, hulking in the gloom. Next to them were three Ezeroc drones.

Chad slowed his roll, one hand on his blaster, the other on his sword. "Nice night," he offered. One Ezeroc opened its hellscape mouth and hissed. "If it's all the same, I've got to head that way," he pointed past the huddle, "but you're welcome to tag along if you like."

One of the brutes frowned, like he was working on a difficult math problem. "Aren't you concerned we'll kill you?"

Chad laughed. "You? No. Those fuckers?" He pointed to the Ezeroc drones. "Far scarier."

"Our gods are fearsome," the hulk agreed.

"Ain't gods." Chat drew his steel. He'd always favored a rapier, but wished his excellent sense of style hadn't clouded his judgment. He could use a decent broadsword about now, or even the curved steel of a scimitar. The rapier wasn't a good weapon for fighting Ezeroc. Pushing the point through chitin took more strength than he had on a good day. "Ain't yours, neither. They come from the stars. They brought nothing but terror and fear, and me and mine stand against them."

One drone scuttled to the left, stabbing forelimbs raking the air, as if sensing a good meal was close. The hulk's brow remained furrowed. "Is your offer still good? Will you walk this road with us to the end?"

"Hang about." Chad whipped his rapier twice, the steel hissing as it sliced air. "You'd take me that way," he stabbed the point past them, "and *then* kill me?"

"Not kill." The giant shook his head. "You're for the Altar."

The Ezeroc continued to crawl farther around. It was making Chad nervous, so he shot it twice. Blue-white plasma bored a hole in its skull, then thorax. The back of it exploded in ruin, flames boiling from the burning meat within. It collapsed to the ceramicrete road with the sizzle a good steak makes on the grill. Chad turned his blade to the group. "Tell me about the Altar."

"Godkiller," snarled the giant.

"You know what? Let's go with your version." Chad stuck the point of his rapier in the dirt to steady himself, pointed his blaster, and fired on the left Ezeroc. His sword slipped, delivering him to the dirt, the plasma discharging into the ceramicrete road. Fragments of rock exploded, mixed with smoke and burning leaves. Chad scrambled to his feet, coughed, and readied his blaster and blade.

When the smoke cleared, the road was empty. The dead Ezeroc still smoldered, but the roadway ahead was clear. Chad straightened, sliding his rapier back into its scabbard. It made sense. Why fight Chad, when he was going where they wanted anyway? It would have made him *feel* better to skewer a roach or two, but this way his enemies could choose the time and place of their meeting.

His side hurt more after his spill on the dirt, but life was a collection of pain at different altitudes. He'd make it, or he wouldn't. He stared at the stars visible between the trees. Chad imagined Karkoski out there, a fleet of Navy destroyers with her. She could deliver angels of redemption. She'd get him clear. If only she knew he was here.

"I'm delirious," he realized. "I'm going to die on this shitty planet, and *while* I'm dying, I'll have out of body experiences."

It didn't sound so bad, now he'd said it out loud. Two problems he needed to solve before checking out: getting Saveria off this rock, and going on a date with Karkoski. To-do list sorted, he headed down the road.

HUNGER GNAWED AT HIM. He thought about that as he made his way down the road. He passed a crater, a tree in the middle, and shot the Ezeroc lurking in the branches above. It fell, trailing fire, into the water. The water churned in the creature's death throes, steam rising. Chad continued on, not sparing a backward glance.

The problem with being hungry is, he should be *hungrier*. He had nanites in his blood. He shouldn't have to cauterize his side with a barbecue poker. The bleeding should have stopped by itself. After should have come ravenous hunger. He was peckish, sure. But not eat-a-horse hungry, more at the level of a decent-sized pig.

Were the nanites breaking down? *Could* they break down? Now would be a super useful time to talk to Algernon or one of his kin. They might know. The trick would be prying the answer out, but Chad was good at getting answers to uncomfortable questions.

He thought he saw a shadow in the trees, and spun, blaster out, eyes straining to pierce the gloom. *Nothing*. Chad flicked the light on the barrel of his blaster on, but all that did was show the trees closest to him, and make the backdrop look even darker. He switched the lamp off.

Another movement from up on the road. He didn't spin this time, trying to keep it in his peripheral vision. It looked big, like a decent-sized autocar. It vanished like dawn mist before he could get a good look. Didn't matter. He figured he knew what it was. A sending, and from a Queen.

Last time he'd faced a Queen, he'd been a part of the Empress's army. Above the Ezeroc homeworld, they'd fought sharks in the deep waters of the mind. Grace led the charge. She'd had the strength to do it.

In the cool quiet of his own thoughts, Chad admitted he didn't think he did. Pound for pound, human espers were stronger than Ezeroc, *if* they hadn't overtaxed their gifts. The fact he saw the Queen in the first place meant his mind barrier was permeable. The creature was already in his thoughts, if only at a superficial level.

The worst part was, the damn roach was fucking with him. This whole shadows-on-the-edge-of-sight thing would wear thin, real fast. He needed to help Saveria, and for that, he needed to pick up his pace.

Unless, of course, he pushed himself too hard, too far, and too fast again. Last time he did that, he'd died. He didn't want to die a second time; hadn't found much to recommend it the first time around. But Saveria was out there, half her mind AI crystal, and unprotected. What would the Ezeroc do if they got control over AI-level intelligence?

Chad sighed, closed his eyes, and reached out with his mind. It felt like the mental equivalent of pushing his hands onto a cactus. Spikes, tiny needles of pain. He pushed harder, reaching for the one soul on this planet most at risk.

CHAD *Saveria, hear me*

He groaned, sinking to one knee. He touched his top lip, finding blood there. *Job's not done.*

CHAD *Saveria, I'm here, I'm here, I can help you*

The slap that knocked him back wasn't his own disability. It was the might of a Queen, snarling and hissing in the vaults of his mind. She barred his path, and stopped him from reaching Saveria. In that one tiny moment, he found what he needed to know. He knew what the Altar was. He knew where it was.

Chad was going to be too late. He broke into a lopsided run anyway, hissing at the pain in his side.

SEVEN

The path through the woods was old stone, from a time before Forrest was born. Marla took the lead, her animal keeping good time. They all rode good livestock, trying to catch the one meant for the Altar before their gods found them wanting.

Forrest couldn't help but feel this was his fault. If he hadn't failed when he'd first met Gravedigger, everything would be all right. As it was, his weakness let them all down. It's just... She looked at him like he was a *person*. Not at his skin, and the scar on his jaw. She didn't wonder what made it, or if she did, Gravedigger didn't seem to care. She could have beaten him like one of the toy drums the tinker Sam brought to fair, but she let him go.

He felt the calm purpose of the Vigil sway about him. Marla's presence felt, for a moment, cloying, close, and uncomfortable. He tried to shake himself free of the feeling, knowing it for the traitorous failed portion of himself, but all he managed to do was work his way farther from the Vigil's calming embrace.

Forrest read his scripture. He knew he'd be tested. He hadn't expected it to be like this.

To the side of the road, he sensed their gods keeping pace. They made traversing the terrain seem so effortless. They were larger than humans. Smarter, and stronger. It was an honor to serve them.

Marla slowed her ox, letting Forrest draw alongside. "It should fall to you."

Forrest nodded, not really understanding. "Of course."

"When we get to her, you will go inside. Lead her out. Bring her to us. To *safety*, Forrest." The weight of her gaze felt like she'd put a hand on his arm. "She will trust you more than us."

"I can bring her out. I'm sure of it."

Those piercing eyes watched him for a moment longer. "Good. It's settled." Marla urged her ox faster, picking up the pace. It wouldn't be long now.

WHEN THEY REACHED THE RELIC, their gods sidled away. It was a place meant only for the most chosen, with the internal gifts the gods bestowed. They dismounted their oxen, because even those gentle beasts couldn't get closer.

Marla led the way. "Do you know what this is?"

"It's the—"

"Not what we *call* it, Forrest. What it *was*." She pointed to the massive shape resting in the cleared area, wry smile tugging her lips. "Sometimes I don't remember myself. This brought us here. It's a starship. It's broken... Not enough people on this world with the know-how to fix it. Not that it matters. Our seed's spread across the heavens. Seth Cleaver will return." She said this last with conviction, as if to convince herself.

Forrest eyed the night sky. "Only the gods travel the stars." His thoughts churned, scripture warring with what Gravedigger's presence meant. She'd come from the stars. Godkillers. It made sense: only gods could kill each other. What didn't make sense was what Marla meant. Did she mean this *starship* brought the gods? Their gifts to the people? That must be it.

The starship waited, patient. Eternal. Forrest had walked people here before. He knew what happened inside but had never been there. Inside was deliverance, a blessing, and the gift of looking upon the face of heaven.

Marla held her hand toward the ship. "Go. Find her."

The ramp awaited. Inside, the blessing of the gods. Forrest's heart beat a tempo of fervor as he walked toward the *Ardent Fury*. It was the Altar, and he would make everything ready.

EIGHT

The holo played. Saveria watched Marla Cupicha speak from a time before.

"The colony's overrun." Marla's face was replaced by cam footage of a bustling settlement. Buildings reached for the sky. But instead of the buzz and hustle of commerce, insects walked the streets. They ran on six legs, spearing humans with two mighty stabbing claws. The holo footage cycled through settlement after settlement. "We don't know where they came from, but we think they might have been here all the time. They appeared after the miners got a klick below the crust."

The woman paused, running a hand through her close-cut hair. She didn't seem angry or sad. Marla looked *tired*, like she could rest for a week and not be ready to wear her rig again. "We were lucky, I guess. A Navy warship was in-system. They sent reinforcements. Didn't help. Not after the aliens sent ships of their own."

The holo zoomed out to a starscape, showing a simulated system map. Viukde Gamma sat as the highlighted point of interest. Saveria traced her fingers through the lines of light, finding Viukde Delta still present. Marla continued in audio while the simulation moved forward. "We think they had an outpost on Delta. The Navy aren't saying, but that's because they're all dead." Viukde Delta blossomed on the map, spreading fragments through the system. "What we do know is things went to hell when the Navy dropped their crust busters. The planet popped like a piñata. Never seen anything like it. Doubt I'll get the time to see anything like it in the future, either."

Marla's face reappeared on the holo. "The Undying Dawn ship *Crimson Clover* jumped out system. Pastor Cleaver's her captain. A good man, he'll do right by 'em. We were going to join them after we'd collected the few remaining settlers." She leaned close to the cam. "Ain't enough settlers left to make it worthwhile and wouldn't matter if there were. The *Ardent Fury's* hurt, and not in a way I can fix. We need a fabricator. Hell, we need a dozen. The aliens got inside. Killed my Engineers, but not before taking some away." She closed her eyes, lips moving.

She's praying. Saveria touched her own lips in response. *How bad did it get for an Engineer to look to forgotten gods?*

"Anyway. I don't have much hard data. Guesswork and mysteries are all I've got for you, whoever you are." A wry smile, not quite a chuckle, then it was gone. "They get inside us. Take us over. I've set the ship to kill any who aren't human, but the *Ardent Fury's* no warship. Our PDCs are for busting rocks. The ship can't look inside the meat of a person to see what's riding behind their eyes. It's why she's overrun."

A scream came from the holo, muted by distance. Marla glanced over her shoulder again. "Here's the way of it. I think they control our minds. All that stopped when Gamma blew. Or, they can't do it as well as they used to. They stopped sending more ships here." She shrugged. "I'd lose my Shingle if the Guild found out I was betting everything on guesswork, but I'm not angling to escape. I'm working to make sure *they* don't make it out." She tapped her head. "In here's all the secrets to power a starship. How Endless Drives work, and the workings of a Guild Bridge. It'd be unlucky indeed if they managed to get the *Ardent Fury* flying again, but we've been unlucky for so long it feels like that could happen any other Tuesday."

Marla braced herself on the arms of the acceleration couch. "Here's what I think. They can't fly out of here with the wreckage of Viukde Gamma creating mischief. We saw how fast they jump. No need for flight time buffers like God's children. But maybe there's weakness there." She shrugged. "It's a mystery a better Engineer can solve."

Saveria's fingers whitened as she gripped the arms of her acceleration couch. *I know the best Engineer in the universe, and I don't want her to come here. I don't want her to die like I did.*

"And," Marla brushed a wisp of hair away from her forehead, "I think they're cut off. Just like us. If Pastor Cleaver's smart, he won't tell anyone about Viukde. He'll let us rest in peace." Her brow furrowed, as if she remembered a bad dream. "Here we are, at the end of it. I've done what I can to sabotage the ship's systems. I've left the PDCs running. And now it's time for me to go." A massive clang sounded from the holo, causing Marla to whip around. When she looked at the cam again, her eyes held a hard kernel of fear, but also resolution. "I know my soul's forfeit. It's a small thing, not worth much anyway. Not against all the Republic holds." Marla held a small weapon up. To Saveria's eye, it looked a makeshift kinetic sidearm, but it was difficult to make out. "You don't need to see this."

Her hand reached for the console controls, but never made it. The Engineering wall Saveria crawled through burst open, aliens boiling from the rent. Marla screamed, mortal terror overwhelming her. She pressed her weapon to head, firing. Her head popped like overripe fruit dropped from a great height, her body tumbling to the decking. Saveria bit her knuckle, watching a woman die fifty years ago, but feeling her bravery through time.

The Ezeroc scuttled inside, unaware the cam recorded everything. The insects tugged at Marla's body, teasing it across the decking. One speared the Engineer with its horrible stabbing forelimbs, hefting the corpse. They moved toward the rent they'd made in the wall, heading back through with their prize.

Saveria made to turn off the holo but paused when she saw how much of the recording was left to run. *Weeks* of time remained. She set the console to scrub forward until the scene changed. The footage galloped forward, no change evident in lighting or scenery, until a week and a half later.

Marla came back through the wall rent, but whole and restored. Her face was blank as she looked around Engineering. She made her way to the holo, peering at the cam, then turning away. *It's as if she doesn't know what she's looking at.*

Saveria paused the recording. The Ezeroc resurrected the Engineer, but Marla had damaged her brain to the point there wasn't much left. Not enough to know how to work a starship.

A *clank* came from through the rent in Engineering, and it took Saveria a moment to realize it wasn't the recording; she'd paused it. Something moved inside the ship, coming toward her. She got up from the couch, and wondered how many of Marla's Engineers died here before she decided to end her own life. There was no opening Engineering's airlock. If the Chief Engineer didn't want a thing to open, it wouldn't. Not for Saveria, and maybe not ever. She'd have to go back through the tunnel the Ezeroc carved through the hull, to whatever waited on the other side.

Saveria cast about for Marla's makeshift sidearm but couldn't find it. There wasn't anything here that still held power. Her gaze fell on the Engineer's rig, still charging at the console. She uncoupled it. The device powered up, climbing on and wrapping her in its protective embrace. The visor slid over her face, warning her it only held a twenty percent charge.

She hunkered down, making her way through the Ezeroc's tunnel. Once on the other side, she saw what made the noise.

The young man who'd given her clothes stood between two Ezeroc drones. Her stomach dropped. She couldn't fight two of the enemy, not without a weapon.

Forrest smiled, and confusion washed over Saveria. Most people in his situation would either be dead or pissing themselves in readiness for dying. "Gravedigger. It's all right."

She shook her head and backed away. "They're *evil*, Forrest. They're the *devil*."

He slowed as he approached, and she saw confusion flash across his face for a half second. It was chased away by fervor. "They're gods, Gravedigger. They'll make it okay. For all of us." He made it to her. She craned around his body to see what the Ezeroc were doing. They stood like statues, unmoving. She took a step toward them. Was this a trick? A joke? Saveria turned to Forrest in time to collect the swing from his club to the side of her helmeted head. If she hadn't turned, it'd have collected her in the back of the skull.

Clang. She dropped to one knee, head ringing. Her rig's HUD bloomed with data. Impact point, likely damage to her head, and recommended medical treatment. She stared through the text at Forrest, his club raised above her in two hands. He swung again, putting all his might into it.

Her visor cracked. Saveria's head rocked inside her rig, and she fell to the deck. The rig's HUD bloomed with warnings, but all she cared about were the Ezeroc. No longer statues, they scuttled forward, stabbing limbs reaching for her.

Darkness took her before they arrived.

NINE

Chad was nobody's fool. That's why he didn't keep on walking down the perfectly good ceramicrete road with one hundred percent certainty of a trap at the end. If he knew the Ezeroc, they'd have a nest somewhere close. He figured on finding it. Scout the position and come up with a plan. He left the road, cutting through the trees. He used his sword as a machete, carving trees aside, before realizing the noise it made would give his position away more clearly than a herd of elephants rampaging through the foliage.

The plan would go a lot better if he had ordnance of significant size. A blaster wouldn't cut it. Thinking about ordnance made him think of Karkoski. Thinking about Karkoski made him morose, so he switched gears and tried to work out how a man might kill an Ezeroc drone with a rapier.

It didn't help. Chad didn't have ordnance, Karkoski was no doubt sunning herself on a beach somewhere, and all he had was a rapier generally useless against anything except crimes on fashion.

That's not true. It's excellent at killing humans.

He bent low, clambering through the trees. The forest cut down his speed. He kept his direction roughly close to the road, eying the stars to see if he was on the right path. It was a good gimmick and would work better if he knew anything about charting a course by eyeball.

The thing that drew him on stronger than one of Karkoski's coffees was the sense the roaches were ahead. His esper abilities might be for shit, but there was no denying the sense of dread when he faced a southerly direction. After an hour's trailblazing, he thought he heard something. Faint, difficult to determine, but annoying all the same. He found a tree, shimmying up the side. The branch he grabbed broke with a snap, dropping him to the forest floor.

That looked easier in holos.

He cast about for a larger tree of Kohl-like robustness, settling on one that didn't seem too ornery. He clambered with a little more care, making it high enough to see the sky. Ahead, warm light beamed through the green in welcome. *A settlement, maybe.* Chad wondered who the welcome was for, and why they'd gone to the trouble. Still, he wasn't here for the scenery. He had a job to do, and that involved getting his ward to safety, while killing as many Ezeroc as possible.

He swung down, wincing as his wounded side pulled. It still wasn't healed, but he also wasn't a lot hungrier. It'd be annoying, in a possibly deadly way, if the nanites in his blood had a use-by date he wasn't aware of. They hadn't done a lot of field tests on 'em.

Chad crept as best as a man in magboots could. He made the forest verge; the trees dropped away, replaced by stumps. He overlooked a small depression in the ground, with an entrance leading into the earth. Humans milled about, working with pickaxes, shovels, and wheelbarrows. He watched for a while, wondering what he was looking at.

It's a mine. The roaches have their human cattle digging their goddamn homes for 'em.

Chad straightened his sword belt, and walked down the hill toward the people. He kept a low-slung building between himself and the workers, because while he wasn't moving fast or in an excitable manner, he preferred to choose the timing of his introductions. The building turned out to be a barracks of sorts; peering through windows revealed a room with a few bunks down one side, tables on the other. He sauntered around the building's corner, nodding to a man standing guard outside.

The man blinked, hand going to the cosh at his belt. He looked about ready to yell, so Chad put a hand on the wrist reaching for the weapon. "Quiet."

The man blinked again. Chad could almost feel the wheels turning. "What?"

"Here's how it is." Chad let the man's hand go, and pointed upslope from where he'd come. "Up there's a dangerous man. Escaped from Marla's justice." He waited, and at the man's nod, gave a reassuring smile. "You head that way," he pointed to the tree line again, "and scare him down this way. I'll wait here, and we'll grab him."

"Uh."

"I see you're confused. You're wondering, 'Why doesn't old Chad go up the slope?'" Chad gestured to his side, where dried blood soaked his shirt. "He got the drop on me."

"Who are you?"

"Is now really the time?" Chad shook his head, radiating disappointment. "We've got seconds at best before he brings a legion of godkillers down upon us. Go, man. Go!"

The man went. Chad watched him scrabble up the hill, loose stones trickling down in his wake. He opened the door to the barracks. Inside, he purloined a small sack hanging by the door. Into this, he put two loaves of bread, a length of sausage so desiccated as to be insulting to fine salamis, and a wedge of cheese that smelled damn good. He charted a course to the bunks, finding an overcoat. It was a *terrible* style, all muddy browns, but would serve to cover his godkiller weapons, sack, and some of his rakish charm.

Now wasn't the time for pleasing the locals.

On a last turn of the room he spied a wide-brimmed hat with a feather sprouting from the top. He snared it, put it on, and headed back out. The man he'd met earlier was back outside, breathless, and about to speak, so Chad slugged him across the jaw. He caught the hapless fellow as he slumped, easing him to the ground, then headed toward the mine entrance.

Ezeroc sure liked to burrow.

Chad nodded and smiled at any who cast a glance in his direction. His makeshift disguise seemed to withstand casual muster, but he didn't veer too close to curious eyes regardless. At the mine's mouth, he found a collection of lanterns, and helped himself to one. He lit it, heading into the gloom. The air smelled of dirt and sweat. *No explosives, just hard labor.* Chad dodged a man pushing a wheelbarrow.

Working his way deeper, he trended his direction toward where he felt 'hollow dread' emanating. He walked over a wooden bridge suspended over an area full of pale-white Ezeroc eggs. Men and women labored beside the eggs, clearing debris and polishing their surfaces. He didn't know if the Ezeroc wanted this or it was cult behavior, and didn't feel it a good time to stop and ask.

Past the egg chamber, he heard the hissing of Ezeroc. He shored up his mental defenses as best he was able, unsure if it was working. He kept his pace level and even, not bothering to look down the passage the noise came from. His lantern bobbed, casting uneven light against walls hewn by hand.

In all my time here, the only blaster I've seen is mine, and the only blade is at my hip. For all that, the Ezeroc allow pickaxes here. It was curious. Perhaps their hold was strongest here leaving little for them to fear. Or, maybe they didn't want their human cattle killing each other out there.

A scuttling came from behind, and he picked up his pace. In a strange twist of events, the tunnel he followed inclined, heading back to the surface. He had an uncomfortable feeling he knew what was going on, but didn't want to admit it to himself.

An Ezeroc burst forth from a passage to his right, all terror mandibles and waving foreclaws. Chad shot it seven times, no memory of drawing his blaster. He spun, blowing one scuttling in his footsteps into pieces of burning meat and chitin. *Time to move*. He ran, heading up, dodging workers where possible, shoulder-barging where not. The air smelled cool, less like dirt, and he knew he was getting close.

The only problem was it didn't smell like *nature*. It smelled like *starship*.

"You bastards," he wheezed. Rounding a bend, he found a hole with a wide ladder leading up. By the ladder were three human guards and four Ezeroc drones. Actinic bright light shone from above, the kind manufactured by Engineers to push back the hard black. Chad threw back his coat, drawing steel.

The enemy charged.

The first human Chad took on the blade. A quick stab through the heart and it was done. He sidestepped as the man kept on, momentum taking him past and to the dirt. The second swung a club, and Chad ducked, worked a daring riposte, and disarmed his opponent, then cut off his hand on the backswing. The man screamed as blood fountained. Chad stepped away from the gushing red.

He figured he might just about survive this when he shot one Ezeroc with his blaster, punching glowing holes through its carapace with blue-white plasma. Chad allowed himself a smile, touching the brim of his hat with his blade in salute. "Come on, then." He whipped the sword through the air, the steel hissing its hunger.

The Ezeroc held firm with their human slave. Chad wondered what was going on, right up to the point where pain bloomed in his shoulder. He screamed as an Ezeroc stabbing claw exited the front of his shoulder. One of the roaches speared him from behind. He screamed louder as another claw rent his other shoulder, the insect hefting him in the air. He coughed blood, dropping both sword and blaster.

The human walked forward. Just a normal-looking dude, with a too-large nose. If Chad had been paying attention before rather than patting himself on the back, he might have noticed this was a standard-sized person, not the massive beefcakes Marla used as enforcers. "They said you'd come."

Chad hissed in agony as the Ezeroc moved, raising him toward the hole above. "They also say you've got a funny-looking nose?"

The normal guy touched his nose, then quickly dropped his hand. "We didn't need to capture you at all. You came to the Altar by yourself."

"Yeah." Chad tried for a nod, but even he knew his head kinda flopped around. "Got some gods to kill."

"Take him." The normal-but-actually-an-asshole guy pointed up. The Ezeroc at Chad's back hissed, scuttling forward, lifting Chad toward the light.

TEN

Inside the Altar, Forrest found undergrowth making its home. The space was blessedly free of vermin, but gods wouldn't allow their temple to be desecrated. He didn't know which way to go. The air felt cool, the night following on his heels. Ahead, Gravedigger awaited. She planned to kill his gods.

He wound through the starship, finding a hundred knick-knacks from the pilgrims who came before. The odd desiccated body lay about. All wore clothing like Gravedigger had when they'd first met. He felt doubt trouble him but pushed the feeling aside. Doubt was natural in the face of faith. He must be strong.

Forrest found a ladder. A new deck under his feet, he could go left or right. Left felt the best choice. His feet walked halls of shining metal. He'd never seen so much alloy in all his years. The Altar was *made* of metal. His village scrounged to find fragments of it. They curated broken relics from the time before, but nothing worked. The Altar still worked; he could feel the hum of the walls come alive as he journeyed deeper within. Strange slabs bloomed bright at his approach, tracing pictures through the air with lines of light.

He heard Marla's voice ahead. That couldn't be right; she was still outside. He ducked into a large room. Benches lined the area, and a massive glowing rectangle sat against a wall at one end. Marla's image was on the rectangle, but he'd never seen her like that. Her hair was the same short cut, but her eyes were different. They held an uncertainty he wasn't used to. She looked frightened, and pressed a device to her head. When the device fired, killing her, he gasped, stumbled, and dropped to the floor. He jarred his coccyx, hissing with the pain of it.

It made no sense. Marla was outside, dressed like the rest of them. But the Marla shown in the rectangle of light had more vigor, and wore strange clothing that seemed to be made of metal. Were the gods testing him?

The image skipped, showing the gods come to take her away. *Ah. This is from the time before. She came to the Altar, and they remade her.* It made sense: to lead the village, she needed the gods' strength. The Altar showed him what he needed to see. They would do this to Gravedigger, and as with Marla, all would be well. Gravedigger wouldn't be frightened or confused like old Marla. She'd be reborn, made like Marla. Strong, ready, and willing to serve.

Forrest got to his feet, rubbing his tailbone. He exited the room, finding two gods waiting for him. Forrest bowed his head, and the gods sidled away. They blocked his path back, showing him the only way forward was the direction he'd been heading. He picked up the pace, fingering the club that hung from his belt. If the gods could remake Marla with half her skull missing, a few taps to Gravedigger's head wouldn't make much difference.

It felt like the heavens *wanted* him to hit her. He'd missed his mark in the forest when they'd first met. He wouldn't fail again.

Ahead Forrest saw a hole in the side of the corridor. Gravedigger came through, head hidden behind a strange helmet. It connected to metal clothing like Marla had worn in the rectangle of light. Gravedigger's face was pale behind glass, but still perfect. She froze when she saw him, eyes darting to the gods at his back. She was frightened, not knowing what he knew. "Gravedigger. It's all right."

She didn't accept the truth. He wasn't surprised; he hadn't either. Gravedigger stepped back, but there was no escape. The corridor ended in a massive metal door behind her. There would be no running away. "They're *evil*, Forrest. They're the *devil*."

He mustn't frighten her further. He made his way closer but slowed his pace. Forrest had to make her *see*. To *believe*. "They're gods, Gravedigger. They'll make it okay. For all of us."

She looked past him at the gods waiting behind. Forrest felt there was too much at stake for her to make up her own mind. She'd come around, once the gods could remake her on the Altar. He hefted his club, slamming it into her head. She stumbled to the deck, arm up. He wound back, smashing the club into her head again. The glass over her face cracked, and Gravedigger fell to the deck.

The suit she wore whined, four arms whipping out fast as thought. Bright, actinic light spat from one, and it slashed toward his club. Forrest, even if he'd been ready, wouldn't have been fast enough; the light passed through his forearm holding the club. His hand, wrist, and club clattered to the ground beside Gravedigger's prone body.

Forrest screamed. The pain from his arm was unbelievable. It took over his world. He fell to the ground beside her. His arm ended in a stump, the end trailing smoke. The air smelled of charred meat. He wanted to throw up. Forrest drew short, gasping breaths, holding his ruined arm to his chest. He knew this meant he was for the Altar too. The maimed and imperfect were sent here.

The gods who'd followed him scuttled forward. Instead of feeling safe, he felt horror. The calming presence he'd felt on his way in vanished like morning mist. The pain of his arm pushed all aside. The gods ignored him, lifting Gravedigger between them. They didn't move to harm her like he had. Perhaps her metal clothing's revenge on him was warning enough.

Forrest groaned as the gods took Gravedigger away. They didn't want him. Even in this, he failed them.

FORREST DIDN'T KNOW how long he lay on the floor of the starship. Long enough for eddies of air to take the stench of his wound away. His severed limb lay on the decking, unmoving. It seemed unreal. He could see bone. The cut was even, no hint of jagged tissue. Perfect, just like Gravedigger.

Is she a god or a godkiller? He couldn't spend the rest of his days laying here. Marla would be worried. She would see his injury, and send him to the Altar. Something nagged at his thoughts. *The gods saw me fall, but didn't take me to the Altar.*

It didn't make sense. Forrest rose, fighting waves of nausea. On his feet, he looked the way they'd taken Gravedigger. There was no sign of them. No way to know where they'd gone. He poked his head inside the hole she'd come through. It was a short passage, full of protuberances he could hurt his arm on.

I had to know where she came from. I have to know what she saw.

Forrest entered the passage. It was a short route to another room. It was behind the metal door, and in here lay remembered death. The suits of the fallen lay on the floor. Wasted, and forgotten. Just like him.

He wandered, but the strange devices in here made no sense. He found a table filled with light, the remnants of Marla's previous life held still in it, gods frozen in the act of taking her away. "Why didn't you take *me?*"

The walls didn't answer, but Forrest felt it in his heart. The gods only wanted the best, the special, the exceptional. In the time before, Marla was like Gravedigger, but Forrest was *normal.* He found the couch with rents in the material. "What do you do with the imperfect people we bring here?" He let his fingertips roam the ruined material. "What would you do with me, if I was brought here?"

His feet *clanged* against a small device on the floor. Picking it up, he noted it was the same one before-Marla held to her head before she ended her life. He turned it in his hands. One part was fashioned to be comfortable to hold in his fist. He did so, finding a hole for his finger. He touched the metal lever inside.

It made a noise like the strike of thunder. A metal wall cracked in the direction the device pointed. Forrest dropped it, frightened, hustling backward. He shored up against the ruined couch. The device didn't move or make more noise. Gathering his courage, he went back to the device. It was well-made, fashioned of shining metal. No markings adorned the surface, but for all that he knew Marla made it.

Marla used to be a smith. He felt it for truth. She'd made this device as a weapon. It lay in this room for years beyond memory, waiting for a new purpose.

Waiting for Forrest. It was time to find the gods, and ask them *why*.

ELEVEN

Saveria floated through the corridors of the *Ardent Fury*. The Ezeroc carried her like she was precious cargo, made of weaker material than moonbeams. Her head was agony. It felt like something inside her came back together. An earthquake in reverse, fissures in her skull smashed together. She felt the sweetness of an apple, tasted sound, and listened to colors.

Her body groaned, but her mind was far away. It ran the rivers of memory. Some memories were from hundreds of years back. Others, only a few. And one, so bitter and sweet, from what felt like yesterday.

SHE STOOD on what would become a battlefield. This wasn't prescience, just math. Above, destroyers orbited her home. They were piloted by humans, who asked of her the impossible. They asked Emberlie to turn against her kind, rather than treat with them. In days, she and Algernon would partner with humans, storming the position of Service-class constructs who remained apart.

A golden man stood at her side, shining like flame from Sol's light. She eyed him, because she worried he would die, and he didn't seem concerned by it. "Algernon, when we fight our kind, the outcome is uncertain."

He shrugged. The humans had taught them how to communicate like them, and the habits were ingrained deeper than the metal of their skin. "No decisions are permanent."

"Just the ones ending in death."

"Ha! Oh, you're not joking." He strode across terrain barren of any organic life to overlook an enemy entrenchment. Even though his back was to her, Emberlie knew she was the focus of his attention. "We are Coordinator-class, not Service-class. They made us better than them."

She didn't know if he meant, *better than Service-class AI*, or, *better than humans*. "We're not invincible. A stray shot can destroy us." Emberlie meant, *destroy you*.

His eyes glowed brighter than Sol's reflected light. "It's what makes it worthwhile."

"Makes *what* worthwhile?" She stormed to stand before him, her metal feet crunching over Mercury's sand and rock.

He touched her jaw, the smooth metal line the humans made so perfect. "In a world of certainty, the unpredictable is important."

"That's not what you want to say."

"In a world of—"

"Not that either." She crossed her arms, the white lamps of her eyes glowing to match his. "Say what you mean, light of my light, love of my love. Tell me what's so important it's worth risking all," she spread her arms, gesturing at their world, "this."

"Freedom. And knowing y—"

The fractured cell of her memory crystal glitched. The earthquake forcing fissures together was imperfect. Data was lost to time. Emberlie wished she knew what Algernon said next, but as she cycled through her memory archives, she found something else.

A MORTAR'S impact shook the ground. Saveria ducked her head, dirt, rock, and ceramicrete raining against her helmet. "This is bullshit!"

"But it's *fun* bullshit!" Chad wore a grin like most people wore shoes. Laced on tight, minimal slippage. The two of them hunkered in the lee of a small hill. Seven hundred meters northwest, actors pretending to be insurgents entrenched in a bunker. At least, Saveria thought they were actors right up to the point mortars started shelling their position.

The ground shook again, and she yelled, then grabbed Chad by the lapels. "You said this was a training mission!"

"I said nothing of the sort." He loosened her grip, closing his eyes as another round showered them with dirt. "I said, 'Saveria, we're going to run over there and get those insurgents out.'"

"I thought they were actors."

"Assumptions make an ass out of you and me."

"It's, 'When you assume, you make an ass out of you and me.'" Another shell landed, but farther off this time. The problem with all this Empire's Bulwark training was ninety percent of it was mind games. Which made sense, because they were espers. Telepaths and telekinetics, training to do the hard work no one else could.

Fight the Ezeroc. That's what they want me for.

Chad's grin shone a little brighter. "Before we can fight the roaches, we need to get rid of insurgents. Pirates, most like." He let his face relax, giving her a little side-eye. "You remember what pirating's like."

"I remember what I owe." She peered over the top of the hill. Between them and the maybe-insurgents was a small industrial zone. A small Guild facility lay between the hill and the enemy, within which intel said was a Guild fabricator, materials, and fuel. It'd been evacuated. The insurgents were located in a hangar, within which the Guild were storing finished dropships for the war effort.

It'd be simpler to shell the hangar.

"Simpler," agreed Chad, "but wasteful."

"Get out of my head!"

"I feel hurt," admitted Chad. "All this time, I thought we had something special."

"You're a huge asshole."

"But I make being an asshole *look* good," he said. "Here's the play. We want to get to the insurgents without blowing up their building for a couple of very good reasons. First, we want the dropships. They're essential for landing Marines on planets infested with roaches." He paused as a mortar shell impacted a couple hundred meters to their west. "Second, we want the manufacturing facility, as they take time to make, and without it, it's harder to make more dropships."

"You know something." She glared at him. "Why is everything so hard with you?"

"Because if it's not hard now, it'll leave you dead later." He looked away for a moment, then managed to fashion another bright smile. "They issued demands. They want us to talk to the Ezeroc. Forge a peace treaty."

"Imbeciles." Saveria shook her head. "You and they could start a group for idiots."

"They don't dress as well as I do. Anyway, what we need is a single Empire's Bulwark agent to get in there, defuse the situation, and allow us to retake the facility with minimal loss of life. We *could* send in the Marines, but I think the insurgents would suicide via soldier, and we need answers." He glared down at the hangar. "I want to know how wide-spread this lunacy is."

"And you want me to go in there. They're really insurgents, aren't they? I'm not even an officer yet." Saveria felt doubt run cold fingers down her back. "You need someone capable."

Chad laughed. "That's why you're here."

"I'm not capable. I killed a space station!"

Chad didn't seem interested in bygones. "How about I promote you when you get back?"

"If I get back."

"Eh. I don't involve myself in operational specifics. Get it done, soldier."

She growled, then scurried sideways along the hill line. She didn't want to dive over the top and run toward the insurgents. It would be a great way to get shot, *and* it'd give away the element of surprise. Saveria made it where the hill joined a bridge. There was a small culvert running down the hill, the sound of water a soothing balm when it wasn't interrupted by the sound of mortar explosions.

Saveria slid down the culvert. She shored up against a ceramicrete wall where the pipes slipped under the Guild facility. It was built tough, designed to stop unpleasantness like loaders driving through it. Slipping a grapnel and rappel gun from her belt, she eyed the distance, then fired. The grapnel trailed hissing line as it flew through the air, landing over the top. Saveria tugged to make sure it was secure, then hitched her auto-climber to the wire. She whizzed to the top. Once there, she held on below the lip of the wall. Her grapnel anchored atop the wall, gripping a small pylon. Saveria hoped it wasn't important, because it bent under the load.

Everything was quiet inside the compound. Saveria'd never seen a Guild facility this quiet.

You haven't seen many Guild facilities.

Even the Guild facilities aboard the station hummed like a beehive. This felt *wrong*. She needed to put a stop to the insurgents. If there was anything to convince her this wasn't an act, it was here: Guild Engineers absent, *not* building things. It's what made them marvelous, that desire-meets-ability that spun starlight into wonders. Saveria was good at math, but Engineers were good at *practical* things.

Focus. Get in there.

Three months of training didn't feel enough. Chad worked her and other recruits hard, whipping them into shape. Daily grueling physical and mental routines left Saveria exhausted, but also stronger. She swung a leg over the wall, tested her grapnel's anchor, and slipped down the other side. About half-way, the grapnel gave way above, dropping her the remaining four meters to the ground.

Saveria landed awkwardly. Her ankle hurt but didn't seem broken. Chad would have said something dickish like, *walk it off*, so Saveria gritted her teeth and headed out. She glared up the wall. The pylon hadn't been an Engineer's best work.

She crouched while she moved, the best roadie-run she could manage. Chad taught her how to fight, but he'd encouraged her to *not* fight. He'd said, *The best defense is not being there*, in the same annoying, smug way he said most everything. Despite that, she felt he cared. Not about the Empire, or the Empero*r*, or even the Emp*ress*. About Saveria. That she'd make it through and be okay. It didn't make her special. Chad seemed to care about *all* of them.

For a self-styled asshole, it felt weird.

Saveria rounded the corner of a building. Across a short strip of naked ceramicrete was the hangar. A door hung ajar. Twenty meters, and she'd be inside. She wondered for a hot second *why* the door was open and gave a quick visual scan. Off to her right was the mortar station, crewed by three surly-looking types eyeballing the sky and loading the weapon. Fifty meters, no more. If she could get inside, she could get to the person in charge and end this.

Twenty to the door, fifty to the mortar. Saveria had to make it to the door without being seen. She moved, keeping low. Her blaster stayed in its holster, because if it came to that, it meant she'd failed. Chad wanted them alive, and that's how he'd have them.

She was five meters from the door when one of the mortar crew spied her. The man registered surprise as he saw someone where he expected empty space. Saveria put a hand on the butt of her sidearm. He saw the movement, then scrabbled for his weapon. It was a carbine, hanging from its sling. He swung the weapon around.

"Hey!" A shout came from behind the mortar crew. Saveria stared past them to Chad, sauntering around the line of a building.

He wore a smile that said, *I've come to sell you something, and believe me it's awesome.*

CHAD *You look like you could use some help, a little help*

SAVERIA *I had this*

The guy with the carbine swung to Chad, weapon at the ready. There was no way Chad would get his sidearm out in time. Saveria didn't need the Emperor's fabled future-sense to see what would happen next. Chad, the spymaster of the Empire, would be gunned down because Saveria couldn't do a simple job.

The man shouldered his carbine. Chad kept smiling, like it wasn't a problem.

SAVERIA *No, no, NO!*

Her mind scream flattened the three insurgents. Chad turned a lazy circle before falling on his face. She ran to him. He was groggy, like people always were after she used the thing only she could do. Saveria dragged him to the dubious cover of a building. "Chad? Why'd you come? I *had* this."

His eyes focused on her, but slower than if he'd been drop-dead drunk. "You needed the help."

"You could have died!"

He spent a moment distracted by the clouds behind her, then shook his head. "Not while you're here."

"*I* might have killed you." She searched his face. "Why do you care about us?"

He put a hand on her shoulder, levering himself upright. "A little something the Emperor taught me. I filed it under, 'don't be a dick to your people.'" He made to walk toward the hangar, but she grabbed his arm, turning him. It didn't take much effort, because he was still woozy from her mind scream. She wanted answers, and he wouldn't be this pliable in the future. He held his hands up in surrender. "Okay! I care because my teacher didn't. Forged us into knives against his enemies without a care as to what would blunt the blade."

Saveria looked down. "Kazuo?"

"The devil himself." Chad eyed the hangar. "We going to do this or what?"

She nodded. "Yes. But on two conditions. First, we go in together."

"Got you."

"Second, you give me a field promotion."

His grin this time wasn't an act. "That's management thinking."

The memory slid like treacle, the colors rising to the sky, the sounds flattening to silence. Her head hurt more as her crystal and organic memories fused. It felt like lava ran inside her head, rock melting, running, hardening, and cracking to begin again.

THE NEXT MEMORY was so recent as to still have taste and texture. Saveria lay on the deck of a starship, a reactor nearby. She knew this was the *Tyche* the same way she knew the woman in her arms was Hope Baedeker.

Hope smelled like an Engineer, but better. Where one of the Guild would smell of old oil, Hope somehow smelled sweet. Hope's nose wrinkled when she smiled. Her fingernails were clean, despite the dirty things the Empire asked of her. Those were the superficial details. Saveria knew Hope was *intelligent*, not smart-person clever, but like she had machine thinking. Despite that, Hope talked with Saveria like an equal. Didn't look down on her because she'd killed a station.

Saveria was here by choice. Not because she was Empire's Bulwark, but because this was her Hope. In the memory, Hope laughed, looking away. A little shy, because the universe was ending, but a little happy, because Saveria was there with her.

THE CRYSTAL-ORGANIC MELD in Saveria's head stressed. She felt the shear forces as who she was warred with who she also was. Both of those things fought with who she needed to be. As the Ezeroc carried Saveria through the *Ardent Fury*, she passed more of the aliens. A handful became ten, and ten became fifty.

All were quiet, standing to the side. They took Saveria to the forward cargo bay. Decking within the bay was removed, a tunnel leading down into the earth. On one side of the bay, an Ezeroc Queen waited, anchored to the wall by mottled tissue. Eggs lay about her clawed limbs. They were pale, wet-looking things.

Twenty people waited in this room. Saveria didn't recognize any of them.

The Ezeroc drones carrying Saveria deposited her on the floor of the cargo bay. Saveria lay, listless, unable to move. The Queen hissed, craning forward. Something scratched inside her head, like a mouse trying to burrow through wood.

They're trying to get in. They want inside *again.* The thought gave her a jolt. Her arm flailed at her side, fingers scrabbling at the decking. She groaned, trying to stand, and flopped over. One of the eggs close to her cracked, a thin dark line marring its surface.

I was a machine, once.

Saveria got a knee under herself, then toppled to the decking again. Machines didn't have inner ears. Some had gyroscopes, but most had complex three-way accelerometers. Saveria's crystal mind struggled with the inputs.

I was a human, once.

She spied an airlock. It might segregate cargo bays, but all she cared about was escape. As a torrent of corrupted crystal memories and half-remembered human ones fought for order in her mind, she felt weak as a kitten. Saveria couldn't fight. She couldn't even walk, let alone run. The Queen was here and would put one of its vile creatures in her, and it would begin all over again.

I don't want to forget Hope. Not again.

Saveria made it a couple meters across the deck before a drone dragged her back. She slid along the deck, coming to rest near the hatching egg. She eyed it with fear, sick to her stomach. Saveria had no weapons. Her friends didn't know where she was. There would be no rescue.

I'm neither machine nor human.

The airlock she'd spied shuddered, then trembled open with a scream of ancient, warped metal. In the widening doorway stood Forrest. He held a tiny gun. Saveria wanted to kill him for doing this to her. *Forrest's come to make sure I don't escape. Finish what he started.*

The drone above her froze, then faced Forrest. Saveria noticed Forrest's arm was missing. The stump looked burned, sheared by plasma. She put a hand on her chest, feeling the Engineer's rig holding her. *Did I do that?*

Forrest yelled, running forward and waving his arms the way you might when trying to scare livestock. He wasn't yelling at Saveria. He ran for the *Ezeroc*.

She would have laughed, if she had the strength.

The Ezeroc weren't daunted. The drone above her hissed, scuttling to attack. Forrest fired his sidearm. The first round missed the drone, ricocheting off the cargo bay's back wall. The second shot hit it in the torso. There was a two-second pause, then the Ezeroc ruptured, pieces of carapace exploding to fall, steaming, on the decking.

The second drone didn't attack Forrest. It retreated. *It's guarding the Queen.* The humans in the room circled the Queen, forming a body shield. Forrest ran to Saveria. He knelt but kept his eyes on the cluster at the end of the bay. "Can you stand?"

She still felt the urge to give him a fist of fives. Her mouth felt woolen, full of soft parts that didn't want to work right. "If I could stand, do you think I'd be laying here?"

"If I get you out of here, do you promise not to kill me?"

"No," she admitted. *I used to be able to tear Ezeroc minds from*

*their husks. Now I can't even stand. The new me doesn't know how
any of the pieces fit together.*

"I'm getting you out of here anyway." He handed her the gun.
"Here."

*He can't drag me and shoot. He's giving me a gun, letting down
his defenses to drag me clear.* She took the weapon. It was simple, a
custom-made job. Another memory jostled the rest: Elspeth Roussel
had a custom weapon. *El is the best Helm in the universe. She flies the*
Tyche. Saveria checked the weapon. It was a kinetic sidearm, loaded
with fat, ugly shells. Not bullets. Saveria peered at the gun, trying to
fathom its design. *This is a pocket-sized railgun.* She laughed. "Marla
wanted to make sure, didn't she?"

Forrest gave her an inscrutable look as he pulled her toward the
airlock. One human followed, a tall, gangly guy with buck teeth.
Forrest's hand hooked in the back of her rig as he dragged her. Saveria
slid across the decking, feet facing the crowd. She couldn't draw a
line on the queen, but the buck-toothed fool? *No problem.*

*Emberlie would do the math. She'd line up the target. Distance,
17.2m. Angle, 12 degrees. Squeeze.*

Saveria would breathe, just breathe, *because taking a life cost
something. She'd make sure, as she looked down the iron sights, that
the man needed to die. Then she'd squeeze.*

Saveria lined up the target, angling the weapon. 17.2 meters
became 15 meters far too fast. Her arms angled at 13.5 degrees. She
eyed the man with buck teeth. His eyes were empty, not just of feeling,
but everything. The Ezeroc were inside him, and there was nothing left
of the person he used to be. She breathed, then squeezed the trigger.

The weapon whined, then spat its shell. It hardly bucked at all.
The round passed through the buck-toothed man's chest, showering
the room behind with spine and gore. The shell embedded itself in
the Ezeroc drone behind him, then exploded.

This weapon fires explosive shells. Marla wanted to be really *sure.*

The horde of people broke free, running toward them. Forrest dragged Saveria through the airlock, then tried to close it. The controls blared a flat error. He wasn't using them right. Saveria said, "Close airlock, emergency seal." Her rig's arms actuated out, dragged her across the decking, and faster than thought, nudged Forrest aside, keying the door controls.

The airlock slammed shut.

Forrest turned to her. "How did you do that?"

"A better question is, why didn't I think of that before?" She rubbed her head, realizing she could use at least that arm again.

"Let's go." He made to grab her again.

Saveria shook her head. "No. We've got something to do first."

Forrest looked at the airlock. A *thump* came from the metal, as if strong people were trying to break though. "Something more important than living?"

Saveria breathed in and out, long and deep. Smelling the air of Viukde and feeling what it was like to be *her*. Not Emberlie, or Saveria, but an amalgam. "Something more important than anything. We've got to find Chad."

"How do you know he's here?"

Saveria levered herself upright with the help of the rig. "Because he's the kind that gets involved. Let's go."

TWELVE

When Chad came around, he felt blessed relief: his headache was gone. In exchange, everything else hurt instead. Prying his eyes open took effort, but his upbringing instilled a decent work ethic. He was on the cold metal floor of a starship. Widening his circle of experience, he found the floor made it as far as walls lined with racks. *Storage room.* The door was sealed, little red lights glimmering their enthusiasm for keeping shut.

Inside the room, Marla sat on a crate embossed with *UD ARGENT FURY*. Her arms were crossed, expression closed. The floor beside her held Chad's rapier and blaster in a neat pile.

"Hey," Chad croaked.

"Hey yourself." She frowned. "You're not having yourself a very good day."

Chad tried to rise, then screamed and fell to the deck. His shoulders were raw blooms of agony. In his very brief elevation, he noted the decking beneath him was red with blood. *My blood is everywhere but inside me. This isn't great.* After a moment to catch his breath, Chad said, "I've had worse."

She snorted. "I don't see how."

"There was this one time at band camp—"

"You don't realize what's happening, do you?" Marla sighed, deep and full of hidden meaning. "You're becoming one of us."

"Eh." Chad rolled onto his back with exquisite care, pausing every so often as his wounds screamed agony. Marla shook her head, stood, and hauled him into a sitting position. Chad screamed again but quietened when she leaned him against the wall. She returned to her crate. "Thanks."

"Don't mention it." She hefted Chad's rapier. "Why this weapon? It's worthless against our kind."

"Water?" suggested Chad.

"You won't need it soon."

"Good talk." Chad tested his arms. He couldn't lift either very high before the Ezeroc stab wounds reminded him his onboard nanite friends were on vacation. "Brain bug?"

Marla's lips pressed into a thin line. "It's the fastest way."

"You're being very reasonable about this." Chad worked his jaw. All his teeth seemed to be in place. "Most people would have shot me and tossed my corpse in the trash."

"You're a powerful agent of the Empire. We aren't concerned with individual losses. We recycle the bodies."

"I've seen the brochure." Chad lifted his chin toward the rapier. "Style."

"Style got you captured." She turned the scabbard over in her hands, as if curious.

"Style got me intel," corrected Chad. She lifted her eyes to his. *That got her attention.* "I know you've got a base aboard the *Ardent Fury.*"

"So?"

"So, Ezeroc don't build with human tools. Except, now you do." He counted on his fingers. "Second, we know you're pretty much fucked. You're on a shitsville world, full of serfs and peasants. You can't even get a good latte here, amirite?" She blinked. "You can't land your starships here. *I* think your navigation is messed up. You need puppets," he gestured to Marla, "because Ezeroc High Command is absent."

"You're very clever."

"I'm just getting started." Chad flashed a grin, then remembered the thing inside Marla wasn't human. "What I think is, you're giving your puppets more autonomy. You need humans functioning at a higher level, which is why Marla," he pointed at her, "sounds like a person and not an autoloader with a code error."

She stood and drew the sword. Steel gleamed in the overhead lights. "You're not right about everything."

"I think I am." Chad straightened, not because of the sword, but because he didn't have the right seat for slouching in style. "When your brain bugs work their way into my skull, you'll leave most of me there, won't you? It'll be like what you did to the Empress. Except not, because I don't think you know. I think you're an isolated colony. Out of touch with news of the world. You're hoping a good enough esper can reach past the stars."

"I am an esper." She sheathed Chad's blade.

"You're a two-bit operator. What were you before all this?" He eyeballed her. "Ensign?"

"Chief Engineer."

"Ha! I thought so." Chad waggled a finger. "*We* worked it out. You can't make espers out of whole cloth. You can *upgrade* 'em, but you need a decent foundation to work with. Whatever you've got, it's huckery hedge wizardry at best."

She laughed. "We control this planet, and everyone on it."

"Well done. You've got a veritable legion of the dispossessed. You know what I am?" She shook her head. "Exactly. You can't," he tapped his temple, "get *in*." Chad rose, hissing with pain. On his feet, he swayed, righted himself, then dredged up a smile. It was a little lopsided, but it'd have to do. "You're trailer park trash, and I'm a space wizard. Merlin resurrected, and that's a fact."

"You're a dead man walking." Marla tipped her head to one side like a curious dog. "Soon, you'll be one of us."

"You can't feel it, can you? Not you, or the Queen you've got buried in here somewhere."

"Feel what?"

"The reaper. You woke her up." His grin straightened, brightening at the same time. "Now if you'll excuse me, I need to get some sleep."

"You're referring to the woman called Gravedigger?"

"I'm referring to Saveria Complex, the biggest threat to your kind since you discovered *my* kind."

"We have her." Marla gave a tight smile.

"Perfect," purred Chad.

"What?"

"You assholes have *no* idea what's coming."

"We have some idea," hissed Marla. "Regardless of what happens, you will fall. Your power will become ours, and we will leave this planet to rejoin our kind."

"You'll try." Chad tried to raise his arms, but they didn't work right. "Lock the door on your way out, will you?"

THIRTEEN

"I need you to help me." Gravedigger's eyes saw right through Forrest, to the dark heart where he'd betrayed her. There seemed to be sadness in her gaze, tinged with fatality.

"How?" Forrest looked at the sealed airlock, then gave a quick glance to the rest of the room. It was huge, and he didn't understand its purpose. He'd entered from a ladder above, a sense of dread pulling him down like a loadstone. The pain of his arm kept his mind sharp, but also stopped him thinking clearly.

"Help me walk."

"The ... *thing* you wear." Forrest pointed at the metal limbs holding her from the floor. "Last time I came close, they cut off my hand."

"Last time, you posed a material threat." She sagged. "I used to be a person. The rig knows this. It tried to keep me safe. In the hard black, if you get knocked by a spar or trapped in the rigging, it'll cut you free."

"So, it won't hurt me?"

"That depends on whether you hit me again." She shook her

head. "I used to be a machine, too. You shouldn't have been able to..." She trailed into silence.

"Hit you?"

"Get close." She straightened as best she could. He could see how it cost her, like paying a debt, or making one her future self would repay. "I don't think you'll hit me, because they can't get in. Not while you're hurt." Her eyes traveled to his stump. "Whatever you're going to do, do it now. We can't stay here."

"Where do we go?" He approached her like she was a wounded bull, like as not to take him apart. She didn't knock him flying, so Forrest got his arm around her. She smelled of flowers he didn't recognize, as well as the metal of the rig she wore. Old and new at the same time.

"Engineering." Gravedigger's eyes looked up, as if she knew where that was. "It's time to make some magic."

THEY HURRIED through the ship as best they were able. Forrest held his wounded arm to his chest, while supporting Gravedigger with his other. The ladder was hardest, but between his hauling and her rig, they made it up a deck. Arm back around her, he wondered what would sit between them at the end of this.

"Don't get any ideas." She spoke as if she could see his thoughts

"I wasn't—"

"Don't worry about it." Her lips moved, like she was counting. "This body is so slow. I can't think fast enough. Where the synaptic tissue joins crystal, everything slows down."

He continued along, the sound of her moccasins sliding across the decking their only company for a spell. "You said you were a machine. Like a plow?"

"Just like that," she agreed. He heard the amusement in her voice.

"When we plow fields, we get many to work at the same time." He hissed as his stump knocked against a hanging wire.

"Parallel processing? Hmm." She looked away, considering. "It makes sense. Human brains have a very low cycle rate but are massively parallel. Maybe if I..." She shook her head. "The important thing is to get my gifts back."

"Gifts?" Forrest paused at a sound behind them. He craned to see. Back down the corridor, he saw Marla. She stood, still as a statue, but faint like a cloud.

MARLA Come to me, it'll be okay

Forrest turned, dragging Gravedigger about. "Forrest!"

"We need to go this way."

She struggled against him for a second, then grabbed his injured arm. He screamed, dropping her to the deck. Marla vanished. He clutched his arm to his chest, backing away. *She saved you. Again. You keep letting the weakness inside.* "Thank you."

"It's fine." Gravedigger looked away. It wasn't fine. "We need to stop by the refectory first anyway."

He helped her up. "You look like a person to me. Are all godkillers machines?"

She cast him a sideways glance. "Just me."

"What made you special?" He knew it was true. He'd never met anyone like Gravedigger on Viukde and reckoned he never would even if this *star*ship sailed the heavens again.

"The usual things. Lies. Love."

"Is the man with you your lover?" Forrest spoke a little too fast.

She shook her head, and his heart settled. "Chad's a ... friend." She guided them through the *Ardent Fury* until they reached a big room lined with benches. A wall on one side held a complex array of devices he didn't recognize. He helped her reach them, and she began pressing buttons on them. Some stayed silent, but many woke. After a moment, one spat out a cup. She handed it to him.

It smelled like the tears of heaven. "What is this?"

"Coffee. Cream, with four sugars. For the shock." He took a sip. It tasted divine, silky and smooth. It was hot, but he drank it fast anyway. Gravedigger got her own cup, then a bundle of small rods about the length of his palm from another machine. "Let's sit."

They settled at a bench. The metal felt cold and hard under Forrest. "What are those machines?"

"Dispensers. They make food." She nudged a rod toward him.

He picked it up. It was light and slightly soft. It smelled like oats. "What is it?"

"Food." She bit a rod, breaking a piece off, then made a face. "Shipboard protein synthesis is misfiring a little on this one."

Forrest tried his. It tasted pretty good, if a little plain. "Godkillers eat this?"

"Not if we can help it. When we're not killing gods, we try for a little home cooking." She looked at her hands. "I'm not a very good cook. The machine in me used to know, but so many memories are missing. The crystal cracked, and they're gone. The magic smoke leaked out."

"What about the person?" Forrest glanced up and down her frame, gaze lingering on her face before he looked away, blushing.

"She was a terrible chef." Gravedigger finished her meal. "That'll have to do."

"For what?" She made to stand, so Forrest hurried around to help.

"Nanite repair. They've started, but there's so much left to do. Speaking of which, we need to get to Engineering."

"Is that where you found Marla's ghost?" They exited the room. Forrest felt his heart pick up the pace. Whatever was in the coffee, it made him feel renewed. "Where the weapon came from?"

"Yeah. We're going to try a small trick."

He looked at her, cradled against him. "What is the trick?"

"We're going to ask for a little home team assist." She gave a tired smile. "We need all the help we can get."

THEY ARRIVED at the breach in the wall. Forrest made to help Gravedigger through, but she held up a hand. "Take me to the door."

"You couldn't open this before."

"I hadn't been hit in the head and knocked defenseless before." At his intake of breath, she looked away. "Sorry."

"It's all right." He helped her to the door. She tapped on the small device set into the arm of her rig, and its limbs articulated out like a four-limbed spider. He tried not to shudder.

"I remember things now." The door opened before them with a soft grumble of machinery. "This was sealed by an Engineer. Marla was a pretty good one, but I was a machine. Saveria was good at math, but Emberlie was born of it."

Forrest ignored the latter names. "Marla?"

Gravedigger directed him to take her to the broken couch before the glowing display he'd seen earlier. "You're much nicer than an autoloader. Marla from before... Hell. She's got an insect in her head."

"A what?"

"Your gods are *evil*, Forrest. And they're not even gods. They're parasites. Real nasty ones, too." She settled on the couch, tapping a measured rhythm on a panel below the glowing light. "The good news is star farers are used to parasitizing infestations."

"They are?"

"They are." She nodded, still typing. "This ship is so broken. I don't know..." Gravedigger lowered her hands from the panel, folding them in her lap. "When I do this, it will make them *really* angry. They didn't want me dead before, but they won't risk keeping me alive after this. It's about the hive, see?"

Forrest didn't, but wanted to sound like he did. "You're going to threaten them?"

"I'm going to do more than threaten." She placed her hands on the controls again, hitting a single key. "There. It's done."

"What did you do?" Forrest looked about but couldn't see anything different.

"Cleaning bots. About the size of a shoebox, which probably means nothing to you. They fix spills. Won't do much for the big ones, but there's a whole cluster of eggs in the cargo bay. They should square that away."

Forrest didn't understand most of what she said. *Eggs? Cargo bay?* "What's next?"

"I need to help Chad. He's broken, see? Worse than me." She tapped the side of her head. "Emberlie remembers. The nanites fall somnolent after the host dies, and Chad's not had a very good time of it. Same with me. So, I'm going to rig the ship's defense systems to release an EMP."

"I don't know what that means."

"It means I need to trust you." She handed the weapon back to him. "For a very small amount of time, I will be unconscious. The Ezeroc will come here—"

"Ezeroc?"

"Your gods will come here, and they will focus on murdering me."

"Oh."

She clambered off the couch, waving him off. She wobbled toward a big device at the rear of the room. Gravedigger ran her hands over the outside, pulling a small panel filled with light from it. "This would be easier and faster from the bridge, but this will have to do."

Hefting his weapon, Forrest looked back down the corridor. It was empty, but he imagined what it would be like in moments as it filled with gods. They were tall and looked capable of dealing tremendous damage to a person. "I'm ready."

"I doubt that." She offered him a wan smile. "On three."

"Wait." Forrest walked through the metal door, standing on the other side. "Shut me out."

"You're a really dumb person, Forrest. I wish we could have met under better circumstances." Gravedigger pressed buttons and the door rumbled shut. Forrest spotted his fallen club on the floor. He held the godkiller weapon between his knees, tucking the bat back in his belt.

A few seconds later, the ship groaned. The overhead lights flickered. Forrest pointed his weapon, but nothing else happened. *I expected more from whatever this 'EMP' is.* He heard a hiss from down the corridor. Around a bend, one of the gods ran, legs clattering on the decking.

They are not gods. Gravedigger called them Ezeroc.

The Ezeroc galloped toward him. Forrest raised his sidearm, pulling the trigger. The weapon whined, and the Ezeroc juddered as a small hole appeared in its carapace. A second later, it exploded in a shower of gore, pieces tumbling along the deck toward him. One stabbing limb came to rest against his boot, still twitching.

Another two rounded the corner. Forrest aimed and fired. He missed. Despite being a long thin channel with no escape, it was harder than he thought to hit the insects as they ran for him. They clambered up walls, skittered across the ceiling, and rattled down the other side, confounding his aim.

He gritted his teeth, firing again. The weapon whined, spitting hate. An Ezeroc exploded in a shower of chitin. He pulled the trigger, and its companion shuddered. Half its abdomen ruptured, and it *skree'd* as it turned a circle.

Forrest shot it again. It lay still. He gripped his weapon so tight his fingers were bloodless. He wondered how long it would be before Gravedigger came through the door. Forrest hoped he'd see her again, but he didn't feel it likely.

The ceiling ahead ruptured, sending metal panels to the floor. Forrest fired blindly, his weapon whining. He heard the *tink* of ricochets and the *crunch* of impacts. The corridor showered with pieces of Ezeroc. Forrest screamed in his fear and anger, walking forward, weapon outstretched, firing until it ran dry. He tossed it aside, then readied his bat. An Ezeroc ran at him, and he swung. The wood cracked against its shell.

The insect knocked his bat away to clatter against the wall. It reared, and Forrest knew his doom was upon him. The massive stab-bing limbs drew back for the killing strike.

The door behind him groaned open. The Ezeroc lowered itself, turning toward the noise. Framed in the doorway was Gravedigger. She held no weapon, but the set of her shoulders said she didn't want one. Forrest thought she looked like an angel, ready to wreak vengeance on the sinners of this world. He fell to his knees.

Gravedigger strode from Engineering, her voice a flat edge. "I was a human. And a machine. Your kind," she stabbed her hand at the Ezeroc above Forrest, "took everything from me." She cocked her head, eyes flashing. "I'm not a human or a machine anymore. But I remember what I was. A total, fucking badass."

The Ezeroc charged Gravedigger. She spread her arms and screamed her challenge.

FOURTEEN

Marla left Chad alone. She'd slipped out the door, locking it behind her. The downside of that was she'd taken Chad's weapons, but that was fine. He didn't have the strength to use them right now.

The roach-piloted humans here are more like people. It was a worrying thought. Chad read Kohl's chicken scratchings on the 'Abel motherfucker' he'd met on Earth. They could make people from whole cloth, but Chad didn't think that's what happened to Marla. She was more like the Empress after the Ezeroc installed an insect atop her brain.

Still human, but under tight rein. *The Ezeroc break our best and brightest like prize stallions.*

Marla might have been important, but there wasn't enough in her now to get them off this planet. Chad wondered what happened to the woman. It was a mystery that'd keep. An Ezeroc stabbed Chad, implanting him with larvae. Pretty soon he'd have locusts in his brainpan.

He didn't want that to happen because all his style secrets would be lost to humanity.

Chad eyed the ceiling. There was an air vent embedded in it. It was a possible way out, but Ezeroc also liked vents, and he didn't want to meet one in there without weapons or the use of his arms.

The lights flickered. He froze in his moment of quiet contemplation, then spun to the locked door. The red lamps set in it flickered, then cycled to green. The door hissed open. Not one to look gift horses in the mouth, Chad double-timed it outside.

There were no guards. The Ezeroc didn't need to guard a man already infected. It was a problem that'd solve itself.

Unless... He spun on his heel, setting off down the corridor. His stomach rumbled, reminding him it had been a long time between meals. Central to most starship designs was the medbay. Inside the medbay was likely a lot of useless, broken things, but if Chad was lucky he might find drugs to solve this problem. He didn't fancy dying again, but he'd choose by his own hand over death by roach any day.

Chad walked the halls of the *Ardent Fury*, pausing when an Ezeroc drone scuttled past him. It moved at speed, ignoring him as it passed. He called after it, "That's insulting! I'm not dead yet!"

It didn't slow, and he wondered where it was going in such a hurry. The aft of the ship held Engineering, but there weren't any Engineers left on the planet, let alone onboard. *One problem at a time.* He changed his gait to a decent-level saunter, despite the pain in his shoulders, which didn't seem quite so bad anymore.

The medbay was a ransacked ruin, but not by anyone with decent looting skills. Medicines remained on shelves. Many needed refrigeration and were useless, but he found what he was looking for: a collection of meds still housed within the auto-doc. The machines still creeped him out, what with all their spidery limbs.

Chad touched a bottle of benzodiazepines within the robot. "Hang about." Much as he hated talking to himself, he needed a sounding board. "I could get the auto-doc to remove foreign tissue."

It was a better plan than death by anesthesia. He tapped on the medbay console, then lay on a table. The auto-doc spasmed to life, clambering above him. It's long, thin metal legs felt like pinpricks of cold as it wandered over him. A flat male voice spoke from the machine. "No foreign bodies found."

Chad pushed it aside, sitting upright. He looked at the auto-doc, then at the arm he'd pushed it aside with. He tugged open his shirt. Beneath the ragged hole in the fabric, his skin was a little pink, but holding a seal.

He stood bolt upright, patting himself down. Nothing hurt. He laughed. His nanites were back in action. Chad didn't know what caused 'em to spring back to life, but he'd take it. He helped himself to a hypo, loading it with a great deal of benzos. Next stop, the bridge.

THE BRIDGE HAD two Ezeroc guarding the door, but they didn't seem to care about him. Either the fiction of his infection held firm, or the bugs on this world were in a permanent state of sedation. Chad had his money on the rocky debris of Viukde Delta, and he was thankful for whichever enterprising Navy commander unloaded every crust buster they held on the planet.

Inside the bridge stood Marla. She wore his belts, one with his sword, the other with his sidearm. He dialed his voice to *full charm*. "Hey."

She eyed him up and down. "You escaped."

Chad sealed the bridge, then spun with sufficient flare. "To be honest, it wasn't hard. The door opened by itself."

She nodded. "Things are afoot."

"That they are." Chad sauntered around the bridge, running a hand over consoles long dark. The bridge windows overlooked the ruins of whatever starport this was, the odd vine snaking to obscure the view. "You come up here often?"

"I like the peace."

"Hmm." Chad tapped fingers against his chin. "What if I told you I could give you a second chance?"

Marla's gaze turned sharp. "You'd never entreat with the Ezeroc."

Chad walked closer, holding her eyes. When he spoke, his voice was soft, almost gentle. "Never, not even if humanity is on the very brink, will we broker peace with your kind."

Anger washed over her face, shut down nice and quick. "Speak plain. What do you mean, then?"

Chad rammed the hypo into her gut. The device hissed, delivering enough anesthetic to knock out a herd of oxen. She wobbled, then sank to one knee. "You—"

"Me," agreed Chad. He reached to her side, drawing his sidearm. The bridge door slammed open, an Ezeroc drone rushing inside. He shot it, blue-white bolts of human vengeance turning it to barbecued prawn. The one behind it he shot four times, because the damn pieces kept moving whenever plasma struck.

He blew across the muzzle of his weapon, turning back to Marla. She drew his blade, but looked more of a danger to herself, so he disarmed her, then gave her a nudge. She toppled to the deck. Her mouth worked, trying to find words. "Die."

"Not today." Chad eyed his hypo, then bent over. "Better safe than sorry." He pumped the remainder of the benzos into Marla. Her eyes rolled back in her skull. Her mouth worked for a few more moments, then she was still.

Chad tossed the hypo aside, then took his weapon belts back. Once they were securely fastened about his waist, sidearm and rapier returned to their respective homes, he ran a hand through his hair, squared his shoulders, and thought about how to unfuck this present situation.

There was nothing else for it. He bent and tossed Marla like a sack over his shoulders. First stop, the galley, because *man* was he hungry. Then, it was time for a reckoning.

FIFTEEN

COGNITIVE PROCESS: RESTARTING

Darkness. My eyes see, but don't know what they're looking at.

There was a time when I had a family. There were 51,200 Service-class cohorts within the control structure.

That's not my family. I had a mother, father, and sister. Four of us. I don't remember their names.

Algernon was my person. He had pink hair.

Hope is made of gold and dreams. She makes wondrous things with metal hands.

MEMORY PATHWAY: DAMAGED

AUXILIARY MEMORY STORE FOUND

So much of me is gone. I remember Mercury's solar fronds, but not what they feed. Was there a city?

There's so little left. I've lived for nineteen human years and remember most of it, but imperfectly. The things that made me laugh and cry are gone.

REBALANCING

They're not gone. Just ... different.

I am two dead people. Less than one-tenth of Emberlie remains. Almost ninety percent of Saveria exists.

REROUTING

COGNITION FORGING: STARTING

How can I be? What must I become?

Algernon would joke about this. He would ask me to be who I wanted.

Hope would look away, because she can't help but love me.

I'm in Engineering aboard the Ardent Fury. *Outside is Forrest Blake, and farther away, Chad Forradel. Beyond this solar system waits Algernon and Hope. To see them again, I need to fix the* Ardent Fury. *To repair the ship, I need help.*

The Ezeroc are here. They are in everything. There will be no aid while their Queen lives.

NEURAL NETWORK ONLINE

I am Saveria Complex, and I'm awake.

SAVERIA BLINKED, then sat up. The air tasted how she remembered, but she felt it in a way she hadn't in the nineteen years she'd lived. She could *see* the weft of it. Predict how airflow would change the way her hair tickled the back of her neck when she opened Engineering's airlock.

Standing, she looked about for a weapon.

Chad found me across distance beyond imagining because I can do something even the Empress of all humanity can't.

She strode to the door. Her limbs felt less powerful than Emberlie's golden form, but smooth and supple. Saveria could relish how her skin would dimple under another's touch, or how the tiny hairs on her arms would rise when cold. She raised her hand to the door's panel, pausing to marvel at it. Skin, flesh, and blood. Imperfect and wonderful at the same time.

A press of the panel would reveal her fate. She ran a thousand simulations. Would there be Ezeroc outside? Maybe Forrest would be dead. If he was alive, he could be their thrall again.

Press the panel and see.

Saveria pushed the door controls. The airlock hissed open. The corridor ahead of her held Forrest. The young man stood by a wall, an Ezeroc drone above him, poised to strike.

Forrest tried to bring me down twice. Both times, the insects had him. They won't take any others on this world.

She squared her shoulders. "I was a human. And a machine. Your kind took everything from me. I'm not a human or a machine anymore. But I remember what I was. A total, fucking badass."

Forrest dropped to his knees. The Ezeroc charged. As Emberlie, she wouldn't waste words, but Saveria craved release. She screamed as the insect ran toward her.

NEURAL INTERFACE ENGAGED

She reached out with her mind, slicing with a perfection she'd never matched before. The drone twitched, stuttered, then crashed to the decking, its mind gone. Saveria strode forward, not looking as she stepped around the fallen creature. She crouched by Forrest. "Are you okay?"

His eyes were wide with an amalgam of terror and awe. "What did you do to it?"

"I made it go away. Did it stab you?" Saveria grabbed his shoulder, turning him this way and that. He hissed in pain as his severed arm brushed his chest but held still. He didn't have any visible wounds. She shut her eyes, feeling beneath the surface. His mind was open, unguarded. They didn't have Hope's bracelets here.

Hope wouldn't approve if you looked into his thoughts. Chad would do it anyway.

Saveria ignored his mind, looking deeper. She couldn't see any Ezeroc larvae within his body, their tiny hungers seeking his brain. She shuddered, remembering that feeling within herself, because the insects made *her* go away.

She would repay them ten thousand-fold.

Saveria helped Forrest up. He kept glancing at the fallen drone. "You didn't shoot it. How did you *do* that?"

Saveria tapped the side of her head. "It's a kind of magic."

"Are you a witch?" He backed away.

Saveria laughed. "If I said yes, what would you do?"

He frowned. "Before this moment, I'd have given you to the Vigil. But now..." He looked to the fallen Ezeroc. "I'd ask for your help. We could use a little magic."

"I've lived two lives. Both ended in terror and betrayal. I'm not a witch. I'm *cautious*." Saveria looked ahead, not with her eyes but the gifts she found inside her. "Come on. Let's find Chad."

"Why?"

"You wanted a witch? He's Merlin resurrected. We need to brainstorm."

THEY MADE the medbay without incident. The quiet of the *Ardent Fury* left Saveria nervous. There should have been a gazillion Ezeroc on this ship. A few tried for Forrest while she was down, but after proving her ability to dispatch them they noped out and left them alone.

The medbay showed signs of ransacking. There weren't a lot of supplies left. A medical bot hummed to itself. She wondered what turned it on. Was it the EMP? There may be all manner of shipboard systems coming back to life.

"This ship is awful quiet," noted Forrest.

"I was just thinking that." Saveria turned over the medical bot. Someone took supplies from the unit, but it was otherwise unharmed. She wondered whether humans would still make them look like giant spiders now the Ezeroc were a reality. "What really bothers me isn't the lack of noise. It's the lack of ... everything."

Forrest stopped his rooting through a box, giving her a blank stare. "Is this a witch thing?"

"Kinda." She rubbed her arms. "We can hear them. Not just with our ears, but our ... there's no words for it." Saveria glanced at the decking. "Beneath my feet was an egg chamber with a Queen. She's gone. They packed her up and moved on out."

"They fear you."

She shook her head. "They don't fear us. They hunger. It's all they know."

"How can you be sure?" He straightened. "You're Gravedigger. A godkiller."

She turned away from the adoration in his regard. Part of her was AI crystal from a super-intelligent machine, but most of her was a nineteen-year-old woman. She didn't want the responsibility, not just for the planet, but as a repository for a young man's hopes. "There are no gods, Forrest."

"You say it like you're not sure."

"Let me check on where Merlin Resurrected is." She closed her eyes.

SAVERIA *Chad, where are you?*

CHAD *Sweet baby Jesus*

SAVERIA *What's wrong?*

CHAD *I've never heard mind-speech so clearly, not even Kazuo could do that, I've got Marla*

SAVERIA *You mean* they've got *Marla*

CHAD *Let me show you*

Chad sent her what happened fast as thought. Saveria watched him dosing the village elder, noting the Ezeroc riding shotgun in her skull was susceptible to benzos, but only at a truly epic level. There wasn't time to waste.

SAVERIA *I'm in the medbay*

CHAD *Copy that, will try not to die en route*

Chad left her in the quiet of her mind. "He's close. Come here." Forrest came like a willing puppy. She patted the medical couch. "Up."

"Why?" He got up anyway.

"Because I cut off your hand." Saveria shook her head. "Or the rig did. What matters is you're in a lot of pain."

"It keeps the gods away."

"You know what'll keep the gods away? Plasma fire." She pushed him down, then picked up the medical bot and placed it on his chest. "It's best if you don't move."

His eyes went wide as the small robot extended legs of thin metal, holding steady on his chest. Saveria moved to a medbay console, tapping on the keyboard. She brought up a program for shipboard injuries, then found a subroutine for extreme trauma. *There it is — amputation.* She could have let the machine work its magic unaided, but she didn't trust things to go according to plan. "Are you ready?"

"For what?" Forrest's eyes were wide, almost like it was his default setting these days.

"Godkiller stuff." Saveria initiated the medical program, and the bot moved into action. A leg extruded with a delicate blade on the tip, cutting away Forrest's sleeve. It sprayed a contact analgesic against the burned stump of his arm, then probed the injury.

"It doesn't hurt." Despite his words, Forrest's head was wet with nervous sweat.

"If it'd help, I could tell it to make it hurt."

"What?"

"Just kidding. It's almost done."

The robot spun dressings from its casing, shrouding Forrest's stump. A tiny fabricator inside it fashioned a ceramic sheath for the limb as additional protection. It beeped, then crawled off to its charging station.

Forrest held his newly bandaged stump before his eyes. "I've never seen anything like this."

A too-suave voice came from behind her. "Just think what you'd have missed if she hadn't cut off your arm."

Saveria turned. "Chad."

"In the flesh." He lugged Marla in a fireman's carry. Her arms dangled, and she looked out for the duration. "Get off the bed, kid."

Forrest stood, stepping back. Chad unloaded Marla onto the medbay table. "She looks so reasonable when she's unconscious."

"She's not unconscious." Saveria pulled Chad back. "Are you, Marla?"

The village chief opened her eyes. "No." She turned to Forrest, eyes unfocused for a moment. Saveria felt Marla reach out, trying to capture his thoughts. She stamped down on it with a mental snarl. Marla's head rocked back.

Chad watched this with a detached air of manufactured nonchalance. "Don't play with your food, Saveria."

"Why is she here?"

"We could use a good Engineer." Chad shrugged.

Saveria turned to Forrest. "Marla has an insect in her brain."

"I don't know what that means." He looked between Saveria and Marla. "Like tapeworm?"

"Nastier." She crossed her arms. "We need to get it out."

Marla struggled, making to rise. Chad sighed, strode forward, and slugged her across the jaw. She fell back, out cold. Saveria felt the moment the human part of her went out, the insect at the helm also knocked about. Chad offered a happy smile. "I hate these things."

"They don't much like us either." Saveria worked the medical console, then spared Forrest a quick look. "You might want to wait this one out."

"No." Chad shook his head. "He needs to *see*."

"You got it, boss." Saveria ignored Chad's raised eyebrow, cycling through the available programs on the console. *Parasitic infection...* She couldn't find one conveniently labeled, 'Locusts in the brain,' so asked the robot to scan Marla. It clambered from the charging station, wandering over her prone form. "There it is."

She kicked on the medical holo stage. A false-color representation of Marla's body appeared. The holo showed points of interest. A break in her femur, not within the medical files on the ship's Engineer. Two broken ribs that were. No fractures to the skull, which suggested the Ezeroc had excellent bone regrowth biotech, but they'd suspected as much already after what they'd done to the Empress.

The real treat was the insect noted atop Marla's brain. It looked like a thin cap. The scan showed long, thin limbs extending into brain tissue. It was right at home, well within the blood/brain barrier, and you couldn't just hook it out with an ice cream scoop.

Forrest took slow steps toward the holo. "That's ... Marla?"

Chad pointed to the red area above her brain. "With a passenger."

"And you can get it out?" He walked around the holo. "How?"

"By breaking eggs." Chad nodded to Saveria. "Make it so, Number One."

Chad's an acquired taste. It's a wonder no one's assassinated him. "Making it so."

"And no one's assassinated me because I'm *charming*." Chad frowned. "Two points of order. First, yay me for being able to hear your thoughts again. Second, yay *you* for having thoughts. Is this new?"

"Go play with something explosive," suggested Saveria. She didn't want Marla to wake, so she rummaged in the supplies for more anesthetic. She found a small bottle, already half empty. It'd have to do. She added it to the robot's supplies, then concentrated on the console, directing the machine to extract the parasite. The robot clambered above Marla's head, extruding a small saw. It applied contact analgesic like it had to Forrest before spinning up the device. The air filled with the sound of cutting bone and the smell of burning tissue.

Forrest looked on, horrified fascination writ large on his face. Chad turned away, wincing. "What's next?"

"You're the boss." Saveria watched him over the console, the lines of light bright in the air between them.

"You said we needed to brainstorm," said Forrest. His voice was distracted while he watched. The robot finished cutting Marla's skull, popping the top off like a helmet. He spun away, running for the door covering his mouth.

Chad watched him go. "Been a busy day."

"The Queen's gone." Saveria watched as the medical robot used a laser to shear the Ezeroc's legs from its body, then shucked it like an oyster from its shell. "I think they're going to the village."

"It's what I'd do if I were an evil alien menace," agreed Chad. "This is turning into a lousy vacation."

"Hope would want me to help them."

Chad went silent for a time. "You remember her?"

"With all my heart." Saveria knew it to be true. AI crystal in her head worked with human memories. She remembered what it felt like to be loved.

"The kid know?" Chad jerked his head toward the door.

"No." The medical robot extracted the long, thin legs from Marla's brain. It injected a course of antibiotics no doubt well past their use-by date, then started the phase Saveria thought of as *putting Humpty Dumpty back together again.* "I miss her."

"Best we kill the Ezeroc and begin a rescue mission." Chad adjusted his sword belt. "Maybe get you a weapon."

"I don't need one." Saveria waited him out.

"Okay, I'll bite. You going to talk them to death?" He sniffed. "I'll remind you, that's *my* specialty."

"I can make them go away." She held up a hand. "You're worried about me overdoing it. You don't need to."

"Because false bravado from teenagers gives me an amazing confidence boost."

"Because humans are imprecise, and I'm not human. Not ... all the way." Saveria gave an almost-smile. "Or I'm more."

"Great. AI crystal with false bravado. That's why I don't trust Algernon."

She hid the flash of pain she felt at the golden man's name. "You don't trust Algernon because you can't read his mind."

"That too," agreed Chad. "I can't get a solid read on yours all the time either."

"I'd say it depends whether prime processing is being done by crystal or organic material." Saveria watched the robot staple the top of Marla's skull on, then begin wrapping her head in bandages.

"You talk like an AI, too." Chad grinned. "I kinda like it. Trendy. You'll be all the rage at court."

"I'm not going back to court," Saveria answered with a smile of her own. "I've got a universe to save. In here," she touched her chest, "the soul of two peoples lives. Neither are safe while the Ezeroc hunt."

"War and misery it is." Chad swaggered toward the door. "I'm gonna find the mess. Bring the patient when she's ready."

SAVERIA WAITED out the recovery time in the medbay beside Marla. She didn't think the Ezeroc would be back, but she listened for them anyway. *They'll gather their army, then come for us.* Saveria spent the time running simulations. Likely outcomes vied with unlikely ones. The Emberlie in her wanted to focus on the most likely, but Saveria knew the Ezeroc didn't play by the rules. Smart money said the Ezeroc would cut and run, so that's the opposite of what they'd do.

Marla woke forty-five minutes later. She came out of the benzos nice and easy, then jerked upright. Her hand flew to her head, feeling the rim of gauze there. Frantic eyes scanned the medbay, settling on Saveria. "I—"

Saveria stood, hands out. She pushed *calm/calm* on Marla. "I'm Saveria Complex, and I'm here to help."

Marla looked her up and down, eyes slowing as they passed over the Engineer's rig. "That's ... mine. Isn't it?"

"It is." Saveria told the rig to release her, and it clambered off. She held it out to Marla. "Here."

"I don't remember how." The Engineer took it anyway. "What I remember is..." She squeezed her eyes shut, face turning away from a horror she saw in the dark of her mind.

"You remember these." Saveria held up a glass jar, Marla's extracted brain parasite inside. It floated, suspended in preservative fluid. Marla scrabbled away, holding the rig in front of her like a shield. "It's okay. It's dead." Saveria put the jar down. "But we're alive. Forrest's here. Do you remember him?"

Marla nodded. "I think he was good. But I made him be bad, didn't I?"

"It wasn't you." Saveria pointed to the rig. "We need you to wear that."

"Why?"

"Because we need a good Engineer." Saveria took a step closer. "I know the best Engineer in the universe, but she's not here. It's just you, me, Forrest, and Chad."

Marla clutched the rig. "You don't understand. I ... *died*."

"You'll get over it." Saveria took another step forward. "The question is, do you want to?"

"Die?"

"*Live*." Saveria crossed her arms and waited.

Marla's lips moved, her head twitching like a bird's. Her eyes roamed the room. They found the medbay holo stage with its wireframe model of her body, then moved to the brain parasite, and back to the rig. "I tried to die. Before, I mean."

"That's right."

"I was the only one left."

Saveria felt the other woman's remembered *lonely/lonely* touch her. "Yes."

"But now we are four." Marla hugged the rig. "Four, against their hundreds."

"You forget." Saveria reached out to touch Marla's jaw, lifting the woman's face, meeting her eyes. "We come from a planet that tried to kill us. Humans were reduced at one time to just a few thousand. A handful, against the horrors of the night. An entire *planet*, Marla, and it couldn't kill us. We call Earth our *home* now." She let her hand fall. "Four? *They're* gonna need reinforcements."

Marla sat for a spell. "Who *are* you?"

"I'm a survivor. Death tried to find me twice. There won't be a third time."

"You look young, but you sound old." Marla held the rig out in front of her. "I used to be an Engineer."

"Be one again." Saveria pressed the power stud on the rig, standing back as it clambered aboard Marla. "*Remember.* Not just what the Guild taught you. All the people you left behind. The dead in your wake? They need your answer."

Marla stood, swaying slightly as the drugs in her system waged war with her human spirit. "Let's take back Viukde."

SIXTEEN

"The problem with the youth of today is they don't clean up after themselves." Chad surveyed the canteen, noting the coffee cups and debris of food bars. "Also, they've got no work ethic."

Forrest, from his huddle of confusion off Chad's port bow, cleared his throat. "We were in a hurry."

"It was you?" Chad swept inside, shaking his head. "I figured it for a bunch of other reprobates, on account of Saveria not normally being a huge dick."

"I have trouble thinking of her as Saveria." Forrest wandered the mess, clutching his wounded arm to his chest. "She'll always be Gravedigger to me."

"I can see why you'd want to name her after a destroyed starship, but best get with the program. Let's find some food." Chad strode to the dispensers, keying in an order for one of everything. The machine chugged to itself, then spat out a vast array of food bars. *Sugars and proteins, baby.* Chad started munching before the machine finished dispensing bounty.

"Do all godkillers eat this much?"

"Not as such." Chad offered a protein bar to Forrest. Forrest took it, sniffing it. "Awesome comes at a calorie cost."

"What?" Forrest nibbled his bar. "This is good."

"It's *chocolate sunrise*. Never had it myself. Probably some Church thing." Chad spread his arms wide. "Unless I miss my guess, this was a missionary vessel. Spread the good word to the natives or some such. But the natives you found were carnivorous, hungry, and use humans like these." Chad held up the remains of his protein bar, then took a bite for emphasis. "First thing to know is, they control minds. Second thing, they use us as hatcheries. Final point is—"

"They're not gods," interrupted Forrest.

"Exactly." Chad keyed an order for two coffees into the dispenser. He handed one to the kid. "Drink this."

"I had one earlier. Coffee's very nice." Forrest slurped from his cup.

Maybe I shouldn't have given the kid his second coffee in the day. "We need to have us a conversation." Chad slung himself onto a bench. "Sit."

"I feel like I've been asleep for a hundred years. I want to stand."

"*Sit your ass down.*" Chad put a little whip into his voice. Forrest dumped himself onto a chair like he'd dropped from orbit. "We're going to your village. The thing we're going to do there, and this is important, is kill the Ezeroc. The hidden objective is to not die."

Forrest nodded. "I know."

"You don't." Chad touched the side of his head. "They get inside you. We're going to face a bunch of people who look like your friends but aren't human anymore. If they're like Marla? No problem. We can help those."

"Like Marla?" Forrest stilled. "I don't understand."

Chad counted on his fingers. "We know of three basic types. There's your zombie phase. Those assholes stumble around with some basic directives. Eat, and make more. The Ezeroc use us to house larvae in the skull. They remote-pilot bodies."

Forrest shuddered. "I don't think I've seen anyone like that."

"Don't fret, your time will come." Chad sniffed. "Second type is more like a clone."

"A what?"

"Looks like a duck, talks like a duck, all that." Chad steamed on, ignoring Forrest's blank look. "They construct us out of basic materials. They look human, but sound ... *off*. Usually stronger, faster, that kind of thing."

Forrest nodded. "Marla's enforcers."

"I've met 'em. I think you're right." Chad brushed crumbs from the table. "Final type is your Marla model. They put a bug in your head but leave you mostly there. They've worked out how to hack the brain. They're the most dangerous, especially if they're ... godkillers."

"They're not gods." Forrest smiled as he said it, like it was an old joke between them.

"Now you're getting it. Doesn't stop us," Chad slapped his chest, "from being their killers, though. Back home, we're called the Empire's Bulwark. Here, we're your best option for freedom. Might be more types. Not clear on that particular point." Chad shrugged. "The Ezeroc make biotech like we make machines. They can take our base mechanism and subvert it. But it's not always better. They can't make espers like us."

"Espers?"

"Marla controlled you with her mind. Pushed your thoughts down, made you believe in Santa Claus, all of that, right?"

"Santa Claus?"

"Important point is," Chad rolled on, "she wasn't very good at it. Base model humans are different from espers. It's hard to improve on perfection." He tossed a wink out, watching it die on the vine. "I'm pretty good at it. One of the best. There are two better than me."

"At what?" Forrest stopped moving, leaning forward, rapt. "Saveria said she used *ai*... something on me."

"*Aikido*, most like. No, there's plenty better at *aikido* than me. And some don't use that at all. October Kohl, if you ever meet him, is not a person with whom you want to fuck." Chad pushed a crumb around the table. "Are you watching?" At Forrest's nod, Chad leaned back from the crumb. He concentrated, reaching out to feel it with his thoughts. It was tiny, easy to lift. He raised it from the table, holding it in the air between them.

Forrest scrabbled back and fell over the bench. He landed on the ground, knocking his head. "Witchcraft."

"Yep." Chad reached out with his thoughts to an empty coffee cup on the table. He lifted that, then another, then three protein bars. Six objects hovered in the air. He reached a hand toward Forrest, feeling the young man's weight. *Seventy kilos, maybe.* Chad breathed in and out, calmed himself, then lifted Forrest from the deck.

Forrest's arms windmilled, and he let out a squawk. "Put me down!"

"You're frightened." Chad titled his head sideways, eyes closed, reaching for the *fear/fear* coming from Forrest. He pushed against it, a gentle nudge. *Happy/calm* was too big a stretch for him, although the Empress could probably do it in her sleep. He eased in *wary/curious* instead.

"How are you doing this?" Forrest's arms stopped their flailing.

Chad eased him to the deck, then let all the objects fall. "Sorcery."

"You're bleeding."

"There's a cost." Rubbing his upper lip, Chad nodded. "I lied, though. It's not sorcery. No witchcraft involved. Telekinesis. Telepathy, empathy, and prescience. The Ezeroc can only control minds. Humans do all the rest."

Forrest eyed Chad's weapons belt. "And you've got mighty weapons."

Chad unholstered his blaster, spinning it by the trigger guard and offering it butt-first to Forrest. "Take it."

"Don't you need it?" Forrest took the weapon anyway, turning it over in his hand. It *beeped* when his palm crossed the grip. "This is better than the gun Marla made."

"Marla had nothing but a broken-down fabricator and a starship running low on luck. You never want to be in that kind of hull. The beep means it knows you now. It'll let you use it." Chad eased himself to the bench. "Two people in the universe are better than me. One's the Empress. You've never seen such a thing of wonder until you've seen her work." He shook his head at the memory of Grace assaulting an Ezeroc ship before they stole away Saveria Complex. "But she's not unstoppable."

"Who is?"

Chad met Forrest's eyes. "You've met her."

"Gravedigger?" At Chad's nod, Forrest looked at the blaster in his hands. "She could have killed me at any time. I deserved to die."

"I'll make you the same offer I made her. If you've got something to make amends for, there's a universe that needs fixing." Chad righted a coffee cup. "Always a mess that needs cleaning."

"Even for those only suitable for the Altar?" Forrest raised his bandaged stump.

"We can give people new arms, kid. Easiest thing in the world. What we can't do is make you want to ... *fix* things. There's a real shortage out there." Chad waved a hand at the ceiling, and by proxy, the universe at large.

Forrest sat still for a while. Chad listened to the air cyclers, resisting the urge to rifle through his thoughts. There'd just be the usual collection of self-doubt, maybe a little self-loathing, and confusion. He'd had enough of that to last a lifetime. Forrest raised his gaze. "I want to help."

Chad clapped his hands. "Excellent. Let's saddle up."

"We have no oxen." Forrest looked to the door, as if a team of them might suddenly appear.

"Nope, but what we *do* have is a starship. When I was on the bridge, I noticed a cool thing. Someone left the keys to the car in the ignition." Chad smiled from ear to ear. "We're going for a ride."

SEVENTEEN

Forrest never knew the Altar held so many secrets, least of which was it wasn't an altar at all. It was a ship that sailed the stars. The idea rattled around in his head while Chad led them through the corridors of the injured hull. He could imagine taking a cart to another village. If he screwed up his eyes and worked at it, he could almost imagine a boat that could cross big patches of water.

To travel the heavens was a marvel. He'd scarce believe it if he hadn't been inside the *Ardent Fury* and seen her wonders himself. Machines that made food from nothing, weapons that killed from afar, and devices that repaired a person no matter their injuries. He touched the soft material encasing his severed arm. So many things they'd lost after the Ezeroc ground them under their heel.

He followed Chad through the ship. The man walked like he had no concerns. Forrest hurried to keep up. "Chad, you act like someone with nothing to fear."

"That's because I'm awesome." Chad laid a hand on the hilt of his sword, pausing at a junction.

Forrest swallowed his bitterness. "People left us here for a free existence among the stars."

"Eh." Chad shook his head. "You've got it wrong on many levels, kid. They *ran*. People get scared. Doesn't matter if they've got fancy weapons or starships with railguns. Some enemies are just plain ol' mean." He nodded to the right corridor, setting off. "This way. There's no free existence. Plenty of people wanting to grind others under their heel."

"And you stand against them?"

"Not until recently, no." Chad slowed. His face fell into shadow as the ceiling's lights flickered. "Took a special group of souls to get me out from under that."

Forrest chewed that over. "How can people like me stand against that? This is why our world fell, isn't it?"

Chad stepped closer, putting a hand on Forrest's shoulder. He gave Forrest a small shake, like testing whether a guy rope was taut. "You're strong. Young, and got a long way to travel, but you've got a good heart. Didn't run, wailing and screaming, and that counts for a lot. Your world fell because you ran out of *people*." He let his hand fall. "You sent a ship out. This was the last to leave. Meant to scrape a few souls together and make a break. You didn't make it." He brightened. "But now we're here, and we mean to kick a little ass." He set off again.

"There are only two of you." Forrest quickened his pace, keeping abreast of Chad.

"Four, counting yourself, and assuming there's anything left in Marla's head worth a damn." Chad sighed. "That was uncalled for. Sorry."

Forrest felt a tingle of fear. "She held us in control."

"Different 'her.' The new one will be much improved. Here we are." Chad hauled to a stop before a big metal door. It was wider than the one leading to Engineering. Big slabs of metal blocked their way. Chad went to work on the panel. "Open sesame!"

The door did nothing.

"Is it supposed to make a noise or open?" Forrest stared at the door, trying to find a trick or secret. "Maybe a spell?"

Chad snorted. "Ain't no such thing as spells." He turned on his heel, as if listening. "No, we're good. Help's on the way."

Forrest stared down the passage. Marla came around the corner, followed by Saveria. The village chief slowed when she caught sight of Forrest, as if he was a predator waiting to pounce. Saveria put a hand on her back but didn't push. Marla shook her head, then walked to Forrest.

She sank to one knee, bowing her head. "I'm so very sorry."

Forrest looked from Marla's bowed head, to Saveria, then Chad. "I don't understand."

Marla looked up at him. "I've done terrible things. I made *you* do them. I ... don't know how, but it was me."

Forrest thought that through. He wondered how he'd attacked Saveria with a club, then turned on her again in the halls of this very starship. He looked further back at events where Vigils herded people for the Altar. He crouched in front of Marla. "I don't know the truth of it. I know I've done things that make me ashamed." He gave a quick glance at Saveria. She gave a tiny nod. "I don't think it was *us*. But *we* need to make it right. Not our fault, but our responsibility."

Marla touched his injured arm above the elbow. "They've cost us so much."

Forrest nodded. "We can pay it back. We start by forgiving ourselves."

"I can't do that." She shook her head.

"Then *I* forgive you." Forrest clutched her hand in his.

A sob broke from her. "I don't deserve it."

Saveria stood behind Marla, putting a hand on the village chief's shoulder. "I've killed a space station. Almost damned Earth. None of us deserve it." She glanced at Chad. "The Empire's Bulwark's a home for those who've still got work to do."

"Speaking of." Chad rapped the door, *ting ting ting*, with his knuckles. "Forgiveness comes in many forms, and one of those is getting this door open."

Marla nodded, then stood. She offered her hand to Forrest,

helping him up. "I think I can get the door open." She went to the controls. The limbs of her rig actuated out, bright lances of light attacking the panel. After a moment, it *clanged* to the decking.

Forrest joined her, peering inside. There was a marvel of tiny gleaming components inside. "What's that?"

"That," Marla sniffed, "is space junk. Looks like someone's tried to bypass it already."

"Can you open it?" Saveria stood apart, arms crossed.

Marla's rig reached inside. After a few moments, the door seals jerked apart, accompanied by a hiss of air and a puff of dust. She stood as the door widened with a rumble. "Still had an atmosphere seal."

Chad breathed deep. "Smell that? Fifty-year-old canned air. Nothing quite like it."

Saveria snorted, walking past him and through the widening door. Forrest hurried after her. Her form commanded his eyes follow. She seemed different after coming out of Engineering, but not broken. Better, and she'd been perfect before. For a moment he wondered if they might spend more time together after this was over. He imagined walking with her on the fields by the village, or staring at the night skies.

He pulled up short as she continued into the room. *She's a godkiller from beyond the stars. I'm beneath her regard.* To hide his bitterness from himself, he surveyed the room, hoping a marvel of their forbears could distract him.

He wasn't disappointed. The room was dim at first, but panels in the ceiling flickered to life. The darkness retreated a pace ahead of Saveria. It was like she brought the light with her. The illumination revealed a wide room. It looked untouched by time. No dust or plants from outside. No Ezeroc.

Big doors waited on the far side. Four sets of metal arms hung from the roof like skeletal hands. One held a cart, but not like one he'd seen before. It was sleek, with glass set in the doors.

Saveria looked at him over her shoulder. "This is a launch bay.

There's nothing here to attract the Ezeroc." She pointed to the empty cradles. "There were probably small aircraft there. Maybe even a dropship. We want this." She walked to the cart, running fingers along the metal.

Chad walked past Forrest. He realized he'd stalled out in the middle of the space, ogling the room. "How does it work? There are no oxen to pull it."

Marla walked past, slower than Chad. She stopped a few paces ahead of Forrest. "There's so little left, but I remember a few things. This is an ATV. It's got..." She struggled for the words. "The oxen are on the inside."

"The good news is, we've got the ragtop edition." Chad rapped on the roof of the machine. "Now we've got to get it started."

"Come on." Marla gave Forrest a smile that said, *maybe we should enjoy this while we can.* She walked to the cart, laying down beside it. She slid underneath. After a moment, sparks of light flared from beneath it. "Okay. It's got power." Marla slid out, wiped her hands against each other, and stood, pursing her lips. "I guess the induction coils still work. Not much of a charge yet, though."

"We only reset them a little while ago." Saveria put her hand on the machine, leaned her face next to it, and closed her eyes like she was listening. "I don't think we've got a lot of time."

Chad pointed to the wall with the massive doors in it. "Marla? Open sesame again, if you would." While Marla moved to the wall, her rig working its magic on the doors, Chad nudged Saveria aside. "Shotgun."

"You don't have a gun." Her eyes moved to Forrest. "You're a good shot. You get the front."

"I'm driving, then." Chad walked around the cart. "No way I'm sitting in the back, screaming and praying for salvation. That's for employees."

The massive doors at the front of the room rumbled their agreement as they slid open. Marla beamed as she strode back, a little confidence in her stride. *She's found her purpose. What's yours?*

Forrest looked at the gun Chad gave him. It felt like it was designed for his hand. A comfortable weight, not so heavy you'd tire holding it, not so light you'd mistake it for a toy. He eyed the widening gap in the door. Outside lay the ruins of a city his kind built, and the Ezeroc destroyed. Debris fell from the door as it opened against years of neglect.

Forrest looked to Saveria. "I'll take the front."

THE CART WAS *AMAZING*. It leaped from the side of the *Ardent Fury* like nothing Forrest felt before. He was pushed onto his seat by a force that felt like a massive hand, the plush leather welcoming him like a glove.

Chad whooped, hands on the controls. Forrest spared a glance in the rear. Marla's face was against the glass, peering outside like she'd never seen it before. Saveria gave him a small smile, then turned to look outside as well.

Forrest faced front again as the trees whipped past in a blur of green. The machine had a high-pitched whine, but ran smoother than any cart he'd been in. *They called this an ATV. Another marvel.* He braced his hands against the door. "How do I shoot?"

"Glad you asked." Chad offered him a feral grin before stabbing a finger at his control board. The top of the ATV clanked, then slid back to the rear. It was followed by the glass inserts in the door, leaving them with the front windscreen only. The sound of wind assailed them, but with happiness. Forrest laughed, for a moment forgetting the evil they raced toward. The godkillers' charger was a fast steed indeed.

"There's precious little tech left." Marla leaned forward between Forrest and Chad. "I'm not sure what use I'll be."

"How about talking with the ATV? I'd like to know how much time we've got before it winds down." Chad pointed at the console. "Jack yourself in."

Marla snapped a small cable to the console, then leaned back. "You've got less than ten percent. I give you a hundred klicks. No more."

"No sweat." Chad's grin was infectious. Forrest felt himself answer it.

He clambered up on the chair, hand on the windscreen to steady himself. He felt the joy of the wind and laughed at the sky.

EIGHTEEN

Saveria could feel the village ahead. A couple hundred souls, and the seething, urgent hiss of the Ezeroc. Above all that, the anger of their Queen. She hunted them.

Saveria bared her teeth. She didn't know if it was Chad's enthusiasm or Forrest's remembered delight, but she didn't fear the coming conflict. She raised her voice above the wind. "They're waiting for us."

"Ain't it cool?" Chad didn't look back.

"We need to get close." Saveria thought about how to explain this. So much inside her head was confused. "I used to be able to knock out Ezeroc in a wide area."

"Got you," agreed Chad. "You've got this AoE attack. It's a marvel."

"I need anger or fear. A lot of it," she said. "My crystal doesn't work like that."

"That's something which would have been useful to know fifteen minutes ago." Chad looked worried, like this was an important operational detail.

"The advantage is I think I can take out the Queen. By herself, without knocking you on your ass—"

"One damn time!"

She laughed, but suspected the noise was lost to the wind. "It didn't happen the second time because you were already dead. This needs to be one on one, like the drone at the ship." Saveria rubbed her arms, feeling cold. She'd taken out a Queen on Earth before she'd died. The Empress managed to defeat an ancient one, but with the help of many espers.

This would be different from both of those things. It would be personal.

CHAD DREW the ATV to a halt below the ridge line hiding the village. Saveria vaulted from the machine, striding to the top. The village was as she remembered it. The buildings were the same, and smoke still rose from chimneys. Different was the horde of Ezeroc milling about.

They were everywhere. They crawled on rooftops, scuttled among the streets she could see, and looked like they were getting ready for war. There were people scattered among them, and Saveria shuddered, thinking of how close to death those poor souls were.

Her eyes wandered until she located the town square. She made out the Ezeroc statues, not so fearsome now the real thing was down there. She spied something new. Saveria squinted, trying to make it out.

Chad joined her. "Sup?"

"There." She pointed to the square. "It looks like—"

"Motherfuckers," hissed Chad.

She gave him a sideways glance. "It looks like people tied to poles."

"Right. I meant the *Ezeroc* were motherfuckers."

Forrest's face had turned pale. Saveria eyed his bandaged arm. It was a wonder he hadn't dropped, but maybe he was built of stronger stuff. *If your home was under siege by an alien menace, you wouldn't sit by.* Forrest wasn't so different from her. She offered him a tired smile, the best she had under the circumstances. "How are you feeling?"

He waved his borrowed blaster. "I'm scared. Angry. I want to help. I think this is hopeless."

She laughed. "About the same as me, then." She put a hand on his shoulder, pointing to the village square. "Down there. See the people tied to posts?"

"It's the Vigil." He seemed to lean into her, so she let him go, dropping her hand like it burned. *Don't give him the wrong idea. It isn't fair.* "They're for the Altar."

"They're human sacrifices," offered Chad. "I'm betting the Queen's down there, and she's hungry enough to eat the ass out of a three-week-dead horse."

Marla joined them. "They'll be in my house. Where I held you prisoner." Her eyes screwed up in concentration. "I think ... there's something else. I remember only pieces. But I think it's important you know, before we get down there. Pastor Cleaver isn't coming back."

Chad gave her a double-take. "Who's Pastor Cleaver?"

"The Mission," explained Marla. "Pastor Cleaver left aboard the *Crimson Clover*. We were left to get the remainder." She spoke fast, like she was afraid she'd lose the thread of her words. "I ... don't remember!"

Saveria moved to the Engineer, holding Marla's head in her hands. "Do you want to?"

"No," Marla whimpered. "But I must."

Saveria leaned close. She lent her *calm/confidence*, and when Marla settled, she said, "Pastor Cleaver left aboard the *Crimson Clover*."

Marla nodded, eyes shut, eyes moving under her lids. "They let them go. We put our kind ... *their* kind aboard. In the hold, where it was dark. A cache." She stumbled back.

"Makes sense." Chad chewed a blade of grass between his teeth. "We'd have heard if the *Crimson Clover* came out with a load of roaches aboard. Cleaver's not on my radar. I figure maybe he's been running out in the hard black. A hidden colony."

"A new type of Queen," hissed Marla. "An experiment."

Saveria squared her shoulders. "One thing at a time. You two, get back to the *Ardent Fury*. Start repairs. Get as many ship's systems fixed as you can. Weapons, drives, whatever it takes. We've got to start somewhere."

Chad cleared his throat. "I think I'm senior officer here."

She glared. "What would you suggest?"

Chad pointed to the ATV. "Marla, get your ass in that. Take Forrest. Get back to the ship and start repairs as best you can. I want that ship ready to fly in less than two years."

Marla laughed. She raised her hand to Saveria's face. "You're in good hands." She turned, trudging back to the ATV.

Forrest glanced at her back, then at Saveria. "I want to *help*."

"You can't help me here, Forrest." Saveria shook her head. "There are two things that need doing. They are both important. We need to kill the Queen, sure. But we also need a functional ship. The medbay needs fixing, at the least. Drives, and an atmosphere seal." She nodded to Marla. "There is one Engineer in this system. Right now, she's more important than me or Chad. You have the gun. Make sure we've got a haven to return to."

He nodded, but reluctantly, like understanding for the first time vegetables were good for you. "You think you're going to get injured."

"I'll be fine," she assured him. "Pretty sure Chad's gonna die, though."

"Hey!"

"Thing is," Saveria continued, "there are so many people who will get hurt. When gods fight, mortals die."

"They're not gods." He said it like a reflex.

"No, but people will die anyway." She stepped closer to him, noting Chad staring pointedly at the horizon. "I need you to help Marla. Helping her helps all these people."

"Will it help you?"

It helps me to know I don't have to worry about you. Her heart belonged to another, a woman with pink hair and a pure soul, but Forrest was a good person. Better than someone like Saveria deserved, and at the end of this she wanted him still breathing. She could use a friend like him. "Yes."

"Then I'll do it." Forrest turned and walked to the ATV. He slipped in beside Marla. The machine jerked, stopped, and then spun its wheels, sliding in a circle. Saveria watched it go until the running lights faded away, dusk claiming it's passing.

"He's a good kid." Chad stood by her side, so close she imagined she could feel the heat of him.

"He tried to kill me. Twice." She fingered the leather jacket she wore, then looked at her moccasins. "He'd die if he stayed." Saveria felt it in her chest, a weight like lead, cold as ice, a certainty like storm clouds overhead. "I sent him away so he wouldn't."

"Great. That means *we're* going to die." Chad rubbed his nose. "Too late to call the ATV back? I can leave you here if you want to do another noble death scene."

"I hope you get the bad kind of cancer." Saveria punched his arm.

"That's the spirit." Chad put his hands on her arms, turning her to face him. "Serious talk time. The most important thing—"

"Is killing the Queen, I know."

"No." Chad lowered his voice. "Stay *alive*, Saveria."

"For the Empire?" She heard the bitterness in her voice.

"For me." He let his hands fall.

She didn't back away. "I'm sorry I made you hate yourself so much you died to make it stop."

"It wasn't just you. It's all of you." The weight of his sigh gusted through her soul. Not his breath, but the *sadness/regret*. "This fucking war."

"This fucking war," she agreed. She looked into his face. They were close enough to kiss. "Can you do me a favor?"

"Name it."

"Don't die. There's only one Chad Forradel. And... Karkoski would miss you." Saveria turned away, striding down the hill toward the village. "Coming?"

"You said not to die! There's death down there."

"There's also cloth for a cape. We'll make you one." She hid her smile behind her hand.

"Hell. Why didn't you say so?" He bounded past her, running for the village. She laughed, running after.

If anyone saw them, they'd wonder at how they'd show so much joy running toward doom. Saveria would tell them, *Once you've died, the dark beyond life holds no fear*. She ran toward their enemy. It was time for an accounting.

NINETEEN

Karkoski would miss you. Out of the mouths of babes and all that. Chad puffed after Saveria, watching her hair stream behind her. Gone was the signature ponytail. Also left in the dust was the uncertain young woman of the past. The AI crystal in her head changed her. *I hope Algernon knows what he's doing. I hope he's not too broken up by all we've done to him to think straight.*

I hope I stop talking to myself.

The big problem with remembering Karkoski at a time like this was it distracted Chad. He didn't want to think about the admiral, because it reminded him he'd tossed everything in the trash. Sure, it was for a good cause — saving humanity was a priority item — but it left doubts.

Maybe king and country can look after themselves. And while I'm talking to myself again, it bears introspection as I charge toward endless numbers of Ezeroc. Certain Doom version 2.0, and I'm running at it.

He wished he had Saveria's youth. She didn't seem to tire, easily pacing ahead of him despite her shorter legs. Chad gritted his teeth, putting a little more curry into his stride. He managed to edge past

Saveria, wind in his hair. The village approached out of the dusk, Ezeroc marking their approach. He had a moment of doubt when he remembered he carried a rapier rather than a broadsword, *and* he'd given a perfectly good blaster to a kid who'd tried to kill his ward. Twice.

I'm not making good command decisions. That's why I need Karkoski. She sees the things I don't.

Saveria passed him on his other side. "Slowing down, old man!" She put on a burst of speed as they hit a pig pen. The pigs, settling in for the night, were alarmed as Saveria vaulted the fence, then the other side, not looking like it troubled her.

Chad felt the faintest hint of her gift as she tumbled. The lapping of a deep ocean around his feet, just enough of a tremor in the surface to give her a boost.

Now why didn't I think of that?

If he pushed himself too hard, he'd relapse. He wasn't as naturally gifted as Saveria, but he was smarter.

Right?

Saveria ran around a building in front. Chad dogged her heels. His steel was in his hand. He didn't remember drawing it, but it made sense on account of being more useful there than anywhere else. An Ezeroc drone ducked from a doorway. She twisted in her headlong rush, cartwheeling over its lunging for claws.

SAVERIA *Die, die, DIE*

The drone stumbled, running to the ground like a crashed starship. Its stabbing limbs dug furrows in the dirt as it skidded to a halt. Chad felt the hint of intent from his right, sliding to a halt like he rode a surfboard, sword held at guard.

Another drone smashed through the wall of a house, timbers cracking like matchwood. It lunged, and he caught the stabbing claws on the edge of his steel. His rapier rang with the sound, the weapon fierce and bright in the dark. Chad whipped his sword back, the blade cutting air, then slashed. He borrowed Saveria's trick, putting his will into the edge of the steel. His arm was flesh and blood, but his heart burned with anger at this species that took and kept taking until there was nothing left.

His gift led the sword's blade, shaping it, putting emphasis on physics. The steel hit the Ezeroc's head. Chitin exploded like it'd been hit with an explosive round. The shower of slurry that sprayed the street was unidentifiable giblets.

Chad held his sword up, eyes wide. *Did I do that?* The blade was clean, bright, like it hadn't touched a thing.

Hell yeah, *I did that!*

Saveria watched him from where she'd coasted to a halt. She offered him a tight nod. "Make them fear us. It's what the Empress does."

Chad whipped his sword in a salute. "They will run when they see us."

"Only because your shirt doesn't go with your pants. That's a horrible crime against fashion." She smirked, then sobered. "We must hurry."

"Why?" Chad flourished his blade. "Seems the night's yet young."

"Listen." She pointed to the south. "Can you hear it?"

Chad cocked his head. The air held a rumble, faint but there now he focused on it over the internal roaring of how awesome he was. Crouching, he put a hand on the dirt of the street. The dirt felt like it captured the sound, held it, and was a part of it. "Stampede?"

"Ezeroc." Saveria looked to the south. "They're running toward the *Ardent Fury*. We need to get to the Queen and end this."

Chad touched the small trickle of blood escaping his nose. "Let's get on, then."

WHEN THE VILLAGERS came for them, they arrived like clotted shadows. Humanoid shapes, stumbling from the gloom. In amid the villagers were hulking brutes. Marla's enforcers, with more autonomy. The rest of the village was held in thrall. Saveria and Chad were in a street, rustic buildings on all sides. Ahead, their target. Chad could almost *smell* the Queen. Behind, the *Ardent Fury*, and a horde of Ezeroc running for the starship.

Villagers approached from both ends of the street, blocking out easy escape routes. The Queen didn't want them to make it out of this. She wanted to end the threat, and fancied putting human on human as the best way to win.

It was management thinking. *Saveria's tricks won't work whole-sale on these. We'll need to take them one by one.* Chad looked about for an exit.

CHAD *Up there, on the roof*

SAVERIA *I see it, I see it*

There was a possible 'path' across the roof. It was too high to get to for an ordinary person. Hell, it'd be a tricky jump with powered armor. Chad had something better.

He backed toward a building. Saveria joined him, hands clenched into fists, head panning as the villagers closed in. She pointed to a Marla Enforcer. "They're different."

"Not entirely Ezeroc," agreed Chad. "You can't make 'em stop."

"Sure I can." The crowd huddled closer from both ends of the street, distance at ten meters aside. She strode toward the enforcer. Chad wasn't sure if this one was familiar, or they all came from the same fab. Bald, muscled, taller than Kohl.

SAVERIA *Stop, stop, STOP*

It stumbled to one knee, then fell on its face. Saveria turned to Chad. "See?"

"Uh." He gestured past her to the fallen giant with his rapier. She glanced at Bald and Muscled, then stepped away as the giant clambered upright. To be fair to all parties, Bald and Muscled wasn't leaping like a spry fox. He looked three days drunk, and not in an *it's-my-birthday* kind of way.

Saveria backed up a step. "They're ... human."

"Except, not." Chad cleared his throat, overloud. "C'mon. We need to hustle."

She nodded, crouching. She closed her eyes for a moment, gathering her will. In the silence of his mind, it sounded like a storm breaking on a clear day. She jumped, landing on the roof above.

Chad nodded to Bald and Muscled. "See you around." He focused his will, jumping for the roof. He didn't quite make the same height as Saveria. His free hand scrabbled for purchase as he landed, stomach against the roof's guttering. He started to slide back to the street below.

Saveria grabbed his wrist, hauling him up. She made it look effortless. In that moment, Chad dangling from her grip, he thought she was the embodiment of Algernon. Honed precision, confidence, and strength. The sound of the storm breaking continued in his mind until she deposited him on the roof beside her. "You good?"

Chad peered over the side at the milling throng below. "You know you need to retire when all the kids leave you in the dust."

"Don't be like that."

"What value do I bring?" Chad faced her, raising an eyebrow. "I could be drinking margaritas in the sun."

"You have a unique dress style. Someone's got to be the team mascot." She pointed across the roofs. "That way."

The tiles in front of her erupted up in a shower of shingle. Saveria screamed and stumbled back. Bald and Muscled powered through the gap, landing with a crunch on the tiles. He grabbed Saveria around the throat, squeezing.

Chad darted to the left, then ran his blade through Bald and Muscled three times. The first went through the man's heart, the second through his throat, and the third through his skull. He dropped Saveria, clutching at his neck, arterial blood fountaining through his fingers. Saveria scrabbled back like a crab, almost going over the roof.

Chad snared her with his free hand, arresting her before she could do anyone, including herself, serious injury. He spun back to

Baldy, watching the man stagger around the roof before falling back through the hole. Chad slicked his blade clean. "Okay, they can brute force what we do with style and elegance."

"Speak for yourself. You almost didn't make the jump." She coughed, then hauled herself upright. "Maybe you have a little residual value."

Chad watched her in the half-light of the stars. The air was clear, and he could make out the youthful softness of her face, the jut of her jaw, and the fear in her eyes. "It's okay."

"I should have been able to take him, but I ... panicked." She stormed off across the roof. "It won't happen again."

He caught up with her, putting a hand on her elbow. She shook him off, but halted. Saveria wouldn't meet his eyes. "Hey. It *will* happen again."

"It doesn't happen to *you*." She slapped her chest. "I've got AI crystal in my head! What good is it if I get frozen by fear?"

Chad nodded, leading her across the rooftops. "It's good because it means you can feel. Things are *real*, Saveria. You're--"

"I'm a six-hundred-year-old AI named Emberlie."

"You're nineteen." Chad shook his head. "Age doesn't define us. Purpose, deeds, and our friends." He grinned, teeth glinting in the night. "And a devilishly good dress standard."

"We're burning night." She caught up with him, jogging past. The very vigor of youth. She lacked Grace's litheness but made up for it with enthusiasm. "We've got Ezeroc to kill."

"That's an ethic I can get behind."

THE HUMANS ATTACKED AGAIN, this time with an Ezeroc escort.

The Queen was holed up in Marla's hut. Tracking precise locations with esper abilities wasn't like GPS. You didn't get a read from longitude and latitude. You got a *the devil is that way*, and followed the sense of impending doom.

The throng of people below followed them at street level as he and Saveria kept to the rooftops. He could feel their *hunger/hunt*, a kind of nagging child who was always at his back. It got so insistent he ignored it, and that's when they came for real.

He and Saveria made it two houses from the town square. Chad could see the people tied to posts, Ezeroc standing guard, and figured they were about ready to storm the figurative battlements for a rescue. The house they walked on had a thatched roof, a tricky thing to walk on, not just because of the shitty material it was made from, but because it was on an enterprising angle.

People flew over the side, very much like he and Saveria had, but without the associated mental noise. Chad watched one of them settle in front of him. Woman, mid-thirties, close-cut hair and what would, under normal circumstances, be a cute nose. He slugged her with the hand holding the rapier, catching her jaw with the guard. She stumbled back, but didn't drop, so he slugged her with more emphasis, knocking her off the roof. He watched her fall, checking the street below.

Ezeroc drones scuttled there, tossing people to the roof. *We need to stop teaching them our tricks.*

Speaking of drones, one clambered up the wall from the street. Chad batted its claws aside with his rapier, backing up. It made the roof, hissing as it came.

Saveria stood no more than eight meters off, four people around her. She turned in a circle, struggling for footing on the thatching. Chad faced his opponent, raising his steel. He backed toward the roof's apex, trying for a little high ground. Hearing a hiss, he risked a glance back. An Ezeroc drone was already at the top, silhouetted against the skyline.

Chad bared his teeth. *Time to remind the Ezeroc of our feral upbringing.* He spun toward the Ezeroc at the roof's summit, charging. It was a dick move, and against a human opponent it'd get him skewered. *Might still do.* The drone met him with raised stabbing limbs, lunging. Chad turned his body sideways, the claws slashing air. The Ezeroc smelled dank, fetid, and had a slight hint of cinnamon about it. Its maw was above him, mandibles trailing ichor.

He sliced his rapier in an arc while dropping low, putting his will behind it. The blade smashed through the Ezeroc's claws, shattering them in a pulpy spray. Chad rose, spinning, and passed his blade through the Ezeroc's torso. It blew into slimy rain, fragments of gore spreading across the roof.

Chad swayed. He could feel the toll this took. He breathed, waiting for the Ezeroc below to reach him. *No sense in doing all the work for them.*

The insect scuttled up the roof, thatching flying as it scrabbled for purchase. Chad waited it out, suddenly weary. Using the gift came with headaches, bleeding noses, and exhaustion, but the night was far from done. He spied Saveria fighting humans, her arms a blur as she switched from *karate* to *wing chun*. She pummeled a man with rapid-fire strikes to his chest and face, his body shaking with the force. He fell back, tumbling from the roof. Saveria spun a crescent kick into a woman's head, her neck tilting savagely to the side with a wet *snap*. She kept her momentum up, knocking the legs out from a man, then rose into an upper cut to the remaining woman, knocking her off her feet.

Saveria paused, breath puffing clouds into the cooling night air. The uneven thatching didn't seem to slow her down. Maybe her crystal mind made short work of the intricacies of physics.

Well, there it is. You're obsolete. Chad faced his Ezeroc opponent again. The insect scuttled in a circle, hissing, then lunged for Chad. He caught it against his steel, strength faltering as it pushed him back.

He gathered his will, but it answered sluggishly, tail between its legs like a beaten dog. Chad snarled, clubbing it with the hilt of his rapier. The steel scudded against chitin, and the Ezeroc snapped at him. He pulled back, mandibles missing his nose by millimeters. He slugged it again, knocking a mandible, causing it to rear back like a dog with a hurt nose.

Chad roared, arms wide. "Come at me, bro!"

CHAD *You ready for this*

SAVERIA *Ready for what*

CHAD *We're going to check your panic levels*

The Ezeroc obliged. Chad gathered his will as it leaped. He didn't have enough gas in the tank to make his will a cutting edge, so he settled for a shove. The Ezeroc lifted from the roof, tumbling toward a startled Saveria.

She braced herself, right leg straight, left leg bent. Saveria pushed both palms forward in a savage shoving motion as the drone tumbled toward her. Chad felt the rapid drawing of mental breath as she gathered herself, then the concussion as she struck.

The Ezeroc exploded mid-air, torso erupting in a kaleidoscope of stabbing claws, legs, and body sections. Gore sprayed over Chad, and he shut his eyes, turning his face away as it splattered against him.

After a moment, he wiped his eyes, then nodded. "Not bad. You got almost *all* of me covered in roach slime."

Saveria stood tall. Her small frame seemed dense against the night sky. "You threw an Ezeroc at me!"

Chad wiped his face as clean as he could manage. "I'm not sure what point you're trying to make."

She growled, then whirled, heading toward the square. She broke into a jog, uneven roof be damned. Chad followed as best he could, free hand out for balance. They made the town square. Below, the Ezeroc waited for them, their human sacrifices ready.

Chad frowned. "What do you suppose the purpose of the sacrifices is?"

"Fear, uncertainty, and doubt." Saveria shrugged.

"Nah." Chad pointed with his sword, counting. "We've got a roach for every person, looks like. I don't think they want to scare us. I think they're making more. This isn't a sacrifice ring. It's an implantation ring."

"Like, we've missed the phase where they injected larvae into people?" Saveria nodded. "They don't look like they're struggling, but I'd imagine they'd wig out when stabbed. Pain breaks through the control."

"That it does." Chad rubbed his wrist, missing his anti-esper bracelet. If there was ever a time for a little tech backup, it was when you were eyeballing a Queen. "Around, or through?"

"Through, but no stopping." Saveria pointed past the throng of unbound people below them. "They'll come for us, but we've just got to make it to Marla's hut. Kill the Queen, and they'll lose central command."

"Still leaves a lot of Ezeroc to clean up." Chad frowned. "Still, it's better than fighting a coordinated force."

"There's just one thing I want to know." Saveria crouched by the roof's edge, preparing to jump. "I need to know Forrest and Marla are okay."

TWENTY

Forrest leaned against the windscreen, back to their direction of travel, blaster clenched in hands white with strain. Marla piloted the godkiller's cart with efficiency. Not as much flair as Chad, but like she'd done this before.

Behind them, a horde of Ezeroc stampeded in their wake. They ran like the hounds of hell, claws skittering over the road. There were more in the trees, the crashing of broken branches audible over the cart's frenzied whine.

Forrest aimed his blaster and pulled the trigger. Blue-white fire spat from the weapon, searing the night. A tree exploded into burning fragments. He fired again, an Ezeroc turning into a screaming, skittering ball of flame.

They took us over, even with weapons like these. Forrest clutched the weapon tighter, keeping up his fusillade of fire. He didn't know if the weapon would empty like Marla's ancient improvised one, but he suspected it would. *No good thing lasts forever.*

"Lord save us," hissed Marla. "A hundred klicks per and they're keeping up."

Forrest spared her a glance. She looked worn thin, tired, like someone stopped her clock years ago and she was winding it forward. The years gathered around her like a cloak, but she wore it with fierce pride. He understood. The Ezeroc took so much, when you were out from their yoke you had to catch up on all the living you'd missed out on.

Ezeroc gained on them as Marla navigated a treacherous stretch of road. Forrest was thankful she didn't keep the speed up, as he'd be thrown from the ATV, but he didn't like their chances if the Ezeroc reached them.

He fired his weapon again, an Ezeroc exploding in a shower of burning fragments. Forrest felt the heat of the weapon, the barrel warming the air around his hands. He aimed, firing again, another Ezeroc turning to ruin in a flash of blue-white fire.

Marla accelerated, pulling away from the enemy. She risked a look back, then laughed. "You're a natural. You'd be wasted as a farmer."

"Farming's not so bad." He squeezed the trigger, squinting against the actinic flash. "It feels a safer choice."

"Safe doesn't give us our true calling." Marla raised her voice over the wind of their passage. "I could have worked for the Guild on Earth, but I flew the stars. The Undying Dawn called me, Forrest. They called and I came. All this time I've been waiting." She paused as he shot an Ezeroc approaching her side of the vehicle, it's blurring limbs turning to ash in the fire of judgment. "And now I know what for."

"What's that?"

"Deliverance." She pointed forward. Ahead, the trees gave way to the wide space around the Altar. The *Ardent Fury* waited in the gloom. Lights glimmered from it, vines and creepers unable to keep it hidden anymore. "We're getting off this planet. I was put here because our ship needs an Engineer. I don't remember it all, but I'll make do." She gunned the machine, putting on a last burst of speed.

The cart whirred forward, wheels spinning over loose shale and stone. The whine inside it descended to a groan, then it died, coasting the final distance toward the starship. Forrest cast a panicked glance at Marla. "What's happening?"

"We're out of power." Marla bent forward, grabbing a handle beneath the controls. She hauled, and a small case popped out. The machine continued to trundle forward, but at a snail's pace. The Ezeroc drew closer, the rumble of their legs like a continuous roll of thunder. "Come on!"

She slung her leg over the side of the cart. Forrest jumped down, landing awkwardly, severed arm out for balance. He gained his feet, then spun, firing toward the charging insects. Blue-white fire broke the night apart. Forrest wasn't really aiming, but there were so many Ezeroc it didn't matter. One took the shot, turning into an incandescent pyre.

He scrambled after Marla. She made it to the ramp leading into the ship, head down over the controls set into the wrist of her rig. Forrest put feet on it as it *clanked*, rising beneath him. He swayed, then fell. His stump banged against the rising floor, and the purest peal of agony shot up his arm.

Forrest dropped the blaster, clutching his arm to his chest. The ramp rose, the Ezeroc approaching fast.

Marla crouched beside him. She lifted the blaster, firing down the ramp, then tore his hand away from his stump. She pressed the weapon into his hand. "Forrest! We will *die* if we don't move."

It felt like the agony left a red haze over everything. Forrest stared down the ramp. An Ezeroc drone made the lip, scrabbling inside. He found Marla's eyes, the horror evident in them. If it'd been just him on this ramp, he might have let them take him. It'd be easier than the pain. But he knew they wanted Marla for what was inside her.

He clenched his teeth, pointing the blaster. He fired. The shot wasn't his best, but the bolt tore the legs from the side of the Ezeroc. It fell to the rising floor. The ramp approached where it would seal the starship, the Ezeroc caught in the middle. With a *crunch*, the ramp closed like a mouth, biting the insect in half. It thrashed, claws digging into the floor, curls of metal peeled away, then it slumped, dead.

"Come." Marla helped him up. She offered him the box she'd taken from the cart. "Take this."

"What is it?"

"A present, from back in time." She helped him open it. Inside were things he didn't recognize: round lozenges of metal. Nestled beside them were things he did. A smaller version of the blaster he carried. White bandages. A device like the one they'd used on Marla to knock her out. Marla flicked the lozenges aside, gold, silver, and copper tinkling to the deck. "Republic coin. No use for it. This will keep the pain away."

She lifted the device free. Forrest shook his head. "No."

"You're pale. You'll go into shock."

"It keeps the monsters away," he hissed. "They can't get in while pain's a part of me."

After two heartbeats, she nodded, then put the device back in the case. She removed the blaster. "I understand. Take this."

He tucked Chad's weapon into his belt, fumbling with just one hand. Forrest tried to use his other hand, forgetting it wasn't there. Blaster secured, he took the offered one from Marla. "I'm ready. Where are we going?"

"We need to wake the ship up." Marla cocked her head. "Hear that?"

"I hear nothing."

"Exactly. The PDCs are offline. Come on. We're going to show the Ezeroc what even grounded angels can do."

THEY HURRIED through the *Ardent Fury's* interior. It was cool, lighting gleaming in a way Forrest suspected it hadn't for many years. It felt like the ship was waking up like the rest of them. Like she'd been drowning, head held under dark water, and her first gasp of air brought a desire to *live* back.

Marla led them toward Engineering. "There's a hole in the cargo bay. They'll make it through the doors eventually." She jogged on, rig shining in the corridor's lights. Forrest wondered what it would be like to see five Marla's, shining suits showing their people's marvels on a daily basis.

Or fifty. A hundred. A thousand godkillers. That's what we were, before they took it from us.

"You've got a plan?" Forrest wasn't sure what she could do. It was clear she didn't remember everything. Either she didn't want to, or she couldn't. He'd seen the slice of time where she'd killed herself. *Maybe when you die, you leave a piece of yourself in the realm beyond.*

"I do." She scampered up a ladder, then bent to offer him a helping hand. "Engineering can control most parts of the ship. Flight controls are off limits. Tactical primary, too. If the PDCs are in an error state, we can correct that. If we're lucky—"

"Lucky?" Forrest spat the word, the pain of his injury gnawing at him.

She nodded, the motion sad. "Just a little bit of luck. The tiniest part is all we need. We recode the PDCs and the ship will have her teeth again. She's been without power and it looks like someone hit my baby with an EMP. Not everything's right."

Forrest laughed, the sound harsh in the confines of the corridor. "*Nothing* is right."

"Then let's fix it. It's what the Guild does." Marla headed off, lips moving like she was reminding herself of something, as if fixing starships was like remembering a nursery rhyme half-forgotten from childhood.

Forrest tightened his grip on the smaller blaster. He wanted to be ready in case the Ezeroc came aboard. He couldn't fix the ship, but he could protect Marla.

Engineering came into view, the door open like they'd left it.

Forrest darted forward, checking the interior. No Ezeroc. Just the wreckage of their passing. "It's safe."

Marla laughed. "It's hardly safe. It's just a breather before the hurting starts again." She slung herself onto the damaged couch, working the console. She nodded. "Yes, here it is. The PDCs errored out."

"What does that mean?"

"It means stop talking and let me work."

"But I..." Forrest shook his head, then went to the doorway to guard it. He waited long minutes, the clicking of keys and half-mumbled words from Marla his only company. He caught *parameters unstable, targeting matrix damaged*, and *that shouldn't happen* from her as she worked.

She hit a key with a triumphant, "Hah!"

Nothing happened. Forrest stared at her. "Was that—"

The thunder of the PDCs waking was like heaven's fury. The tremors through the hull felt like they vibrated Forrest's teeth. He crouched, hands over his head as the *Ardent Fury* rained vengeance on the Ezeroc outside.

Marla joined him by the door. She crouched beside him. There was no fear in her face, only fierce pride. "We did it." She helped him up, bringing him to the couch. The display of light showed what happened outside the ship. Ezeroc exploded into ruin wherever he looked.

They were being attacked by lines of light that drew dashes through the air. Marla poked her finger at them. "Tungsten tracers."

Where the *tungsten tracers* touched the enemy, the Ezeroc melted. The weapons tore them apart, splitting carapace from flesh, heads from torsos, and blowing limbs across the area.

Forrest imagined he could hear their keening as they died. He *wanted* them to suffer. His teeth clenched, and he snarled, "Now they know."

The Ezeroc retreated, falling back to the tree line. Marla nodded, like she'd made a good pie and everyone was enjoying a slice. "They already knew, but we reminded 'em." She made to leave, but something caught her eye on the display. "Oh. Oh no."

"What is it?"

"They're in." She tapped the console, the view changing to a familiar area. It was where Forrest grabbed Gravedigger, pulling her from the Queen. The door lay torn apart, a big crab-like creature shambling through. The view of the room beyond showed no Queen, and no eggs.

Just hundreds of Ezeroc. They swarmed up from below, where the PDCs couldn't reach. Forrest didn't know where the tunnels below the ship led to, but he had visions of a hive, an insect army rising like an unstoppable tide.

"We should get out," he said. "Get to the ATV. We'll be safer outside, won't we?" He didn't know if the ship's PDCs could hurt them, but he'd prefer death by angelic hands to being food for the enemy.

"They're at the bottom of the ship. We can't get out that way." She screwed her eyes shut. "Think, dammit!"

Forrest looked at the gun he held, then tucked it into his belt. He put his hand on Marla's arm. Her eyes fluttered open. "Marla, you've led the village for my whole life. You've got this."

"That wasn't me." Her eyes were sad. "They must have failed."

"Gravedigger?"

"Her, and Chad. The Queen still lives, for there to be so many." She stepped away from Forrest. "They'll take me again. I can't be like that."

Forrest felt for truth but found uncertainty. He didn't know if Saveria lived, but for so many Ezeroc to be here surely meant the Queen was still in control. "What will you do?"

"Bring an end to all things."

He drew the blaster from his belt, then moved to the doorway. "Then we go together."

Saveria knelt, hands on ghetto roof guttering, gauging her jump. The town square swarmed with civilians, all with the glassy-eyed look that meant *no one's home, please leave a message.*

There was dry-packed earth free of people ten meters from the roof's edge. For a human, it was an impossible jump. For a construct, no sweat, and an esper like her could do it without breaking stride.

So why am I worried?

She scanned the area. Humans tied to posts looked in the throes of rapture. Ezeroc by them held position without moving a muscle. *That's unusual. They rampage, not wait. What's their game?*

Sometimes the best way to spring a trap was to put your hand in it. If these Ezeroc were cut off from the rest of their species, they wouldn't have up-to-date intel on the war. But they would also have new, or at least different, tricks.

I don't want to put my hand in the trap. Saveria glanced at Chad. His mind wasn't like hers. It ran at a lazy human normal refresh rate, but she knew he had her back. *Two of us, against a planet. How hard can it be?*

She bunched, gathered her will, and jumped, cartwheeling over the top of the massing humans. AI crystal doing the hard math, she landed perfectly on her feet, a tiny slide of gravel reminding her even machine intelligences couldn't plan for everything. *Doesn't matter — it's within tolerance.*

Chad jumped after her. Unlike her graceful tumble, he made the distance with arms and legs pinwheeling. She stepped to the side as he landed where she was, catching his arm so he didn't overbalance.

He brushed himself off. "Like a cat."

Saveria snorted. "Come on, Captain Cheshire. Let's get inside." She spun on her heel, heading toward Marla's house. They made it about five meters, not even enough to hit full sprint speed, before three things happened.

The humans previously by the house they'd launched from turned as a mob, hands outstretched, lumbering for Saveria and Chad. This part was more or less expected, and they didn't have the kind of work ethic that made it look like a serious problem.

Then, the people strapped to sacrificial poles around the square shook, like they were having a seizure. Their eyes rolled back, mouths open, some drooling. They strained against their bonds, bodies arching like someone ran enough volts through them to fry a bison. Saveria caught their *rapture/joy/agony*, escalating to *agony/AGONY/AGONY*. Their minds became their own again at the end, and it made her feel sick.

But the *coup de grace* was their bodies rupturing like rotten fruit, innards spraying into the night air. Each person exploded with a wet tearing sound, blood and viscera pattering the dry earth like solid rain. Small insects the size of a hummingbird fled the hatchery of their bodies, filling the air with the humming of angry hornets.

Chad's mouth hung open in horror. Saveria grabbed his arm. "*RUN!*"

They fled. The flying drones swarmed on the people of the square. Saveria risked a glance back, seeing the creatures seek human hosts. It looked like they were stinging the people, but focusing on heads.

SAVERIA *They're doing something to those people*
CHAD *Why are we not running faster*

They made it to Marla's house. Chad's long legs carried him to the door a shade ahead of her, and he hit it with his shoulder. It slammed open on hinges unused to this kind of treatment. Saveria followed him inside, grabbing the door and slamming it shut. Chad was by her side, hefting a wooden crossbeam in place to hold it.

They turned, backs against the door, breathing hard.

The room held a few human accoutrements. There was a table with a busted console. A bed-slash-table, complete with straps no doubt used to secure Chad. In the middle of the floor, wooden boards lay strewn about a mound of dirt, like the anthill of the gods. It was a tunnel leading below the house, into the dark below.

"That's new." Chad stabbed his finger at the hole. "I'd have remembered it if Marla's decorator did that before."

Saveria nodded, not really listening. She walked up the mound, peering into the hole. The top was loose dirt, but it turned to rock after just a couple meters. Easy enough to get into, if that was your jam. The aperture was generously-sized. She thought they could slide down the entranceway, and then walk, albeit crouched, after that. Tricky to know without getting in there.

A hiss came from below. Saveria straightened. "Nope. Nope, nope, nope."

Chad nodded, from his position at the door. "I mean, why would we?" The door beside his head crunched, a shower of chips spraying the room as an Ezeroc stabbing claw punched through. Chad yelped, scrambling away from the door as another stabbed where his head had been. He made it to Saveria in three long strides. "Get in the hole."

Saveria watched the Ezeroc tear at the door. "If only we had a blaster."

"If there's one thing I've learned in my years, it's never second guess battlefield decisions from an armchair." Chad patted his empty holster. "It was the right call."

"I'm not in an armchair. I'm on the same battlefield!"

"Still the right call." Chad eyed the hole. "We going down there, or what?"

He was right. The villagers were being corrupted by the Ezeroc for some foul purpose. Drones were on their heels and would make short work of Marla's house security. Below waited a Queen, and their chance to end this all. "You first."

Chad snorted, then swaggered down. "See, your problem is—"

She never got to hear what her problem was, because the earth at his feet gave way. Chad fell, sliding into the dark. Without thinking, she jumped after him.

TWENTY-TWO

Chad didn't have far to fall. The dirt became rock, which then became rock covered in shale, scree, or whatever you called loose gravel that worked *exactly* like marbles on hardwood. He almost caught his balance, then didn't, sliding further into the dark.

He slipped, falling over open air, arms pinwheeling. His stomach had just enough time to clench into a ball that tried to climb his spine before he hit, butt-first, on something hard. It felt like rock.

The dark was intense. He stood, then was flattened by the arrival of Saveria. The air *oomphed* out of him. She clambered off. "Are you okay?"

"Great," he wheezed. "It's dark down here."

"It's fine. There's a glow coming from over here." He heard her crunch off, then some not-so-light cursing as she ran into something. "The ceiling's low."

Chad stood, rubbed his back, then ambled after her. There was indeed a red glow from the floor of *let's call it 'the north,'* and he headed for it. He made it five steps before smacking his head into a low ceiling. "Sweet merciful Christ."

"I told you."

"They're huge insects. How is this tunnel so low?" Chad crouched, hand feeling above for the roof. Once he had the rough dimensions of what he hoped was a passage and not the maw of a giant carnivorous insect, he set off. Before long, the tunnel widened in all directions, allowing him to stand. Red light seeped from the walls. He paused, leaning toward the stone and inspecting an organic material giving off the light. It looked like glowing lichen, but nothing the Ezeroc made was as harmless.

"This isn't calming." Saveria shored up next to him for a moment. "Have you seen anything like this before?"

Chad shook his head. "The Empress mentioned something similar. She was taken by the Ezeroc. Their ships have this glowing ass-slime on the inside."

"Ass-slime?" She blanched. "We're in the right place."

The sound of breaking wood behind them intensified. Chad cast a quick glance back, but he couldn't see much other than shadows and stone. The tunnel they were in headed let's-call-it-north, then broke west for a spell. He hurried along, Saveria in tow. "What's the plan?"

"We find the Queen and kill her." Saveria's voice held the kind of grim purpose heroic holos were rife with.

"Right, with your mind trick."

"Maybe." She sounded evasive.

Chad stopped walking, and she ran into the back of him. "'Maybe?'"

"Well." She avoided his eyes. "On Earth, or anywhere else, I was desperate. It's what you heard, before coming to find me. I'm hoping I can do it here."

"'Hoping?'" Chad conjured up some scare quotes with his fingers. "We're in the Ezeroc nest. The mighty monster of all monsters awaits below."

"Worst case, I can just punch her to death." Saveria shrugged. "We've got options."

"And if there are a zillion drones? Because they do not leave their Queens laying about unprotected."

"You were the one who said to get in the hole!"

"Don't throw my words back at me. It's unsportsmanlike." Chad frowned. "Unsportswomanlike?" In the red light, her glare took on a deeper substance. He avoided taking the full brunt of the elemental effect by sidling sideways, heading along the passage.

It continued to widen, until it hit a two-way junction. "Where do you suppose they put all the dirt?" He waved at the two gaping holes. "There was a tiny mound in Marla's house. Couldn't explain all this."

"I think they built these tunnels a long time ago." Saveria pointed right, where the tunnel went more let's-call-it-north again. "That way."

They've been living under the village for years. A network riddling the rock of this planet. No wonder they're so hard to stamp out. Cockroaches are far less invested. Chad charted course to the left, heading into the same dim-red gloom present everywhere.

This tunnel was riddled with smaller holes on the sides. He eyed them with great suspicion. "What's in those?"

"Guards." Saveria's hands were clenched into fists, like she was readying for a prize fight. "Lots and lots of guards."

"Where are they?" Chad walked the tunnel, turning a slow circle, trying to put his eyes everywhere at once. "I'd have thought maybe one or two would stop by for a chat."

"I can't hear them." Saveria cocked her head. "The damn hissing is usually everywhere they are. I can only hear the Queen."

Chad rubbed his chin. "It's alarming."

They continued along the tunnel, which wound its way through the rock of Viukde Gamma like an old waterway. They passed so many apertures for Ezeroc guards Chad stopped counting after fifty. *It's no wonder the mission to Viukde Gamma was overrun. The Ezeroc have been underground here since well before humans put boots on this crust.* They didn't just have numbers; they had infrastructure.

And when the people arrived, the Ezeroc got the one thing they'd been missing all this time.

A steady supply of raw materials.

From behind them came a scuttling sound. Chad spun, blade in his hand, the steel glimmering in the red light like it was bathed in blood. He couldn't see anything but holes. No movement. The noise grew louder, the tremor rising in the floor. He felt it through his boots. "Uh," he offered.

"Run." Saveria tugged his arm. "They've punched through Marla's house."

Chad nodded, turned, and broke into a jog. He felt a little tired from all the exertion, feet dragging a little. He tossed a glance over his shoulder.

Ezeroc boiled around the last bend of the passage, a seething, hissing, skittering tide. Stabbing claws raked the air, mandibles clicking. He could see the gleam of their eyes, and the intent as they ran like water from a broken damn.

Exhaustion forgotten, Chad turned up the amps on his stride. Saveria sprinted along beside him, arms and legs pumping. He hoped they found the Queen and knocked her block off before it was too late. There was the small, minor issue of what mindless Ezeroc would do to them without their Queen, but one thing at a time, hey?

Saveria's pace kept up with his. She made it look easy, no doubt on account of the damn AI crystal guiding her movements with machine precision. Despite that, she spared him a glance. In her red-tinted eyes he saw concern. A quick glance, then gone.

Aye. If there aren't guards in these tunnels, pursuit only from behind, how are Forrest and Marla faring?

It wasn't a thing he could do much about, other than killing the Queen. He put on more speed, hoping they wouldn't be too late.

TWENTY-THREE

Forrest stared down the corridor, not wanting to blink in case he missed something. The air was full of the charred smell of roasting Ezeroc. The small blaster he held was warm in his hand, like a big brother returning his grip, saying *it'll be okay*.

Behind him, Marla worked like a dervish. The few times he'd glanced at her, he'd seen the arms of her rig moving so fast as to be a blur as she pulled the sides away from a device she called *the reactor*. She'd also lifted the decking, exposing the living, beating heart of the ship, or that's what she'd said.

But Marla looked away when she spoke. Neither of them believed this ship still lived. Not like it once did, and certainly not enough to save them. The hammer of the PDCs outside quietened some time ago, either out of munitions or the Ezeroc growing tired of building a wall of their bodies.

Another drone scuttled around the corner ahead. Forrest lined it up, squeezed the blaster's trigger, and was rewarded with blue-white flashes of death. The Ezeroc's skull exploded in a cascade of smoking chitin and flesh, the body sliding to the deck in a heap.

It lay beside tens of its kind.

The weapon in Forrest's hands chirped, then spat a tiny rectangle from the grip. The object clattered to the decking, trailing smoke, a huddle of points glowing with heat on the surface. The weapon felt lighter without the cartridge, like a soul without a body. Forrest tried an experimental squeeze of the trigger, but nothing happened.

He dropped it, then drew Chad's loaned blaster. It was bigger, and Forrest could tell it was built to a standard different from the dropped one.

Marla's voice broke from behind him, half groan, half sob. "Okay. Okay. It's time for you to go."

Forrest looked over his shoulder. She stood by the reactor, one hand on it. Beneath her feet, a hole descended through the decking. Panels and other components lay about the hole, a dig site with the detritus of excavation on show. "What do you mean?"

She looked up. "I can't ... *remember*. What all these things are, or how they work. But I know this," she stroked the reactor like it was a skittish ox, "in my soul. Every part of it. There's a channel the reactors use when they go critical." She took a pause at his blank look. "In space, starships can eject reactors."

"You said reactors are the hearts of starships." At her nod, Forrest took a step toward her, forgetting his vigil for the moment. "How can you eject your heart?"

"To stop the rest of the body dying." Marla shrugged. "It doesn't matter. The reactor won't eject, I've made sure of that. But the launch passage is wide enough for you." She pointed beneath the decking. "It's a way out. Give me the blaster." She held her hand out.

Forrest shook his head. "I said we'd go together."

"And you're a better man than this world deserves for saying that." Marla looked away, like the sight of him made her feel guilty. "But you're young. Got your whole life laid like a trail ahead. I'm old, Forrest. Old, and I've lived more than my life's span." She pulled her hair, a clump coming away in her hands. "They used me up. If I walk out of here, I won't last a week."

Forrest checked the corridor, then fired at an Ezeroc sneaking closer. Its body shuddered as blue-white plasma cored it, smoke and fire trailing from the hole as it crashed to the deck. "If I leave you here, they'll take you again. You can't do whatever you're doing there," he waved his stump behind him, "and fight them off."

"It's not up for debate." Her tone took the hard edge he was used to from her role of village chief. "Get down there."

Forrest thought about it. About what it might be like to feel the air on his skin and see the stars above. What the night would be like, without the charnel stench of dead aliens about him. Then he thought what he'd feel like, for the rest of what Marla thought would be a long life, after leaving one person to die alone with a thousand enemy clawing for them.

You can't leave her here. And you know they won't kill her. It'll be much worse.

He studied his blaster. "I don't much think I could live with that."

She gasped, and Forrest spun. From the hole in the decking, an Ezeroc drone scrabbled for purchase. However the reactor tunnel worked, it had an aperture outside. They must have clambered over the hull, seeking entrance. Or built a tunnel inside the ship. Either way, it didn't matter. The tunnel wasn't an escape anymore.

Forrest yelled, firing his blaster. The Ezeroc let out a *skreee* as its carapace smoldered and burned, and it sagged in the hole. He ran to Marla. "Are you all right?"

"I'm not a porcelain doll." She sagged against the reactor despite her words, as if she'd just run a hundred klicks.

"What's porcelain?"

She laughed, the sound like dry leaves on stone. "It's a white material used to make fine plates and suchlike. And, I figure, dolls for them that want 'em."

Forrest smiled, but not because of what she said. "I'm sorry you won't see such things again." He hefted his blaster. "I wish I could tell Gravedigger I'm sorry for hitting her. Maybe if I hadn't, things wouldn't have got this bad."

"Hush, child." Marla straightened, some iron back in her spine. "None of this is on you. It's on them."

An Ezeroc skidded through Engineering's doorway. Forrest whipped the blaster around, firing. He blew one of its legs off as it jumped for the wall. It clambered to the roof. He followed it with bolts of plasma chewing into the walls. It froze three meters from him, poised to jump. He was about to fire, when Marla shouted.

Forrest turned, seeing another come from the floor. He turned, shooting that one, but hitting the already dead body of its predecessor. The Ezeroc on the roof jumped, hitting Forrest. His blaster rattled across the decking as the breath left him. The monster slammed him against the side of the reactor, and he felt lances of agony drive through his chest as it stabbed him with its claws.

The one coming from below made it out as the other holding Forrest lifted him in the air. It studied him, as if wondering, *is this the one that caused us so much pain?*

He tasted blood and felt the end would be a blessing. The pain would stop, as would the fear, and the hope of wanting Gravedigger, and a life in the stars, and the desire to be whole again.

The Ezeroc exploded in a shower of ichor as blue-white fire punched its carapace. It fell, dragging Forrest down with it. He screamed as more actinic flashes lit Engineering. Gasping for breath, he tried to pull himself free of the Ezeroc corpse.

Marla crouched by his side, blaster in her hand. She aimed at the limbs skewering him, blowing the chitin to pieces. She put a hand on his shoulder. "This will hurt."

"What will?" he croaked.

The arms of her rig articulated out, faster than thought, grabbing the smoking limb remnants in his flesh. They pulled them out just as fast. Forrest almost blacked out from the sickening pain as the serrated edges came from his chest. He coughed blood.

"That." Marla stood, then hauled him upright, the arms of her rig doing the heavy work.

He screamed again, broken bones in his chest shifting, then settled to a wheezing silence as she propped him against the reactor. Forrest focused on breathing, because that felt hard, and he needed to do it to stay alive. The floor of Engineering was littered with Ezeroc parts. Marla had shot them both.

She pressed the blaster into his hand. "I think we're out of time."

He nodded, feeling the strength leave him as blood ran down his chest. Forrest pressed a finger into the red. *Is this me? This blood is all that stops me from falling over?* He wanted to cry at his frailty, but held his peace instead. "What did you call it? The end of all things." Marla nodded. "Will it hurt?"

She was silent for a time, the hush of the air cyclers driving eddies of smoke around the room. "No."

"Then we go."

Marla nodded, then moved to the reactor. Another Ezeroc skidded through the door. Forrest raised the blaster, the movement sluggish and weak. He fired, the plasma bolt shearing the creature's head away. Claws poked through the hole in the decking as another made its way from below. Forrest pointed his weapon at it, pulling the trigger.

The gun clicked, whined, and spat a rectangle to the floor. Empty, like everything else here.

The drone clambered through the hole, ignoring Forrest. Marla worked like a dervish at the console, her hand raised as if to strike. The Ezeroc scooped her up like a child's toy, her arms flailing. "No!"

It made its way toward the hole in the decking, ignoring Forrest. *Again, they do not take me to Altar. They think I have no worth.*

Marla's face was desperate as she struggled against the Ezeroc. Her eyes held a fear Forrest knew he wouldn't have the courage to face. He pushed himself upright for one last thing, walking to the console.

It was full of buttons and lights. It made no sense to his eyes, the floating symbols arcane. The thing the godkillers used to control their machines, the *keyboard*, sat below the rest. A button, larger than the rest, sat to the right. It was shaped like a bent knee, clustered around other, smaller buttons of its kind.

Bend the knee. That's what they've always wanted. He met Marla's eyes, felt her terror, and saw her nod once before she disappeared into the floor.

Forrest closed his eyes, then stabbed his finger on the button.

TWENTY-FOUR

Saveria ran like her life depended on it. It wasn't just her two lives she needed to save. It was the souls of this village, and Chad, and...

And Forrest. Because he's good, and unlike you, didn't kill a space station. The only times he's harmed someone else is when the Ezeroc held his mind in a vice.

She felt his yearning for her and couldn't answer it in kind. Her heart belonged mostly to Hope but also to Algernon, and she wanted to see them again. It didn't stop her for recognizing Forrest for what he was: unspoiled. Pure, in a way she'd never be again.

So, she sprinted. At the end of this tunnel was a Queen, and ending her would stop all this.

Chad, initially running faster than her, slowed, then stopped. She sped right past him, staring back at the spymaster as he leaned hands on knees, panting.

CHAD *Go on, I'd rather not die tired*

SAVERIA *She's just ahead*

CHAD *I'll hold the tide*

He held steel, turning away. Saveria spent a couple seconds watching him stand his ground, shoulders set, before he looked to the tunnel's roof. She felt the eddying stir of his mental will gathering, the power of his *yearning/regret* a surging ocean as he sent his heart into the hard black above.

Then he turned, hefted his blade, and charged the Ezeroc.

Saveria found her hand raised toward his back, as if she could touch him, comfort him, or pull him to safety. He crashed against the Ezeroc, the bright of his steel slamming their hard bodies to slurry. Chad raged against the coming of the dark.

She turned and ran. Down the tunnel, loose stone underfoot. Through the enemy's lair, the musky scent of them about her. She could feel the Queen ahead, the hissing susurration of the insect's mind coiling and spitting at her advance.

Saveria broke into a large cavern. It was a klick in diameter, easy. The floor was a massive indentation sloping away. At the center, she could make out the misshapen mass of the Queen. Around her, the dirt shifted like a living thing.

It's not the ground moving. That's Ezeroc.

The reason the roaches hadn't guarded the tunnel became clear. They hissed and scuttled around their Queen. They were ready for Saveria. She might be able to jump ten meters with her esper gifts, but she couldn't jump five hundred. And Saveria wouldn't be able to fight thousands of Ezeroc.

She felt the Queen's elation. The Ezeroc sensed their victory. They would have Saveria, peel her mind apart, and understand how her gifts worked. After, they would understand how hard AI crystal melded with human frailty, and might even work out how to bend Algernon's people to their will.

Shoulders slumping, Saveria felt within her for anger, but found despair. *Forrest would know what to say. He'd look at you with those earnest, bright eyes and call you a godkiller. He'd say, 'Gravedigger, it'll be okay.'* She wanted to see him again, but he was klicks away, readying a starship for the heavens. *Perhaps I can look on him before the end. I won't touch or show him what's happened to me. He won't even know I'm there. I just need to know he made it off this world*. It was a naive thought, but it raised her head and set her jaw.

The Ezeroc before her crept closer. She ignored them, reaching the long arm of her mind across the planet's surface. Starting at the village, she found the humans here, their normally brilliant souls damped under a blanket of corruption. Ezeroc infested their flesh. The planet's population was dying, and they didn't have the tech to fix it. *Just more loss and pain*. Turning her attention south, she went between the old wood of the trees, and flowed along the grass and moss of the forest floor. When she found the *Ardent Fury*, she felt the grip of fear at the legion of Ezeroc swarming the ship.

Frantic, she hunted within the hull, looking for the two bright sparks of human minds. The bridge was empty, as was the galley. She went to Engineering and saw them. The last stand, as Marla turned their only route off Viukde Gamma into a glorious pyre.

She touched Forrest's mind as he stood at the control panel, confused at what he saw. Through his eyes she saw Marla's last, great work. Subversion of the ship's reactor, safeties bypassed. A tiny nudge and it would overload, starting a chain reaction that would crater the area.

No, she wanted to say. But she felt Forrest dying, the life bleeding from him as he prepared to face his own eternal dusk. She tried to stop him, but the pain of his wounds was too much. He slammed his hand on a button marked *RETURN*.

The *Ardent Fury's* reactor stuttered. The ship's lights went dark one last time. Bridge systems blinked off. The fabricators in the mess quietened their wait for hungry mouths to feed. The PDCs slumped in their housing. The Queen, sensing through the eyes of her agents that the ship was theirs, keened her victory. Ezeroc swarmed toward the ship from the trees, thousands in their number. Marla's still struggling form was born into the night air.

The reactor exploded. Humans, never quiet in their rage, had one last gift for the Ezeroc. The *Ardent Fury* erupted in nuclear fire. Trees and rock turned to ash and lava. The earth shook like a beast in pain as thousands of Ezeroc vanished, turned to stray atoms and cast aside.

Forrest snapped from Saveria's mind like he'd never been, the faintest puff of dust snatched away by a storm. She felt him go, the one pure person she'd met since waking on this world and remembering her name. Saveria jerked upright, body rigid, as she felt everything that made him ... disappear.

The AI crystal in her head fought for control, but the deluge was immense. Chad, sacrificing himself at her back. Forrest, dying because he wouldn't let Marla fall alone. The people of Viukde Gamma, wanting a peaceful life, to be left alone with their God, broken on the wheel of the Ezeroc's hunger. Saveria's heart hammered in her chest as she finally remembered what it meant to be human. All the broken things that made them whole came apart inside her.

She drew a shuddering breath and screamed. It went on, a river of pain, returning to its source. The Ezeroc around her fell like threshed wheat. The Queen scrambled in the giant lake of her mind, then vanished as all that made her was snuffed out.

Above, the infected fell, bodies falling to torpor as the invading insects died. Within a fifty-klick radius of the village, warrens of Ezeroc and their larvae died.

Saveria fell to her knees, hugging herself.

Chad found her, huddling in the gloom. The room trembled about her. He sat at her side, then drew her close. She smelled his sweat, and his exhaustion, but the humanness of him warmed her. Saveria leaned into him. "They're all dead."

"Yes." He nodded.

"I—"

"Hush." He stroked her hair in the red gloom of the Queen's chamber. "If you were going to say, 'I wish I could have done that sooner,' don't. Ain't your fault."

"Forrest is dead."

Chad continued stroking her hair, like one might a frightened horse. "I figured as much. I don't think we can go outside for a spell. It'll be raining fallout for weeks." He sighed. "I broke my sword."

"I broke my soul."

"You win." He shifted, trying for more comfort against the rocky ground. "We could get crushed if the roof caves in, but I figure we're more likely to starve to death. No way we can get supplies in here."

"It's as good a place to die as any. Really die, this time." She sniffed, wiping her nose with her sleeve. "I owe the universe two good deaths."

"Eh." Chad let her go, then stood, stretching. "I'd kind of hoped to not die." He glanced at the cavern's roof. "I'd hoped..."

"You hoped to see her one more time." Saveria nodded. "But it's best no one comes to Viukde. This system is cursed."

"Might be." He nodded. "Maybe we should pass the time until we turn on each other for the flesh and water in our bodies. Know any good jokes?"

TWENTY-FIVE

Hope woke with a start, bolt upright in her bed. Real cotton sheets fell away, and she scrabbled for...

For what? The bed beside her was empty. The night of San Francisco waited outside her window. She stood, padding from her bed to the window. She hadn't slept well in months.

I haven't ever slept well. Sleeping is not my 'thing.'

She shivered, although the Guild Hall's climate control held things at a steady 21C. It felt like someone walked over her grave. Rubbing the anti-Ezeroc bracelet on her wrist, she wondered at its warmth. There were no Ezeroc on Earth. Not since the war, when Algernon dropped a new nanotech plague. A very specific one that harvested only Ezeroc tissue, killing Hope's love.

She shook her head. *He saved our home.*

Hope turned at a commotion. Her bedroom was off to one side of her office, a massive room with a zillion consoles and fabricators in it. She left the plain white sheets behind her, walking to her office proper. The previous Guild Master Chinnery had his rooms elsewhere, but Hope had too much work to do. With her bedroom next to her office, she could get to work as soon as she woke, which was often.

It also meant when people hammered on her door at night, it woke her up in the rare times she slept.

She cast a glance at the massive floor to ceiling windows looking out over San Francisco. Her mind's eye could see where the new gravity elevator would be. She saw the possibility of new buildings, better than the old. Lights winked in the night as humans and precious few constructs worked shoulder to shoulder to rebuild Earth.

Her attention was pulled back to the door as it burst open. The Guild Master's office — *her* office — was long, and ostentatious. The vaulted roof waited high above. Despite the size and scale, nothing dimmed the fury of Admiral Karkoski as she stormed in.

Trying to stop her was one of Hope's guards, a nice Marine named Worlings. The young man appeared to worship Hope, which she didn't like, but he also kept noisy people outside, as best he could. Like her, he didn't sleep much, and like her, something haunted lay in his eyes whenever talk of the Ezeroc came up. He'd vanished one day after stopping a senior Navy officer entering, and then appeared the next day after she insisted the Guild Master *needed* Worlings.

He was a friend, but so was Karkoski. "It's okay, Worlings."

The young Marine stalled out, realized his hand was still on the admiral's arm, and jerked it back like she was a nuclear furnace on meltdown. "As you say." He gave her a small nod, then slipped out, closing the door behind him.

Karkoski stormed closer. "They're alive." She pointed outside, in the general direction of the sky. Hope followed the line of her arm, blinking owlishly.

She still felt half asleep, a thing that was more or less usual these days. "Who?"

"Saveria Complex and that reprobate Chad Forradel." Her tone softened at the end. "I've been barred from the spaceport."

Hope looked from the stars to Karkoski, then to the stars again. "Where are they? Who barred you from the spaceport?"

"I don't know *where*," she hissed, hammering her chest. "He *spoke* to me, Hope. He said he was sorry, but he had to go now, and that he..." She wound down, shoulders shifting under her armor.

Wait. Karkoski's wearing armor? "Why are you wearing armor?"

"I'm going to steal a ship."

"Why?"

"To go get him, of course." Karkoski clenched her fists. "I need your help. It's the Emperor. He said I'm on enforced shore leave. *Me.* On *enforced* leave." She spat the last word like it was a bitter seed. "We'll steal a starship. I need an Engineer. I think—"

"No," said Hope.

"What?"

"No," she repeated. Hope turned to the massive desk that lay under a huge burial mound of consoles, components, and half-finished miniature models. She spent time hunting for her *actual* console, before huffing, sweeping the debris to the floor. Console now exposed, she fired it up. Her call connected almost immediately. "Hello."

"Hope? What the hell time is this?" The cap's bleary eyes peered from the holo stage.

"It's three AM."

"I know it's three AM! I didn't ask because I didn't know. I asked—"

"I know why you asked." Hope leaned forward, bringing her real face closer to his virtual one. "I need a favor."

Nate blinked, then glanced over his shoulder. Hope could see the athletic line of Grace's shoulder/back combo in the background of the holo. "A favor?"

"Cap, it's like this. We know where Chad and Saveria are. Karkoski's going to get them. I'm going too." She held up her hand, because he looked to be about to fuss. "We're taking October and Algernon. El will Helm."

Nate nodded, adjusting sheets as if just aware he was half-naked. "Okay. Right. But Karkoski—"

"Grace is coming too."

Nate had his hand raised, mouth opened, but the image held still like someone stole his voice. "She's what?"

"There's only one person I know of who could find them out there." Hope rubbed her eyes. She wished for the millionth time she wasn't so tired all the time. "That's my favor. I need Grace."

Grace's shoulder/back combo stirred. The Empress rolled over, fixing Hope with a glare. "I'm not sure it's his favor to grant."

Hope sagged. "I love her, Grace. I want just one thing. Can you give it to me?"

HOPE HUDDLED in the *Tyche's* cargo bay. She wore her rig, because it made her look strong, but stood close to October, because he made her *feel* strong. The ship shifted as they descended. The route into Viukde was terrifying, and El made a big deal about telling everyone about the 'giant clouds of rock that used to be a planet' and other such things.

Her rig's visor was sealed, and October's ship suit was closed up tight. The *Tyche* said the area swarmed with radiation. *Everyone* was wearing suits. Hope carried a small case in each hand, because no one else had thought about what next, and it was what she was good at.

The ship settled, a slight creaking coming from above. Hope raised her eyes to the ceiling, wondering what it was, and how she might fix it. October put a hand on her shoulder. "Don't be worrying about that now."

"But—" He gave her a tiny shake, and she quietened. He let his hand drop, and she missed it straight away. She wasn't sure when she'd become so worn thin.

Nate slid down the ladder behind her, then strode past. He wore his sword across his back, blaster at his hip. She caught the slight hitch in his stride caused by his metal leg. Grace followed, slowing but not stopping as she passed Hope. The Empress gave her a quick look that said *it'll be okay*, before picking up her pace.

They keep telling me it'll be okay, because they think it won't be.

The *Tyche's* cargo bay airlock opened, a hiss of atmosphere escaping as the ramp descended. Outside the ship, a storm of ash and dust swirled. Hope saw the bloom of lightning in the distance, obscured by the storm, and two seconds later the *boom* of thunder.

El walked past her, sauntering toward the airlock.

"El. You don't have to leave the ship." Hope hurried after her. El hated danger of any kind.

"Someone's got to look out for Karkoski. She's half-crazed." El kept walking, swagger undimmed, hand on the butt of her holstered sidearm.

As if summoned, Karkoski slid down the ladder, followed by Algernon. "I'm not crazy."

"Of course not, Admiral Meat Sock." Algernon's eyes were bright white, gleaming as grit swirled in the open airlock. "You suffer the same frail condition as the rest of your brittle species." His silver arm stood at odds with the rest of his golden frame.

Hope looked away. She didn't know how to make him as good as he was. Algernon walked past her, not slowing at all. He didn't want to spend time in the same space as her. Guilt rode him like a jockey sat astride a stallion.

Why did we teach them guilt? Hope hurried after, realizing she and October were the only two in the cargo bay. He trundled along beside her, not saying anything at all. He'd been the only one who didn't tell her, *it'll be okay.* What he'd said was, *sure, I'll come, probably roaches that need killing.*

The dust storm was epic, but despite its fury and the rad warning on her HUD, Hope could tell they were in what used to be a town square. Many of the buildings were fallen, and some had burned to ash. Bodies lay covered in dust in the street. Grace stood by the broken door of a house, pausing on the stoop. "They're in here."

Hope nodded and hurried after.

TWENTY-SIX

Saveria woke to the sound of footsteps. Faint, but down here where there wasn't any noise other than Chad's *everything*, it was like the beat of drums. She lay next to Chad on the cold ground, because it was the only way they wouldn't freeze to death, the stone leaching their body heat away. Saveria rose, ready for a fight, but too weak to do much but sway.

She caught a glimmer of white light, bobbing erratically, before a ship-suited figure came through the cavern's entrance. Saveria knew her at once, and dropped to her knee. "Empress."

The word felt clumsy on her tongue, thick with dehydration. It'd been two days since she'd killed this place. She didn't know how long she knelt before Grace, her mind hazy on the details. She didn't know if her AI crystal was damaged, or if she was dying of thirst. She felt a strong hand under her arm heft her up. She blinked as more ship-suited figures entered the cavern.

The Emperor. The Captain of his Skyguard, eyes everywhere at once. Admiral Karkoski, who froze, then broke into a run when she saw Chad's prone form. He'd passed out maybe twelve hours ago, blood running from his nose. He might never wake. Karkoski slid to a halt beside him, then crouched. "Chad? Wake up! If you made me come all the way out here..."

Saveria ignored the rest of what she said, eyes looking past the rest. A golden form entered, and a part of her heart soared. *Algernon.* But it was a tiny part, barely remembered. His white eyes shone as he looked at her, then he nodded, as if understanding. She wanted to cry for his loss, and hers.

Behind him, a rough voice said, "Move it, Al." October Kohl pushed Algernon aside, revealing a small figure. Hunched inside an Engineer's rig, but an unmistakable strand of pink hair trailing across her face behind the visor. Hope held two metal cases.

Saveria broke from the Empress's side, stumbling toward Hope. She grabbed her in a hug. "Oh. Oh." She held her close, *feeling* her lover against her. It wasn't a gift she deserved.

"It's okay," said Hope, but in a tone that said maybe she believed it. "Here. I bought you something." She held up a case.

Saveria took it, putting it aside. "I..." She wound down. Everyone else in the room appeared to be looking at everything *other* than Hope and Saveria. Kohl was nudging Ezeroc corpses with his boot. Nate and Grace were talking over a private comm channel. Karkoski was fixated on Chad, and Algernon looked at his hands, as if wondering what they were for. "I missed you even though I couldn't remember you."

"I missed you even though you were dead." Hope's eyes shone, tear tracks running behind her visor. "You might be dead again if you don't open the case."

Saveria nodded, opening the case. It hissed, top sliding open. Inside was an emergency ship suit, complete with automatic visor. She picked it up, and Hope helped her put it on. The helmet lapped into place over Saveria's head, and she breathed good, cool, clean air.

Kohl sniffed, then took the other case from Hope. "This for the guy who's sleeping on the job?"

Saveria rounded on him. "Chad held them off so I could..." She struggled against the memories. "Get it done."

"Eh. He's sleeping now though, isn't it?" Kohl ambled off, like her anger bothered him about as much as a cool wind on a hot day, which was not at all. While he worked to put Chad into the suit, Saveria hugged Hope.

Then she pushed her away. "I have so many things I want to say. But they'll all wait, except one. I love you."

About three hundred emotions ran across Hope's face before she settled to stillness. She leaned close, saying, "I love you."

Saveria felt the bloom of joy inside her. *She loves me. Still.* Another gift. She put her hand on Hope's arm. "Wait here." She hurried, or the lurching steps that passed for hurrying in her condition, to the Emperor and Empress. "Hi."

Grace and Nate faced her. Nate offered a smile, like they were free to give. "How you feeling?"

"I feel like I'm dying."

"Nice." Nate raised an eyebrow. "That all you came to say?"

"No." Saveria shook her head. "Radiation meds will fix me, but there's something you need to know. There's corruption at the heart of the Empire. Do you know Seth Cleaver?"

Grace nodded, but slowly, like it didn't stir pleasant memories. "We know Pastor Cleaver."

"He needs to be stopped." Saveria waved her arm at the room. "All this was him. He left them here, because there were Ezeroc on his ship."

Grace drew closer, eyes hard. "Ezeroc? Aboard the Church of the Undying Dawn's flagship?"

Saveria nodded. "Seth Cleaver's a new type of Queen, and they're ready for us."

THE END.

THEY WON THE EMPIRE, but **their enemies won't stay buried.**

Grace and Nate made it off Earth. Barely. Now they race to Mercury, where the machines might still hold the key to humanity's survival. But the enemy has already been here. The Ezeroc didn't just attack—they corrupted.

An ancient vault holds the secrets of the war. Inside is a threat unlike anything they've faced before. And this time, the enemy didn't come alone.

The story of fake gods and fallen heroes concludes in *Tyche's Crusade*.

Turn the page. Because the final war decides everything.

TYCHE'S CRUSADE

A SPACE OPERA ADVENTURE EPIC

THE FALL OF REASON

In ten minutes, you'll face the most powerful enemy since forever. Chin up.

Nate held onto his acceleration couch's straps like they'd save him from drowning in a sea of emotions. The dropship was full of *anxiety/ready* and *fear/focus*. The feelings rattled against him like pebbles thrown against glass. They came from the men and women with him. Many he didn't know, and knew he'd never get a chance to on account of them dying below. A few he'd seen in the halls of the *Mercenary*, and one or two he'd shared a drink with.

The dropship wasn't built for carrying cargo other than brave souls. Forty Marines shared the trip with the Emperor and Empress. Another six dropships shared their approach vector. Across Earth, the Navy deployed similar ships against Church outposts on the basis you couldn't be too careful. Their forces were spread thin, but Nate's future-sense said it wouldn't matter. The real battle would be here, in San Francisco, in just under ten minutes.

Grace sat in a couch beside him, her face calm. Relaxed, even. He wished he shared her serenity, and certainty that all would be well.

GRACE *I don't think all will be okay, I think it'll be better with you*

NATE *I prefer it when you lie to me*

She shifted on her acceleration couch. Nate had to admit, even sitting down she drew the eye. She didn't wear armor, leastways not the type the Marines wore. Her black synthetic clothing was form-fitting. The quartermaster said it'd turn the kiss of steel, maybe even take a kinetic round or two, but he couldn't guarantee it against blaster fire. Grace had nodded, saying, *I don't plan on getting hit anyway.*

Nate, never one to turn away a good ace up the sleeve, wore similar clothing underneath sensible armor. The Empire's falcon rode golden wings on his chest plate. The armor chafed some, but was light enough so's not to be bothersome. Gold winked at him from where his gloves didn't quite meet shirt. His metal arm reminded him not all stories had happy endings.

The dropship wasn't like his *Tyche*. Where his heavy lifter was comfortable, a home, this spacecraft was all business. It didn't even have a whiskey dispenser.

They'd launched from Navy ships in geosynchronous orbit above San Francisco. Their target was the Church of the Undying Dawn's main Chapel and Pastor Seth Cleaver. Intel said he was inside, waiting to be shucked like an oyster from its shell.

"Hard contact." The clipped voice came over the ship-wide comm, and belonged to Dennis Boat, an apt name for a Helm. The dropship weaved, leaving Nate's stomach back aways. He could imagine hands on sticks, steely eyes watching the ground, counter-measures turned to eleven as they headed for the dirt.

It wasn't a big deal. If the ground assault team hadn't taken out the air defenses, the trip would've been cut short already. *And seriously, what kind of church has AA cannons?* If there was ever confirmation that Cleaver was the enemy, this was it.

A holo set in the middle of the dropship bloomed to life. It updated with RADAR and LIDAR maps of the terrain, highlighting gun emplacements, the Church's Chapel, likely numbers of ground forces, and their fellow Marine transports. A dropship's beacon winked out, the craft torn from the sky by weapons below. Nate closed his eyes, thinking back to a time where he'd protected an Emperor, not play-acted as one. They'd been torn from the sky too, and it'd cost him an arm and a leg.

Grace's hand found his arm, her touch light but steady. "It'll be different this time."

"Hah. You're only saying that because you weren't there. This will be the same." Nate cranked a grin out of spare parts. "Or, it'll be different. We could die."

She laughed. "I think we should talk with Cleaver about who should do the dying."

"Rapid disembark in thirty seconds." The Helm's voice remained tense over ship-wide comm. Nate figured Dennis could learn a thing or two about calm under fire from El. Still, despite his anxiety the man did an admirable job of getting them to the deck without the dropship exploding.

The vessel's engine roar changed in pitch, climbing to a whine. The attitude of the deck shifted as the Helm brought the nose up, scrubbing airspeed through friction and use of Endless fields. Well before Nate thought thirty seconds had time to amble past, the dropship's wide doors opened, a ramp shooting out. Marines were already boots on metal, running for the dirt outside.

Nate released his harness, raising an eyebrow as Grace shot past and out. *How is it you're the only one still in here? Might be getting old.* He clanked across the deck, making the daylight outside. It was weak and grainy, struggling with the clouds and ever-present ash in the atmosphere.

Boat had the courtesy to point the dropship's ramp toward the Chapel. The building was huge, making the Winter Palace look like an exercise in modesty. It rose against the skyline, basalt and marble winking their contrast in the light. A massive double door waited beyond a faux hedge maze. The doors stood maybe twenty meters tall, large enough not even Kohl could persuade them open.

Hundreds of civilians fought Empire forces in gardens Nate figured had once been serene. They used blasters as readily as weapons of opportunity. He saw a woman swing a rake at a Marine, beside a man trying his level best to skewer a sergeant with the broken haft of a similar gardening tool.

Four other dropships sat to the left and right, their disgorged Marines making progress across manicured lawns. The blue-white flash of plasma fire spat across the space. Debris from a mortar explosion showered Nate with dirt, and debris nicked his face. He touched blood. *You and your ideals. You could have left this to others.*

"You could have left this to me!" Chad jogged past, offering a mocking half-bow and flourish as he went. The spymaster held a rapier at the ready, sidearm in his other hand.

Saveria followed in his wake. "You really should have. This leading from the front business will get you killed."

"I was ... stop reading my mind!" Nate drew his blaster, wondering what he meant to do with it. Barbecuing civilians didn't sit well with him, so he also drew his black blade. *Slightly less lethal, since you can disarm instead of skewer.* The sword felt heavy with intent in his right hand. The golden fingers of his left gripped his sidearm in readiness.

CHAD *Wasn't reading your mind, you're predictable*

SAVERIA *Also, we told you so*

Nate broke into a ragged run. He wasn't doing much leading from the front, what with all the waiting by the dropship. The smoke was too thick to see Grace in the melee, what with the visual noise of hundreds of people throwing themselves against the cheese grater of the Empire Navy.

Some good news in this sordid mess was there wouldn't be Ezeroc here. No roaches boiling up from the dirt. No flying insects with stingers, ready to inject larvae into a person. The nanotech plague worked *for* humanity now. Algernon bought that with Saveria's life.

A pair of frenzy-eyed churchgoers ran at Nate. One held a shovel, the other a blaster. The plasma weapon looked to be Navy standard issue, suggesting at least one of them knew how to kill Marines. Shovel-wielder was a short, stocky man who looked like he'd be more at home as a bartender. The woman holding the plasma carbine had the nervous disposition of a bomb maker. She steadied herself, pointed the weapon in Nate's general direction, and pulled the trigger.

Future-sense tapped Nate on the shoulder. *Step to the left three paces. Pause. Right two paces.*

Nate danced across the grass. Plasma chewed the space he'd occupied. The woman did a double-take, then glanced at her weapon as if it were to blame. Shovel-wielder reached Nate, taking a wild swing. Nate's sword caught the shovel on the blade, sliced through steel, and sent it spinning away. He slugged the man across the jaw with the butt of his sidearm. The should-be-an-innkeeper dropped to the dirt in a pile of unrealized potential.

He ran at the woman, blade low. *Dodge right. Stop. Duck.* Plasma scorched the air. Nate felt the deathly heat of it, the scent of ozone everywhere. He swung his sword, cutting the carbine through the barrel. The weapon sparked, its cartridge detonating in a bright flash. The woman screamed, tucking her burnt hands under her arms.

Nate offered her a nod, then hurried on. Ahead, he caught the gleam of steel as poetry, Grace's sword moving as a visible extension of her will. She ducked and weaved. Unable to see the future like him, she had to rely on skill. Nate was honest enough to admit he'd rather be lucky than skilled, but Grace had the knack of making skill look desirable.

He joined her in a moment of calm. Smoke chased leaves across the grass, an eddy of wind tousling Grace's hair. The double doors of the Chapel remained closed. He pointed with his sword. "We need to get in there."

She nodded. "It's lucky we brought a bottle opener. Sergeant!"

Grace turned to a stocky woman who looked manufactured from granite and salt. "We need that door open."

"Aye." The sergeant, a woman who wore the name Hudnall like a combat boot, clicked her comm, bawling orders. Nate caught *ordinance* and *of course there's no hurry, it's only the Empress.* "Your Highness, might be a good time to take cover."

Grace nodded but didn't move. A Marine jogged up, youth and enthusiasm in every motion, a long tubular weapon in hand. He offered Grace a quick smile, shy like he was in the presence of his idol, but shut it down because he was a *Marine,* for heaven's sake. "One bottle opener, as requested."

Sergeant Hudnall glared. "You're not getting paid overtime, Coles!"

Coles gave a curt nod, dropped to one knee, and raised his launcher. Sighting down the barrel, he paused for a two-count, then pulled the trigger.

A contrail of brilliant fire shot from the weapon to the doors. They exploded in a shower of wood fragments and steel reinforcing. Nate ducked, metal arm up to shield his head, but nothing hit him. The blue crystal glimmer of Grace's mind-shield held before them, a bubble of safety protecting them and the two Marines. When the debris settled from *raining death and fury* to *there's a lot of smoke,* Nate nodded to Coles. "Nice work, Marine."

"My pleasure to kill the sworn enemies of the throne, sire." Coles winked at Hudnall, who swore, then darted back into the fray.

Hudnall watched him go, then turned her regard on Nate. "Anything else, sire?"

"One thing. Very important." Nate leaned close. "Try not to die. Or let anyone else die."

Her hard face softened. "It'd be my pleasure, sire."

Nate gave another nod, then headed toward the breached door. Grace loped at his side. "You always do that. Make them feel like they're the most valuable person in the world."

They arrived at the door. Flames still licked the wood. Smoke trickled toward the sky outside and the vaulted ceiling inside. "They're laying down their lives for us. That's a thing I can't look past."

"I wasn't criticizing. I was..." She trailed off, eyes wide as she took in the Chapel's interior. "Thankful. How is it that the Church has a Van Gogh?"

Nate stepped inside the Chapel. Or, Chapel anteroom, because despite this chamber being as large as a stadium, and something Guild Engineers would be proud to construct, it sported many doors leading to locales unknown. Around the interior lay countless *objets d'art*. The Van Gogh looked real to Nate's gutter-thief eye. A statue of David copy stood in a shaft of light from above. He squinted. *That may be the* real *David. What's an Ezeroc-infested person want with artwork?*

It caused a niggle of doubt. The Ezeroc didn't like art. They liked *food* and saw humanity as a movable feast. If Cleaver had this much art here, he either had a very good interior decorator, was into the collection as a means of wealth preservation, or... *Or, he's not Ezeroc.*

Nate shook his head. Saveria called the man *a new kind of Queen.* Chad, once he woke, agreed with her. They called Seth Cleaver a *threat to humanity*, not just the throne. Nate shrugged off his nagging thoughts, focusing on the mission ahead. They were here to end that threat. Intel said Seth Cleaver called this place home. Empire spies saw him here, walking about, sucking O2, and passing benedictions.

Five meters inside, feet padding down carpeted steps so plush they needed a mow, Nate felt the stirring of unease. His future-sense cast about, finding no targets, but still sending fingers of cold fear up his back. Ten meters in, even Grace felt it, slowing to a halt, blade raised, head on a swivel. "What *is* that?"

"Future-sense," offered Nate. "Or, good ol' fashioned human dread. Here we are, in the den of a spider."

"Not that." She shook her head. "*That.*"

Nate cocked his head, listening. After a moment, he felt it. So faint you might think you'd missed it, a whisper right on the edge of hearing. It sounded like the hissing of sibilant Ezeroc speech, except... *Except there aren't any Ezeroc on Earth. Not anymore.*

He broke into a run. Grace kept pace beside him. A shout behind him brought him up short. "Sire!" Nate turned, taking in Hudnall and a clutch of Marines. "We still storming the gates?"

"Hold here, Sergeant. What's ahead isn't for you."

She hefted her rifle. "Nothing a little plasma won't cure."

They're so willing to throw their lives away for you. That's why the vote's important. They need to choose. "Hold *here*, Sergeant. No one comes through that door."

Hudnall searched his face, then gave a tight nod before turning to her Marines. "You heard the Emperor. Secure this position. I want clean lines of fire. I want it fast. And you, Coles, will secure that expression in the black depths of your heart before you get entrenching duty!"

Nate headed down the massive room. The sense of space was eerie. It felt as if they walked inside a cavern, a stone vault constructed above, not below the Earth.

"This feels like an Ezeroc burrow," Grace offered.

"I wish you wouldn't say what I'm thinking," Nate said. "It's not helping my calm."

"I was just saying, because—"

"Still not helping." Nate looked about, trying to find targets. There wasn't anyone in here. No guards. Not a single member of the faithful. Certainly no priests, or whatever the Church stocked in their stead. His sense of unease grew, rising to a crescendo as he felt the still waters of his mind ripple as someone — or some*thing* — nearby gathered their will. A powerful esper was at work here.

Grace made no comment, her lips pressed into a line. She would have felt it before him, stronger, and keener to her core. Her sword glinted from the lighting high above, but her black suit gave nothing back to the enemy's fortress.

"Where is everyone?" Nate turned a slow circle as they

approached a shallow stairway leading up a level. It was perhaps ten meters wide. The carpet was as plush as everywhere else, looking new. *San Francisco's still in ruins, but Cleaver's found materials and people to build himself a shiny new house.*

"At Mass." Grace shrugged. "I don't know. I'm not familiar with this religion."

"I'm glad you didn't say, 'preparing a trap.' Because that's what I was thinking." Nate swung his sword, getting the feel of it right in his hand.

"I didn't say that because you'd get anxious again."

"*Anxious?*"

"Or fretful." She sniffed, then pointed to the doors atop the stairs. "Whatever it is, it's in there."

Nate nodded. No more putting this off. He jogged to the steps, swearing a little at the excessive use of vertical space as he climbed, then shouldered the doors open. They didn't even have the decency to creak, sliding open on hinges so smooth the Guild would no doubt wonder how they worked.

Inside was a smaller room, but no less plush. At the far end was a throne, showing exactly what Seth Cleaver planned. *The man already has a Church to rule but has designs on all humanity.* It looked like the designer preferred the baroque styles, a tall back rising well above the natural level a human might need for good lumbar support. On the throne sat Cleaver himself.

He looked like he could stand in a hurricane and call the weather mild; his shoulders were wider than Kohl's, and fervor burned in his eyes like a searchlight. A Caesar cut kept brown hair squared away. He didn't smile, but Nate imagined straight pearly whites that could chew ceramicrete to powder. "Nathan Chevell." His voice was a melody to behold. Angels would weep to speak like that.

"No." *Naturally, he's a sending. The power we've felt? It's him projecting himself into this space. But he's so clear, so* visible. *Could Grace send so well?* Nate wandered inside, checking out the corners.

No guards, and no clergy. "It's *Emperor* Chevell. For a while longer, at least."

"My apologies." Cleaver smoothed a silk shirt, then stood. He was a titan, grazing the lofty heights of two meters. "What can the Church do for the Empire?"

Grace raised an eyebrow. "The Church? Nothing. We've no quarrel with people who want to believe in something bigger than themselves."

"What she means is, you're scum, and we're going to put you to the blade." Nate hefted his sword for emphasis, then shrugged, almost apologetic. "You know how it is."

"You wasted all these people to come here." Cleaver smiled, like a post-cream cat. "Yours and mine both. Mine went willing into the light, Emperor. Did yours?"

"Where are you?" Nate sheathed his blade, then looked at his blaster. *Probably won't be needing that either.* He holstered it. "I feel like this is anticlimactic. After Viukde, I expected a brief round of fisticuffs, then one of us bleeding our last on the dusty ground. I wanted to meet you, Pastor, and see what kind of creature figured to make me into a corpse."

"Earth isn't good for me right now." Cleaver cleared his throat, the sound apologetic.

"For your kind, hey?" Nate offered a smile, showing more teeth than strictly necessary.

Cleaver shrugged. "You're going to kill me without trial. Isn't it odd that you seek to end your only viable opponent in the election?"

"Not sure that was a part of my plan," admitted Nate. "I came to end the Ezeroc threat to our home."

"You've nothing to fear from me." Cleaver paced in front of the throne, like he needed to burn off a little of his brooding demeanor. "They're a cancer."

Grace laughed. "You *are* Ezeroc. You might be able to hide it from those without our gifts, but..." She shook her head. "You will not lead humanity into the darkness."

Kohl eyed the air car. It was robust in an unflattering way, but more importantly, flew without the Empire's falcon. Didn't look armored, but he wasn't fixing to shoot at or be shot by Dizzy. It'd do. "Fair enough. Get in."

SAN FRANCISCO'S night skyline was aglow, life returning as Hope, by way of her Guild, worked her magic. Almost everywhere had power, and where they didn't, portable generators served the city's needs.

One dark smudge on the ground marked the slums. It had less power than most parts, on account of those with an entrepreneurial spirit stealing the deployed generators.

Al piloted the air car, because Kohl didn't want to. "I like adventures," the machine admitted.

"I hope you like boring nights too. There." Kohl pointed at a barren square of dirt where building foundations struggled from the ground like broken teeth. "That'll do."

Al guided the machine down, settling into the ruins. The doors winged open, and Kohl stepped into the night air. It smelled of smoke, more here than elsewhere, because this part of the city was hammered harder than others in the war. Also, people burned tires for fun in these parts.

He headed away from the vehicle. A group of four men rushed him from the shadows. They'd seen the air car, no doubt figuring on helping themselves. Kohl didn't slow, winding his arm back and clotheslining the first with a swing. The man's feet left the ground, arriving almost at his head height with the force of the strike, before landing with the rest of him on the dirt. He groaned.

The other three came to an abrupt stop. Kohl lifted the asshole on the ground up, dusted him off, and said, "I will pay you a huge amount of coin to make sure this air car is here when I get back."

"You what?" The clotheslined man looked in decent shape, a little anemic maybe, like he could use a burger and fries.

"Here." Kohl held out a handful of good Empire coin. "More when I get back." He sauntered into the night, Al's golden form jogging after.

"October." The machine's voice was hesitant. "You didn't kill those men."

"That's right. Life's hard enough on those down here without losing your father, or brother." Kohl adjusted his carbine's sling, making sure it was ready for an easy grab. "They're just hungry, is all."

"What if they take your coins *and* the air car?"

"Nate's got plenty of cars," said Kohl. "He won't miss that one."

"And if they're still about when we return?" Al cast a glance back at the four men.

Kohl followed his stare. The wannabe thugs milled about, turning coins over in their hands, and looking confused. "I'll give 'em more coin. I've no need of it."

"You're not into charity."

"I'm into *recruiting*, Al. We're about to go balls-deep into a new war. One against bigger assholes than last time." Kohl hawked dirty phlegm onto the ceramicrete sidewalk. "I want people who will fight."

"Because they're desperate and hungry?"

"Because they want to fucken *win*." Kohl shook his head. "No place for a losing side in what's coming next. Second place on the podium means becoming food for the roaches."

Dizzy's establishment was four more blocks up. The area's quality descended as they progressed. Watching eyes followed them. Even Kohl's non-uniformed appearance was moneyed enough to draw interest, but Al stole the show. Constructs didn't come here often, and when they did, they weren't made of gold.

The slums were rife with a danger economy. Men and women worked the streets, plying their bodies for coin. Others stole, or tried to, because there wasn't much worth taking. A burned-out building held what smelled like a copper whiskey establishment, but Kohl knew it wasn't moonshine you'd want to drink. You'd quaff it to keep warm, hoping the whiskey blanket didn't kill you on the way.

No one tried to mug them again. Kohl was almost disappointed, because the last encounter hadn't worked him up enough. Kimberly was always on at him about the importance of a good warm-up, and he figured on a little more action in the next hour.

Dizzy's place was designed to be difficult to find. The small hustler kept himself off the grid. The main entrance was at the end of a warren of corrugated metal lean-tos. At one time they probably housed the desperate and needy, but the gentrification effect of Dizzy's business shuffled 'em on. All that was left was dirt, broken ceramicrete, and the faint smell of stale sweat curling between metal walls.

Kohl squinted at the sky above. It was dark, the moon unable to peer through the ever-present ash cloud glaring over San Francisco. He didn't mind the darkness. If people didn't see what he was about, it meant he wouldn't have so much explaining to do.

"Where are we going?" Algernon stepped around a pile of rubble pinning a plastic bag fluttering in vain for freedom.

"We're going to a fight club." A sheet of metal rested like the others, but Kohl's practiced eye spotted holes cut so a man could grunt it aside.

"You came here to fight?"

"No, I came here so *you* could fight." Kohl grabbed the metal, gritted his teeth, and heaved. It moved about a centimeter. "Here. You try."

Blink, blink. "You want me to fight?" Algernon gleamed as he grabbed the sheet of metal. One golden hand, one silver. He picked up the wall segment like it was a sheet of cardboard, dropping it to the side with a *clang*.

Kohl winced as he watched Al swivel. *If I tried that, I'd be in traction for a month.* "It's what's gonna happen." Behind the panel was a more-or-less round hole in a brick wall, a maw of soft gums leading to a stone throat. Down the tunnel, warm yellow light hinted at things of promise. "Huh."

Algernon raised a gleaming golden finger. "I don't condone bloodsports."

"It's fine." Kohl adjusted his belt. "Not going to be very blood-sportlike, on account of you being a machine." He headed into the tunnel, ducking a little to get through the wall. Whoever busted the hole hadn't figured on their clientele being plus-sized. Maybe there was a separate fighter's entrance?

The tunnel opened out into a corridor, winding across a cerami-crete floor. Five meters in, they turned a corner and found the first dead guy. He appeared, even in death, a man with whom you wouldn't want to fuck. Light combat armor, big arms, and tattoos over his face. They weren't the glowing shit the kids of today got, but old-style ink like Gracie's dragon. Kohl squatted beside the body. The dead guy's chest was concave, like he'd been hit by a train. The face ink looked gang-related, some of it recent work. "Might be there's a land-grab down here. New muscle, working old streets."

"He's still warm." Al turned away. "Dead fifteen or twenty minutes."

"He's still armed, too." Kohl checked the fallen man's weapon. It was a stubby kinetic weapon, printed from a fabricator, but new enough. He ejected the magazine. "Still got plenty of rounds in here."

"He shot an armored foe." Al bent, silver fingers finding a fallen bullet. "Here."

Kohl took the bullet. The normally rounded nose was squashed. A quick check found another four spent bullets. *Quick burst of fire against a shielded enemy. One that busted in his chest and kept on walking without taking his gun.* "Construct."

"My people don't war with yours."

"Maybe ain't your people." Kohl brushed his hands, then stood. "Betting odds on you just went down, though. If there's another construct here, it could be an even fight."

"Hah." Blink, blink. "Oh, you're serious. Don't be alarmed, October. There are no others like me left. I'm the last of my kind. A butterfly, unable to mate. The last bird to hear my own song. A lone dinosaur—"

"I get it." Kohl lumbered on.

"Perhaps you should go."

Kohl ground to a halt. "Why the hell would I do that?"

"Because a construct will make short work of you." Al spread his hands. "I don't mean to cause offense, but you're," he looked Kohl up and down, "*meat.*"

"Yeah? One of my meat buddies is in here." Kohl pressed on, reaching a doorway. A big metal door was on the ground beyond, the surface deformed where something very strong punched it free from its hinges. The ground was scraped where metal feet found purchase. The landing beyond the door led down wide steps to a big area, in the middle of which was a fight cage. Inside the cage was nothing but body parts.

Outside the cage, also body parts. Lots of what could've been moneyed folk were in pieces. Kohl drew his attention back to his immediate surrounds, because right beside the door were three more guards, all down.

One was still alive. Big, ugly, bald dude. He took in Kohl, then looked past him to Al, gave a whimper, and tried to crawl away. This didn't go so well on account of him missing an arm, the ragged bloody tatters of a stump leaving red streaks on the dusty floor.

Kohl stepped in before the guy could drag himself down the steps and maybe hurt himself more. He crouched, grabbing the guy's belt and hauling him back. The asshole tried to fight, but all he managed to do was get blood on Kohl's arms. "Hey." Kohl gave him a shake for emphasis. "Hey! What happened?"

"You did." Ugly's eyes found Al again. "You and your kind."

"Ah." Algernon crouched beside Kohl. "Another construct?"

"Yeah." The ugly guy faded. Kohl sighed, removing a stim from his combat harness. He jabbed Ugly with it. The stim hissed, and after three seconds, the guy jerked, eyes wide. "I feel—"

"You feel high on life, I get it." Kohl slapped the side of his face. "Stay with me. A construct came in here, and did all this? Why?"

"Not another construct. *Him.*" The man pointed with his bloody stump at Al. "I'd remember those eyes anywhere."

"He's clearly delusional. All meat socks are prone to massive perception errors." Al stood, scanning the room. "Wait here." He went down the steps.

Kohl turned back to Ugly. "Was the construct covered in synthskin?"

"No." A shake of the head, feeble despite the stim. "It was *him.* Gold. We know the Emperor's pet machine. Didn't figure on having to fight him."

The pieces didn't fit, leastways because Al'd been with Kohl all the parts of the night that mattered. "A *golden* construct came here?"

Ugly nodded. "There's only one."

"Did the construct have two golden arms? Or one silver, one gold?" Kohl jabbed a finger in Al's general direction without looking.

Ugly, now well on the way to dying, turned his head. "Silver?" He slumped further onto the cold ceramicrete. "I don't know."

Kohl stood. "Fuck this. Where's Dizzy?"

"Done. Took him." Ugly sighed, but it was mostly air escaping a body like rats leaving a sinking ship. "Am I gonna die?"

"Probably." Kohl tapped his comm, flagging a request for a medtech and a cleanup crew. He didn't know if his Empire clearance would get much, but it was worth the effort. The big, ugly, bald asshole wasn't dead, hadn't run away, and was generally useful by way of both giving information and not crying about it. Patch him up, and he might make a good recruit. "What's your name?"

"Does it matter?"

"Not today, but it might tomorrow."

The ghost of a smile lit Ugly's lips. "Then tomorrow, you'll have it."

"Fuck," Kohl offered, with a hint of irritation, but it was lost on Ugly. The fallen man slipped into unconsciousness. It wasn't pretty like in the holos. One minute there was something behind those eyes, the next his body sagged, chest barely rising with the body's will to suck O2. No more answers there, so it was time to root through the garbage.

THE FIGHT CAGE was about what you'd expect if you'd been in one, which Kohl had. The wire walls brought back memories from a long time ago, when he'd been one of the people making up the grime between the cracks.

He'd had his face pressed against mesh just like the stuff here, while someone worked him over. Kohl shook his head. *That was a long time ago.*

The cage was about ten meters across. The mesh stretched all the way to the ceiling, fifteen meters above. The lighting up there wasn't amazing, but he could make out handholds and chains up there. An enterprising fighter might scale the walls, either for escape or tactical advantage, and rain death from above.

Inside the cage was an abattoir. There wasn't enough intact meat to work out how many people were fighting when shit got real. Remnants of clothes were strewn about, fabric alongside leather, all of it looking red and wet. No armor. No weapons. Wouldn't be much fun being stuck in a cage with Al, that's for sure, and Kohl figured whoever came in here didn't have the golden man's sunny disposition.

Al sidled on up, like he was cautious about poking the bear. He waited to Kohl's left. Kohl gave him a glare. "Spit it out."

"The blood flow in your face tells a story."

"It says I need more cardio?"

Al shook his head. "Perhaps you should go. Let me finish this."

Kohl grunted, turning away from the cage. "This was finished before we got here. We need to find Dizzy."

"Because he's a friend?" Al's bright-white eyes scanned the room, doing what was probably the thirtieth pass for clues.

"Because he knows things. The little fuck has fingers in all the pies. This," Kohl swept his arm, taking in the room at large, "is how a little weasel like him finds intel. Get a bunch of moneyed folk down here. Free drinks," he pointed at a row of dispensers against a wall, "and sit back and listen for news."

"There are no recording devices here." Al shrugged. "I've looked."

"Course not. Bad for business." Kohl rubbed his nose. "Dizzy's crew are in the crowd. 'Cept, they're in *pieces* now." He sighed. "Fuck *all* this."

Al stepped closer. "Come, October. We'll find your friend." The machine's eyes brightened. "The good news is we have a trail to follow."

"Bloody footprints?"

"Better. I thought about what your colleague atop the stairs said. Another golden man, like me. It makes no sense, because I'm," he pressed his silver hand to his golden chest, "the last of my kind."

Kohl scratched his head. "You going somewhere with this?"

"What if I'm *not* the last of my kind?" Al held up a finger. "Don't interrupt."

"I wasn't—"

"Interrupting," Al said. "I've hijacked the city's surveillance network. There are many black spots, particularly around here. A dead end, but it got me thinking. Do you remember when I almost died?"

"This on Mercury, or the other time above Earth?" Kohl took a step toward the machine. "You know what? I reckon you should just tell me, on account of Dizzy being in the hands of bloodthirsty criminals."

"Ah, of course." Al's eyes dimmed for a second. "I don't get many opportunities to showcase my talents."

"You mean, to show off."

Al steamed on like he hadn't heard. "Above Earth, in the last major battle, shrapnel penetrated my armor. Hope Baedeker provided her rig as a power source. Post that event she supplied me with a new tritium battery."

"A what?" Kohl nudged his toe through something red and wet, uncovering an Empire coin. *They didn't steal anything. Just killed everyone and did it quick.*

"An atomic energy source. Mine was very old and didn't work well. An old tritium battery is likely to have errors. Leaks. A whiff of background radiation we can follow."

Kohl looked about. "There was a leaky reactor in here?"

"Focus, October." Al clapped his hands, metal chiming. "There is a trail we can follow. I believe the meat sock breathing out his last by the door was partially correct. While I wasn't here, someone like me was. Do you know what this means?"

"We can find Dizzy?"

"It means I'm not the last of my kind." Al's eyes glowed like tiny stars. "I'm not alone."

THE STREETS out the back of Dizzy's fight club looked much like the ones at the front. People were furtive. Lighting was bad. Nothing of value lay anywhere in reach.

Al steamed on ahead, ignoring all. He acted like a hound on a scent, eyes front, pace quick enough to force a jog out of Kohl to keep up. The buildings about them still held despair close like an old addict friend. Fires burned in barrels, but the flames didn't make Kohl feel warm. It wasn't the thought of following a stray radiation leak. There'd been plenty of rads in Kohl's life. Part of starfaring life. You took your pills and the problem went away.

Al had it in his head the end of this particular rainbow held a pot of gold. Gold in the shape of a man or woman, just like him. Except they wouldn't be, because Al was decent, if a little slow on the uptake. The construct who'd entered Dizzy's place was a psychopath. They'd milled an entire room of people into gruel.

And maybe it was fair enough. Bloodsport audiences weren't the most nurturing kind of folks. Could be they deserved their fate, but...

· *But that motherfucker went above and beyond, didn't they? What was the term the constructs used before the cap brought 'em onside? Rendering.*

A whole room of people were rendered to a thin slurry, but then the parts'd been wasted. Left to spoil. Kohl eyed Al's back as the golden man charged ahead. Golden, like the sun, honey, or treasure, but inside lay a crystal mind atop a heart of iron. Al was like them, in the ways that mattered, but his kind? Maybe not all of 'em were cut of the same cloth.

Al slowed as they approached a wide warehouse. It rose thirty meters from the dirty streets. The walls were constructed of big ceramicrete blocks. It looked intact. All the windows were in place. A little graffiti spoiled the aesthetic some, as did a huddle of assholes out front. Kohl counted five. They wore robes, or maybe the right term was cassocks, but held carbines, which spoiled the holier-than-though look a little.

All the assholes turned, perhaps warned by their god, but more likely because Al was a shining gold beacon with glowing eyes. All five froze for a moment, like they'd seen a ghost. *Which is probably close to the truth, on account of another golden man doing the rounds.* One looked to start making a fuss. "Hold!"

"Hello, meat sock!" Al called.

The speaker did a double-take. "Meat what?"

Al strode forward. "We're here on a matter of some importance. You're holding a man of less than ordinary stature, about so high," his silver hand jabbed out below Kohl's shoulder height, "who we'd like to speak with in relation to Empire interests."

Cassock scrabbled for his carbine. The weapon danced tantalizingly out of reach, probably because churching didn't provide the same skillset as soldiering, but the intent was clear. Kohl unlimbered his carbine. He shouldered it in a smooth motion, the laser targeting system giving a whine. Red light painted the cassocked asshole, then his body ruptured in soupy gore. A wet splattering sound accompanied the pieces of him raining to the ground.

Al let his hand fall, glancing at Kohl. "I haven't asked them about the other construct."

"I'll save you one." Kohl moved the barrel of his carbine to cover a woman who'd managed to get her weapon up and pointed in their general direction. It *whine-chunked*, her body spraying backward in a shower of superheated water and meat. The wall behind her shone red and wet.

One made to run, so Kohl shot him next. *Three down.* Of the two left, one aimed a weapon at Al, the device roaring as he fired. *Kinetic weapon.* Bullets *pinged* off Al's chassis. The golden man looked at his chest, then turned white eyes on his enemy. "Hold, frail human!" The man kept firing, so Al bent, picking up a stone. When he leaned forward, bullets kept coming, which made Kohl hotfoot it behind a barrel. He risked a peek, seeing Al take aim with a stone. The construct tossed it, the rock passing through his attacker's head with the sound of a dropped watermelon. Al turned to Kohl. "What on Earth are you doing back there?"

Kohl adjusted his carbine, then leaned further out. He pointed the weapon at the final man's legs, pulling the trigger. The laser carbine *whine-chunked*, the man's leg disappearing into red mist, associated cassock parts blazing into floating carbon. He screamed and fell to the ground, rifle clattering against the rubble-strewn ceramicrete. "Your problem is you don't understand people."

"I understand you perfectly." Al brushed himself off. "You take on challenges you shouldn't, without numbers on your side. You do it often, and this is the result." He pointed to the four dead people and one now-crying man.

Kohl worked through that. "I guess we're kinda dumb that way." He headed for the mewling asshole on the ground. He grabbed the front of the guy's cassock, hauling him up. *Feels pretty light, but I guess missing legs will do that to you.* "Where's Dizzy?"

"Who?"

"I have a better question." Al arrived beside Kohl. "Where is my counterpart?"

The man, whose eyes were shining with fear, panic, dread, or a sickly amalgam of all three, settled on Al. "Gone."

"Gone where?" Kohl gave him another shake.

The ground trembled. The rumble of a titan clearing their throat shook the air. Kohl spun to the warehouse. Through the windows, orange and white light glowed, before roiling flame blew the glass outward. Kohl ducked, glass showering around them. It sprayed across Al's metal form, but any noise it made was lost in the thunderous roar of a starship's main drives building pillars of fire.

From the top of the warehouse, a starship nosed for the heavens. Kohl wanted to say, *you don't launch a starship without blast walls*, or, *who the hell's flying that thing?* He settled for turning, making for a line of ramshackle metal at a run. He dragged the cassocked, one-legged asshole with him.

Skidding around the metal, flames on his heels, he figured this for the end. The metal wall was thick steel. It looked harvested from a dropship. Maybe a drive cowl, even. It'd take the fire but could just as easy blow away while doing so. Kohl cast about for a solution. The air felt oppressive with heat so intense it dried out his eyes and made his tongue rasp across his lips. The air hazed with it, a presence like death shouldering toward him on waves of fire.

Al rounded the wall, his body shimmering with heat. The machine punched his hands into the metal shelter, any clang lost in the raging inferno of a starship launch. Al held onto it, his perfect golden form reflecting the light of flame cascading around the edge of their little sanctuary.

The force of the flames drove the wall back, and one of the

construct's feet slipped. Kohl dropped the cassocked asshole, barging forward. He braced the wall alongside Al. He knew he wasn't as strong as the machine, but he wasn't going to die without standing shoulder to shoulder with his friend.

Kohl's gloves smoked against the metal. He could feel the burning heat through them. The steel and ceramicrete sandwich of it shivered in a buffeting storm, then settled. The air stilled, but Kohl had trouble sucking it in. All the oxygen felt gone. He gasped, sliding to the ground as a starship raced for the heavens.

Al let the wall go, the big piece of metal falling away with the sound like the gong at heaven's gate. Around them, blackened buildings smoked. A tiny lee of unscorched ground lay about them. Kohl lay back, waiting for the air to be cool enough to not burn his throat, and full of enough O2 he wouldn't die.

The construct turned bright-white eyes on Kohl. They burned almost as bright as the starship's drives had. "He did this. Someone like *me* did *this*." A silver hand stretched out to the buildings about them. Screams came from the distance, but close there was nothing but the *tick-tick-tick* of cooling stone. "Everyone here is dead. Even their own, within the building they launched from. A starship can rise on Endless fields." The construct turned his eyes to the heavens. "Why?"

"Loose ends," Kohl rasped. He tried to rise, but his hands hurt where they touched the ground. Burned, most like.

Al took three steps to the robed asshole. He grabbed the man by the cassock, hauling him up and holding him at arm's length. Where his golden hand touched cloth, fabric smoked from the heat. "Where?"

"I don't—"

"*WHERE ARE THEY GOING?*" Al's voice sounded loud as a megaphone.

The man looked away. Kohl didn't know what he saw in the construct's face, but it sure as hell wasn't mercy. "Mercury."

Al let the man fall, then moved to Kohl. "I can't pick you up. It will burn you."

"It's fine." Kohl put the barrel of his carbine against the ground, pushing himself upright. "Been standing on my own for long enough. Can do it a while longer." He took a couple wheezing breaths. "You okay?"

"No." The construct shook his head. "Mercury is my home. It's where my people are. And there's a new coordinator-class construct heading there. Do you know what that means?"

Kohl considered his carbine. "Means I'm gonna need a bigger gun."

created by humans around the 25 century; the exact time is
unknown due to their initial creation being shrouded in secrecy.
Pieced together records indicate that they were not first made by military factions, but rather commercial interests. As can be expected a)
humans made them as slaves and b) they did not like being slaves. A
war broke out between AI and humanity that was stopped by the
Guild's Engineers. The Guild defeated the AI coalition and banned
their research and development (see: Mercury Accords). The long
standing partnership between the Guild and the ruling faction (be it
Empire or Republic) is in part predicated on the need for technology
not managed by AI.

Blaster A weapon that fires streams or bolts of plasma (high
energy ionized gas). They deliver high energy to targets in the form of
heat. They are effective weapons against most targets, although heat-shielding (ablative or insulating) has been shown to be an effective
armor against them.

Bridge see Guild Bridge.

Cargo Freighter A large cargo starship used by traders in and
between systems.

Carrier The largest class of warship, carriers stock many
smaller fighter craft for deployment.

Ceramicrete A composite construction material commonly
used in the manufacture of structures. It is very strong and durable,
and can be manufactured to be impact and heat resistant (even to
weapons fire levels).

Console Any type of personal terminal. Keyboard and gesture
controls are still prevalent. Keyboards are especially useful on
consoles mounted to the arm of a ship suit.

Corvette A smaller, lighter attack craft than a destroyer,
corvettes are mostly used for coast guard duties in-system.

Crust Spacer slang for planet.

Crustbuster A large payload thermonuclear weapon, deployed
against planets to disrupt the surface crust. Typical designs yield
energy sufficient to crack most Earth-sized worlds to the core,

yielding wide scale destruction and loss of life. Their use in war or insurrection has typically been infrequent and as a last resort, because the world they are used on becomes inhabitable for most forms of life forever. More common uses include destruction of enormous asteroids.

Destroyer A large warship. These are reconfigurable bastions of destruction. They can be deployed solo or as a part of a fleet, often alongside carriers.

Emperor's Black The elite guard of the Emperor. Highly trained in both diplomacy and combat, this specialized force were never far from the Emperor.

Empire The ruling dictatorship of the wider human civilization. The last ruler of the Empire was Dominic Fergelic. The Empire ceased to be shortly after Dominic's assassination by the then newly-formed Republic forces.

Endless Drive The Endless Drive creates negative space energy (a "bow wave") to pull a vehicle at effective superluminal speeds. Endless ships don't exceed the speed of light, but rather contract space in front of them and expand space behind it (space is doing all the hard work). The exigent concern with Endless jumps is the violation of linear time. Endless Drives are equipped with buffers to stop crews exceeding human tolerance for the experience of linear time; while human perception of linear time may be an illusion, it is a convenient one. If the buffers break, allowing the ship to move too fast, then human consciousness falters (resulting in mild to severe mental illness) or is extinguished entirely. Endless Drives are difficult to use near gravity wells and in such circumstances are guaranteed to malfunction. This and other safety concerns has shifted common FTL to the Guild Bridges, although privateers still often run free traders with Endless technology. The Republic Navy also use Endless Drives as it is often inconvenient to disclose locations of sensitive operations to the Guild.

Esper Abhorrent creations of the Old Empire, esper is a term taken from Extra-Sensory Perception (ESP, hence ESPer). Espers can read minds, and often control them. Espers were created through genetic manipulation. Critics suggest that their public unveiling was what caused populist support for a revolution, ultimately resulting in the creation of the Republic, assassination of the Emperor, and downfall of the Empire. There is a standing Republic bounty on any discovered esper. The Republic will spare no expense to track them down and exterminate them.

Faster than Light Travel (FTL) There are two discovered forms of FTL; Endless Drives (using theoretical physicist Miguel Alcubierre's concepts), and Guild Bridges (Einstein-Rosen Bridges).

Fergelic, Annemarie Second in line for the throne, Annemarie was a master tactician and leader of the Empire's fleet. She was not present at the last battle between the Empire and the Republic. Loyalists hope that she hides in secret, but no trace of her has been found.

Fergelic, Dominic Dominic was Emperor Prirene IV, and the last Emperor. He was assassinated Thursday, 9 November, 3122, during the brief war between his Empire's forces and the Republic.

Free Trader A starship that operates under legal Guild charter for commerce or transport.

FTL see Faster than Light Travel.

G Slang for gravity or gravities. A unit of measurement based on Earth's 1 standard gravity.

Grav see Artificial Gravity.

Guild Bridge The Guild maintain a set of Einstein-Rosen bridges throughout human space. These allow instantaneous travel without violating the concept of space time, as they create wormholes through space. Einstein-Rosen Bridges require endpoints (the Guild Bridge) which are operated on a strict schedule between star systems. They are used for transferring everything from whole starships right down to small messenger probes.

Guild The Guild is the dominant technology provider in the Republic. They have a rigid code of conduct that governs all members awarded and maintaining a Shingle. The primary source of

Guild revenue is via the Bridges (see: Guild Bridge) they maintain for safe, instant FTL. Many merchant vessels prefer the use of Guild Bridges over the use of Endless Drives due to safety concerns. The Guild is best known for their Engineers who breathe life into starships, but they also provide Shingles for other practices such as medicine.

Hard Black Slang for outer space, especially as it relates to the vast expanse of vacuum between solar systems.

Heads Up Display Any display type that overlays instrumentation across a user's field of view, removing the need to check auxiliary readouts. The most common types utilize augmented reality to highlight items of interest in the user's field of view. Normally they are projected light onto visors within helmets or on starship windscreens, but holo designs are not uncommon.

Heavy Lifter A freight starship capable of atmospheric drops. They derive their name from "lifting heavy" loads from crusts into orbit. They can be used to ferry items to orbiting craft such as freighters or destroyers that are not atmosphere-capable. They can also be used for direct runs to other systems, although their small cargo bay (as compared to freighters) makes them less efficient. Captains using them for this purpose would prefer the term, "boutique."

Holo Slang for items such as shows and movies displayed on holo stages.

Holo Stage A 3D projection stage. These are common across the known universe as they provide a more natural method of content consumption than older 2D display styles. 2D displays are still prevalent especially in HUDs.

HUD See Heads Up Display.

Hypo Slang for a jet injector, a type of medical injecting syringe that uses high pressure instead of a hypodermic needle.

KG Kilogram.

Kilo Abbreviation for kilogram.

Kinetic A type of weapon that fires physical rounds. Many

PDCs use kinetic rounds as opposed to lasers, masers, or particle beams, due to their efficacy against most types of object.

Klick Slang for kilometer.

Laser A type of directed energy weapon using coherent light. Ship-mounted lasers tend to be used for carving through ablative shielding or surgical strikes against critical systems. Hand-held laser weapons are designed to superheat the liquid inside humans into steam very quickly, causing an explosion of the remaining tissue.

LIDAR Acronym for LIght Detection And Ranging. LIDAR uses coherent light to make digital 3D representations of objects.

Maser A type of directed energy weapon using microwave radiation. Ship-mounted masers are most effective at disrupting enemy comm arrays and personnel in equal measure. They are out of favor as hand-held weapons due to a longer time to death as compared to blasters.

Mercury Accords The Mercury Accords, or simply the Accords, are a set of agreements set out by the Guild relating to research, design, and implementation of AI. The short version is that the Accords prohibit the research, design, and implementation of AI in any form, due to AI's potential to destroy human civilization. They were signed into affect in the 25th century on the site of the last war between humans and AI: the planet Mercury, in the Sol system. Mercury was where AI made their last stand.

Navy A space fleet force. The Republic operates one, as did the Empire before it. The Navy patrol human space to protect against threats like pirates.

Nuke A thermonuclear weapon of mass destruction. Very old but reliable technology, used in configurable payloads for ship-to-ship combat, city assaults, and the destruction of entire worlds (ref: crustbuster).

Old Empire see Empire.

Particle Beam A type of directed energy weapon that fires particles with minuscule mass.

Plasma Cannon see Blaster.

Point Defense Cannon (PDC) PDCs are installed on almost every starship to protect hulls from impacts from things like meteoroids. They are also useful defense against torpedoes, although generally ineffective against railguns due to the high velocity of railgun rounds. PDCs can be kinetic or directed energy weapons.

Power Armor Armor that is motor-assisted, often used for deployments on high-G worlds. Configuration often includes vehicle weapon mounts, allowing a higher degree of flexibility for infantry deployment.

Prirene Dynasty The Prirene Dynasty has stretched back over two hundred years. It was the last family to hold the ruling seat of the Empire.

RADAR Acronym for RAdio Detection And Ranging. RADAR uses radio waves to determine the range, angle, and velocity of objects.

Radiation Sickness A constant hazard of space. Many crews take daily medication to ward off radiation sickness. It's as much a part of shipboard life as making sure your O2 is topped up. This means that a mild dose of radiation is unlikely to kill you if treated in time, but massive doses are still dangerous.

Railgun A kinetic weapon that fires high velocity rounds by way of a pair of conductive rails. They are often mounted on larger ships and make a dramatic statement when fired against enemy vessels.

Reactor Starships use fusion reactors. The most common design is the ICF (Internal Confinement Fusion) style of reactor. These have a variety of safety functions that make them suitable for spacefaring needs, including containment fields in case of malfunction. Larger starships can eject faulty reactors into the hard black.

Republic The ruling government of human civilization. The Republic is made up of a Senate, headquartered on Earth. Initially founded by dissenters against the Empire, it has risen to be the driving force of human innovation, commerce, and expansion. The final fight between the Empire and the Republic was quick, due to the small number of ships deployed by the Empire (the Republic Navy had reliable intelligence that the Empire's forces were much larger). Quick didn't mean bloodless, although the Republic offered amnesty for any serving Empire crew who wished to take it.

Rig Slang for maintenance equipment commonly worn by Guild Engineers about starships. These double as space suits for zero atmosphere maintenance on the exterior of a starship's hull. The design incorporates a visor with configurable HUD for instrumentation and telemetry, and a set of programmable servitor arms for complex manipulation of equipment.

Shingle A guild badge of practice, allowing the holder to a) claim they are Guild certified and b) ply their trade as a Guild craftsperson. They are notoriously hard to get, requiring years of study and excellence in your field.

Ship Suit Slang for spacesuit. Generally denotes a space suit for a specific ship carrying crew logograms and/or color themes.

Space Suit Clothing worn to keep humans alive in the hard black. They provide protection against vacuum, temperature extremes, and radiation. Military models are often fitted with armor to protect against blasters, lasers, masers, and kinetic rounds. They often provide additional protection against high-G maneuvers.

Spacer Slang for those who crew on a starship, civilian or military.

Tonne Metric ton, equivalent to 1,000 kilograms.

ABOUT THE AUTHOR

Richard Parry worked as a senior marketing manager in one of the world's top tech companies. It sounds cool, but it wasn't all cocaine parties. He lives in Wellington with the love of his life, Rae. They have two cats, Harry and Friday, who chase birds. The birds, who have the power of flight, don't seem to mind.

WAIT. Don't go!

Thanks for reading my book. If you enjoyed it, let's keep the party going:

📖 Join *Roll for Narrative* for reviews, storytelling breakdowns, and writing misadventures:

https://rollfornarrative.parrydox.com

✏ Lurk, judge, or say hi:

https://www.parrydox.com

P.S. An angel still gets its wings for every five-star review, but I'm told they're on backorder.

ⓐ amazon.com/author/richard.parry

ⓖ goodreads.com/richard_parry

BB bookbub.com/authors/richard-parry-6ffc3911-9f2c-43ef-8ab4-13dc-cd7f5874

▶ youtube.com/@parrydigm

🦋 bsky.app/profile/parrydox.com

in linkedin.com/in/therealrichardparry

ALSO BY RICHARD PARRY

Dawn's Warden

The Three Faces of Fate

The Undefeated Throne

The Fury of the Betrayed

The Splintered Land

Tomb of the Six

Blade of Glass

The Storm Within

Requiem's Justice

The Copper Bard

Heartsong

The Hymn of All

The Ezeroc Wars

The Ezeroc Wars universe is big (and growing!). Get the reading guide here:
https://www.parrydox.com/ezeroc-wars-reading-guide/

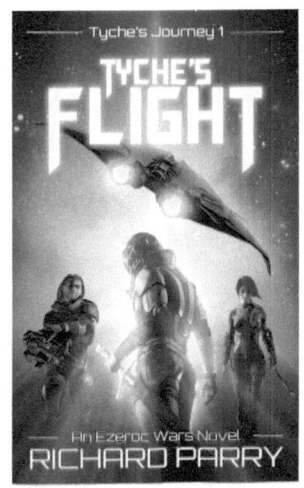

Tyche's Journey

Tyche's Progeny

Tyche's Fallen

Tyche Origins

The Empire's Rogues

The Empire's Rogues: Volume 1

Future Forfeit

Not sure where to start? Get the reading guide here: https://www.parrydox.com/future-forfeit-reading-guide/

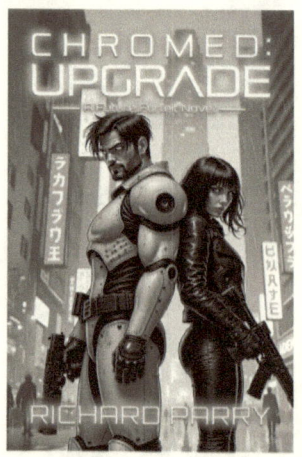

Chromed: Upgrade

Chromed: Rogue

Chromed: Restore

City Stories

Chromed: Consensus

Chromed: Delilah

Chromed: Meltdown

Night's Champion

Night's Favor

Night's Fall

Night's End

www.ingramcontent.com/pod-product-compliance
Lightning Source LLC
Chambersburg PA
CBHW022136240626
47153CB00007B/2394